Ten Thousand Secrets National Park

Book One in the
Tales from Apple Island series

Hilary A.B. Lambert

For Peggy and Oliver, Leslie, Roger, and Deb;
Jim and Duke.
Thank you, Linda.

Table of Contents

Part I
Now and Then

Chapter 1

Ten Thousand Secrets National Park Casino & Entertainment District, Kentucky.

A hot summer night.

On a midnight road in midsummer, our pickup truck rolled quietly, headlights off. In the moonlit sky above, bats swooped for bugs. I was driving and Steve was leaning out the passenger window watching for the beast we were tracking. It loped lithely next to the road, ten feet away. We had tracked it around the park's restaurant zone for about an hour, after surprising it in the dumpster of the Hideaway Café.

"What if we catch it or corner it?" I wondered. I was terrified about the cat, and aggravated at being called out to help.

After one month on the job at Ten Thousand Secrets National Park Casino & Entertainment District, I was not expecting to be yanked into service in the middle of my solitary supper after a long day behind the Visitors Center counter. But the park's science advisor, Steve Roberts, appeared at my apartment door clad in a stealth suit and infragoggles, and tossed me the truck keys.

As a new hire, I was first on the call-down list for emergencies, and had to go. Now we were tracking an actual sabertooth cat along this national park roadway. I had not known any of this fantastic story until an hour earlier, it being one of the many secrets in Ten Thousand Secrets National Park.

"We're keeping it quiet for several reasons," Steve had unhelpfully explained.

Now he shouted a warning and pulled his head in as the animal leaped snarling from the darkness at our truck. Steve's shotgun got stuck in the closing window and through the gap came the cat's yowls and spittle. The truck shook and recoiled as the beast fell into the truck bed, launched itself off the other side, and bounded down the employee road toward the Casino. I lost sight of it in the glare of the Casino's glittering bulk above the screen of trees.

"Go after it!" said Steve. We lurched onto the narrow lane, were caught by the facility's security beam, and came to a screeching halt.

"Approach denied," droned the dashboard console, and somewhere an alarm sounded. I didn't have the clearance codes, so my body shut down, hands inert on the steering wheel. Steve barked numbers at the console and the beam lifted as my paralysis faded. He leaned across me to punch the acceleration and steering panels, and I took back nominal control.

We sped through the trees and emerged onto a circular drive at the rear of the massive Casino. Its music and lights were muted by the half-mile distance to the front entrance, and by its 20-storey height. Pulling up next to a concrete staircase leading down a slope, we saw the big cat's tail vanishing into a small doorway set into the Casino's foundation. The steel-reinforced door stood slightly ajar, lit by a solitary lamp. Its glow illuminated the billowing mist forming as chilled casino air poured out into the hot Kentucky night.

"What is that door doing open!" said Steve. We secured the truck, dashed through the open door, squeezed through a revolving door, pelted down a concrete-floored cinderblock hallway, and emerged onto a narrow landing. Ahead, a metal staircase led down to the Casino's basement levels. I could not see much, and shined my flashlight around the dark, narrow space.

"Where are we?" I asked.

"Just below the main floor of the Casino," called Steve as he ran down the narrow metal staircase, boots banging loudly.

"That cat must be in this basement somewhere," I called down. "I'd feel a whole lot better if we could wait here for Security, and if we could turn on the lights."

"There aren't any lights in this basement," Steve replied. "There's an exit a couple floors down – let's head there. That critter is way beyond us now. I'll submit a report. No one's ever going to find it in here." I reluctantly started down the stairs after him.

Our flashlights showed the way as the narrow staircase made an abrupt left turn. After about ten steps it plummeted to the right, then descended steeply into the murk. I stopped, and called down to Steve.

"Surely a large animal like that can't hide in a building basement for long, and anyway what do you mean there aren't any lights?"

Steve turned to peer up at me.

"Look, this is a really big basement. This is one hell of a basement." He continued downward and I followed, listening for the beast, hearing only water dripping. Below I discerned a red glow and saw the friendly red light of an EXIT sign over a door.

"C'mon!" hissed Steve. We made a noisy run for it, pushing the heavy door open and slamming it behind us, the hair on our necks standing straight up, catching our breaths in the brightly lit cubicle beyond. Steve's green eyes were wide, pupils contracting in the light. I realized the little room was moving. We were in a rising elevator, red dots on a panel moving from BC to B2 to B1, then L. The door opened and we stepped out into the noisy, crowded scene of the Casino at the height of the summer tourist season. My lowly posting as a Park greeter had not brought me here before, and I would have stood staring at the noise and fun if Steve had not yanked me behind a large fluctuating holostatue of a Shawnee brave.

"I can't wear this stuff in here," he said, stripping off his stealth suit. I took the wadded-up suit as he failed to conceal the shotgun under his arm and followed him across the busy, noisy space under the Pleasure Dome, past age-specific entertainment zones.

Security finally caught up with us when we stepped onto the Styx River Bridge. I felt the familiar sag in energy as two uniformed officers approached. All Park visitors and low-level staff surrender the standard federal 30 percent of their free will at the entrance gate, and Security can raise this level upon need. The flush of imposed laziness filled my mind, and I leaned on the bridge railing for support. Steve nodded at the two women. I dreaded their scrutiny, but could only smile weakly.

"Please report," said Park Security Officer Shanice to me. They could not hassle Steve, who was way above their reach, but would happily try to crush me, the newbie.

"Janet Harper reporting. We tracked it. We lost it, down in the basement here." My voice came out in the flat drone of report mode. Security Officers Shanice and Audrey stared at me coldly, waiting for more. I continued, "At 19 hundred hours, office manager Sonny Scott called and instructed me to accompany Steve Roberts. To track this unknown animal. I drove the vehicle. We followed it into the back casino lot. We followed it into the basement. We could not find it. We took the elevator to this floor. We approached the bridge and met you."

I had been trying to develop defenses to this bio-debrief process, but found myself helpless. They probed me for answers about time, location, and impressions, which unreeled from my brain through my voice.

I glanced at the giant Styx Riverboats floating past below, full of excited Casino guests. As everyone knows, this artificial river runs through Ten Thousand Secrets National Park's three Pleasure Domes, stopping at hotels and casino entrances. The raft below glided out of sight, into a tunnel toward the next stop. Children squealed. In the personnel training sessions, I had learned that the park's tamer Secrets were clustered here, in the Family Secrets Entertainment Dome.

"Well, this goes in your record, Janet, and it sure don't look good," said P.S.O. Audrey. "You get on out of here by the front door and don't come back any time soon." She turned to Steve and said, "This new gal isn't supposed to be in here, sir. She doesn't have the trainings or the clearances."

Steve replied, "Thanks, officers, we were just leaving."

The two of us walked down the far side of the bridge, as my energy returned. I followed Steve closely, hemmed in by the crowds. We passed the entrance to Silent as the Tomb (Secret #445), an all-ages attraction, and walked around the crowd of kids lined up, waiting to learn the secrets that people take with them when they die. Not to my taste!

Beyond a tubular corridor punctuated with Pan-Asian snack bars, a cold blast of air came at me from the right. Down the gleaming red corridor I saw a brightly lit room through a glass wall. I glimpsed people standing, sitting, lying down, staff in white lab coats.

"What's *that* one?" I asked.

"Let's pick up the pace," said Steve. "That's the biggie." I had heard about it, Secret #666, adults only, a top attraction. People went in to experience The Ultimate Secret. When they came out, they knew they had finally seen it all – only they could not remember it. The park guaranteed that it was not a drug, or hypnosis, but a real experience in a real place with real people. But it was so secret that visitors had to forget it and be content with the 100 percent guaranteed lifetime aftereffects of thrill and awe. What I saw were people in various stages of recovery. Secret #666 had a two-year reservations backlog.

We approached the front door through crowds of newly arrived bus tours in the Reception Zone, pushed through the jolt of the Security Zone, and emerged into the sticky night air.

Steve pointed to the monorail above us and said: "Take the rail to the VC and change for Park Admin, and do *not* stop at any of the Secrets. Thanks for your help." I made it back to my apartment, did a quick check for intruders, and fell fast asleep in my bed.

Homeland-Interior Region 3 Headquarters, central Ohio.

The next day.

Steve Roberts's long day of troubleshooting in Kentucky was not over. He parked the truck in the staff lot, locked up the gun in the main office, jumped in his car and headed north in the midnight darkness on I-65 toward home and sleep in central Ohio. At 1 p.m. the next day, he kissed his wife and headed out the door to his office, shaved, suited, and mildly sleep-deprived in that pleasantly edgy way. Steve's mind had shifted into crisis management. Urgency seldom intruded into his workplace, the muffled, brightly lit corridors of the mid-Ohio buried fortress that housed Homeland-Interior Region 3 HQ.

But a sabertooth tiger, loose in the nation's premiere Multi-Modal Entertainment & Nature Park? Something was wrong, and had to be investigated and fixed before the public heard about it. He was one of the few people with clearance to know the whole situation. Coffee-fueled and propelled by nervous energy, Steve emerged into sunlight on his brisk morning walk across the restored prairie-savanna to the nearest work Entrance. Cameras and biosensors recorded his every moment. Surveillance monitors compared fresh biodata to his long-term profile as he walked toward the escalator. Planning the park's crisis response, Steve was immune to the charming butterflies and hummingbirds flitting through the native plantings lining the low-impact suspended pathways.

The federal departments of Homeland and Interior had spent twenty years in a close embrace to restore this vast swath of degraded Ohio suburbia and small towns to fully authentic pre-European conditions typical of circa 1400 A.D. Not one expense or detail had been spared in this cooperative program, where ecologists and social scientists from Interior's Division of Ecology for Security worked hand in hand with Homeland's Restoration for Protection Division.

But twenty years is a long time in politics, and change was coming. After all, the Department of Homeland Security is a federal terrorism response and funding process founded after 9/11, and the Department of Interior is a fusty old amalgam of farming, land management, and energy exploitation interests. Certain influential people in the White House administration felt it was time for military interests to prevail, and they had their eyes on a top-secret program. Steve, focused on protecting his park's environmental resources, would soon find this out, the good old-fashioned hard way.

Redundancy is at the heart of security, so Steve's bioreadings were again sucked out through his eyes as he entered the fern-overhung Northeast Entrance. Dodging the waterfall spray, he merged with the flow of early arrivals into the vertical people mover. By the time he was seated in the conference room at 2:30 p.m., two thousand feet below the surface, his identity had been confirmed four times more in a number of ways. The feeling of being in a play, anyway, was second nature. Steve's colleagues regarded documents on their seat monitor screens as he began his report. He invoked acronyms and interagency shorthand, comforting to his supervisor.

"HI344 is complete, and we'll have 4022 and 4023 in your hands by close of business today. We'll mop up with HI900 as soon as the Park security debriefing data has been bio'd."

"Biodecoded": the Casino security interview with Janet went through a series of comparative security runs for maximum quality assurance and clarity indicators. That is, the data sucked out of her pupils and from her and Steve's body language and speech patterns was looked at from several angles. Watching the recording, Steve saw in Janet – the park's new hire, transferred to Kentucky after the disaster at Nevada's newly remodeled multi-modal national park – an intelligent woman, guarded and uneasy. There was a look in her eyes he did not understand. Had he glanced in a mirror, he might have seen the same look in his own eyes.

"But they have not found the big cat?" asked Inge Knowles, Steve's supervisor. "I just don't get it about this basement. How can a five-foot cat vanish in a basement?" she complained.

Homeland rep Stuart Bolles smirked at his Interior counterpart and said to her, "Wink nudge, not your turf, dear gal. Steve knows about that basement, and we'll leave it to him and staff to reconcile their Secrets modulars." Translated, this meant that Steve outranked everyone in the room on his Secrets clearance for that Park, and they had to accept his recommendations.

A thorough security review of this meeting would note a distinct shift in Steve's demeanor as the others discussed his beloved park. He adjusted his legs, crossed and uncrossed his arms, rubbed his face. Ten years earlier, Kentucky's national park had been converted to the new sustainably self-funding casino-entertainment "multi-modal" national park model, and re-named Ten Thousand Secrets National Park Casino & Entertainment District ("10K$" in the four-letter federal parks nomenclature). Thanks to Kentucky's senior Senator Harlan Styce, it was the second of the new-model parks, nationwide. The first one, in Nevada, was closed for repairs.

Within the Federal Parks Program, Steve Roberts was an interagency liaison officer as well as 10K$'s science advisor. He wanted to protect what remained of this park as it became a massive entertainment draw for the public, while also becoming a testing ground for top-secret temporal transfer research (again, thanks to Senator Styce). Steve knew the park – especially that basement – better than anyone. He was determined, off-camera and in his private mind, to protect its wonders.

Eager to move on and leave no lingering curiosity, Steve said, "Staff has the reports under way, and I know the park. The Overlap and Redundancy studies" (the aforementioned 4022 and 4023) "indicate no problem." He stopped, looking pointedly at his watch: lunch would not be denied. People stirred in their seats, blinking when the room lights came up.

"Catching that cat won't take long, I hope," said Inge to Steve as they walked down the wide hallway toward the Commons, which opened around them. The Commons provided an authentic summer day experience for the deeply buried workers. Here they lunched daily in the shade under big umbrellas on the Time Terrace, soaking up the perpetual light breeze and warm air smelling faintly of lavender. The meeting group dispersed, settling around tables and picking up menus, stretching their legs and grabbing some sunshine.

This workplace perk was a product of the ongoing top-secret temporal transfer research, but few knew that when they entered the sunny Commons they walked into a specific summer day in France's Loire Valley, 1873. No one ventured beyond the sunny terrace, ringed with velvet ropes containing alarms that responded if brushed. Steve Roberts had gone off the terrace. He was Homeland-Interior's vetted, trusted, and apparently tame explorer. His leash was long; his cage was large. When first hired, he had been observed continuously for signs of "ferality." Several staff had lost their office culture under pressure from the top-secret fieldwork and had to be tightly managed, or dismissed following a mind-wipe.

Over the years, concerns about Steve had dropped out of his six-month reviews, and his eye scans were cursory. Mimicking office and community behaviors and speech, Steve kept his thoughts deeply covered, and secretly protected his park. He had a wife and family and was mostly content, except for that uncertain look that matched Janet's. But that secret he kept even from himself.

That same day.

Even trusted employees work within wider rings of security. Steve and his co-workers chatting in the long-ago French sunshine were unaware that their crisis-response meeting had been observed by higher-ups who did not give a shit about diligently numbered reports.

"I don't like that guy," said Senator Harlan Styce, leaning back as Ard Sprinkle, his senior aide, blanked the screen. "Roberts is cocky. Disrespectful. Where does he get off, running the meeting from the back seat? Can't you retire him?"

"Steve is our official fly in the ointment, Senator. It's part of his job to irritate." This was Ed Zanetti, the Department of Interior's interagency liaison officer to the top-secret temporal transfer research. Ed had hired the younger, black park ranger into his present interagency post. Steve had soon caught the attention of the Senator, who was – no need to ease around it – a racist. Ed gulped his coffee, anticipating the Senator's standard tirade about "that arrogant boy."

But he was in for a surprise – the Senator had bigger things on his mind. Styce and Sprinkle had shown up without warning at Ed's Department of Interior office in D.C. just when he was coming to grips with work after a 10-day field deployment.

Styce took command of the conversation. "Ed, observing this meeting has helped me make up my mind. It's time we moved forward. Cut the bait. Shit or get off the can. You know where I'm going with this?"

Zanetti swiveled to stare at the big handsome Styce, alarmed at an unusual note in his voice. Why *had* he "just dropped by"? Why was Sprinkle with him?

Styce now had Zanetti's complete attention, and continued: "It's time to pull the plug."

Zanetti was unprepared. To gain time, he interrupted, "Senator, more coff— "

"Now, Ed," steamrolled the older man. "It's time. To. Pull. The. Plug. For twenty years, no, twenty-one, I have put up with this airy-fairy bullshit. We let fucking liberals in to co-manage time travel, and we get over two decades of useless pansy crap. National parks. Sabertooth cats. Reports!" He thumped the desk with his meaty fist. Sprinkle settled back and beamed at the Senator.

Zanetti tried to inject a good word for the programs that were inflaming Styce: "Senator, co-developing the temporal transfer technology as a hybrid Homeland Security-National Park Service project has been sheer genius! The defense applications will benefit enormously from the intellectual and creative depth in the Park Service."

"Exactly! I knew you'd see it my way!" replied the Senator. "It's time to move on – you're thinking what I'm thinking!" He beamed at Zanetti who, fresh from that laid-back working vacation in 1910 Pasadena, was in no shape for this bullying. But he tried to resist.

"Senator, you need to take one of our trips. If you spent just one day in the village of Santa Monica 1910, and felt the sea breeze – " This only fanned Styce's flames.

"All the more reason to bring this shit to a grinding halt, Zanetti. You've been softened up by this fucking humanistic bullpucky. We funded the Parks folks to study time travel for the sole purpose of its defense applicability. OK! We're there! Time's *up*." He and Sprinkle nodded in agreement, staring at Zanetti, whose mind was on that endless beach, stretching from the Mexican border to San Francisco, unimpeded by anything larger than fishing villages and Spanish missions. He was haunted by its otherworldly beauty – and its looming demise.

The Senator rushed in to fill Zanetti's stunned silence. He went for a kindly tone. "Ed, you guys at Homeland-Interior have done a fantastic job. Test project after test project tell us that the past is safe for our military. And now we have proof, with Professor King's research report, that we can change it, without harming the present." Zanetti jerked at the mention of this name, and Styce continued, lowering his voice tenderly, gently.

"Ed, your work has been a total success, and it is time to reap the rewards, for the benefit of the U.S. military, the American people, and our nation's proud history. Just imagine – to be able to right past wrongs and set the record straight! I am very grateful to see this day finally arrive."

Caught up in his own cunning, Styce wiped moist eyes on his sleeve, and picked up his phone.

"I'll set up the meeting, and we can move forward, thank God, at long last," he said, entering a number. Sprinkle was taking notes.

Zanetti spoke, he hoped coolly. "Senator, due respect and all that, but Professor King's report is worthless." Styce ignored him as he phoned to his staff the names needed, the stars of Congressional committees, the top military, the consultants, contractors, and advisors who had all been long awaiting this day. Styce equated making the call from Ed's office with his agreement.

"King's study is nonreplicable, sir," continued Zanetti. "We cannot with any sense of safety manipulate or occupy the past, with only one, flawed study indicating that there are no negative impacts in doing so." There, he had found his voice again.

The Senator muted the phone and turned to stare at Ed. "The study is nonreplicable because you guys are too chickenshit to replicate it," he replied.

Ed had evidently missed his moment to say no with force, so the big meeting was scheduled to take place in two days' time. But he continued the conversation, even though it was fast crumbling into a shouting match.

"We cannot," he said loudly, "act in a manner with potential irreparable results, on the basis of one bad study carried out by a well-known liar. He claims that he went back in time, killed his own grandfather, and that neither he nor the rest of the present world has suffered or changed in any way. Studies are just now getting under way to ascertain if this is in fact the case. These are long-term studies, Harlan. We had to get funding and organize the teams. It would be crazy – "

"Ed, we're old friends," said Styce, as he and Sprinkle rose together and headed toward the door. "I am fully authorized to get Project Retrofit moving forward. I did not have to have this meeting with you today, but did so for sentimental reasons. See you at 10 a.m. Wednesday in the conference room."

Styce handed his phone to Sprinkle, to dial Personnel. He wanted to get Steve Roberts fired while Zanetti was distracted. The door closed behind them. Fully roused from his vacation torpor, Ed pawed through the piles on his desk until he had unearthed Professor Tom "Cat" King's report. With his other hand, he punched in an ally's phone number.

Corning, New York, and environs.

A few months earlier.

Late one night the previous winter, young Brian Owen dejectedly checked his email. He had a social media Web presence notifying the world of his ability to write grant proposals on a free-lance basis, but three months of hoping had not produced many inquiries. So he was surprised to see an "Urgent!" message in his in-box from Maeve@sha.fae.

Dear Mr. Owen:
I am in dire need of your help in writing and submitting a Community Heritage grant proposal for our local project. Our small organization – Special Heritage Area, Inc. – was unprepared for the proposal-writing process, and the deadline is now less than two weeks away. Please contact me at once. We will gladly pay your fee.
Thank you,
Maeve

Brian replied that he would be happy to help, and she sent her phone number.

"Hello, Maeve?"

"Wonderful to talk to you, Brian. We are so grateful that you will help us." Her voice was a stunner – low and melodious. Captivating.

"Maeve, where is your group located? I don't recognize the area code."

"We are not far away. We have a different telephone area code, part of our special heritage area status." Reveling in her voice, Brian thought nothing of this weird remark as she went on.

"In fact, we are just a short drive from where you live. We want to work with a nearby expert who is familiar with our local concerns." Brian was happy to say yes. Though he was swamped with busy little projects, none were profitable.

Maeve sent him the Website link for the federal Community Heritage funding opportunity. The group's project was small-scale, detailed. They were asking for funds to support completion of a roundabout entrance to their heritage area, street and directional signage for visitors and residents, and red neon EXIT and ENTRANCE signs for "the gateway area." The group had a letter of support from their New York Congressman and a list of supporters. During the proposal process, Brian spoke with Maeve on the phone a second time. Her voice was fascinating and attractive, as she replied to the queries on his cleanup list.

"By all means, Brian, if you find the language of our request 'old-fashioned and charmingly anachronistic,' as you put it, please change it as needed. Our Board is not in tune with the larger world. They used the words they are comfortable with."

"All right," he said, "here's a suggested re-write for one particular passage. Your wording states, 'This then we are of a mind to build, three hand-wrought and painted sign-posts for the passageway thence, and one for the woods path.' Is it OK if I change that to, 'We request funding for four medium-sized (each three feet by four feet) directional signs, to be constructed locally. Bids will be sought for competitive pricing per standard practice.'?"

Maeve was silent for a moment before replying, "That will be fine, Brian, though it is surely unattractive and confusing. Is that truly the style of language needed?"

"Well," he said, intrigued with the mocking note at the back of her voice, "in short – yes. It's the jargon that grant proposal writers use. It's not better than how your group said it – only different, and more official-sounding." He realized she was laughing, and stopped speaking to listen. She had a low gurgle of a laugh, smoky, deep, and attractive. She spoke again.

"Mr. Owen, we are certainly fortunate to have found you to work with on this project. You are the ideal man to help us, in our hopelessly old-fashioned situation."

"Ma'am," Brian replied, flustered by her condescension. "I suspect that you are laughing at me and my line of work, just the tiniest bit, but I also hope that I can help you and your community attain your desired ends."

"Bravo, Brian," she replied, "That is a fine and spirited reply to my teasing. But I am also worried about this 'competitive pricing' phrase that you used. Pray, what does that mean?" And so it went. She was both the most sophisticated and least-informed woman young Brian had ever dealt with; and they got the work done.

After the proposal was submitted, they did not communicate for several months. Brian waited with rising tension for news of the grant agency's decision. He had a strong desire to get this grant – for Maeve. He wanted to prove that he was the man for the job, as she had said in her teasing fashion. Although Brian had spoken with her only twice, he was taken by her warmth and charm. He envisioned her as a redhead, but tended to dream a lot about redheads, in his sadly under-active social life. Payment for his work was direct-deposited to his bank account, and Brian spent it. Months went by.

One day when he was feeling especially low and self-pitying, this message appeared on his phone:

Dear Brian:

We have received the grant! Our Board of Directors is overjoyed! We will get to work on this project immediately. I will be back in contact when we have completed the work, as we would love to have you visit to view the fruits of your labor.

Very cordially yours,

Maeve

Brian floated on air for days...and then for weeks, when no further communications followed. She did eventually call, on a cold day in late February.

"Brian! You must dine with me midday at our village inn. Along the route you will see the improvements your efforts have made possible. When can you come?" Her voice was as ripe and beckoning as in their earlier conversations. He was in no state to play hard to get, seeing that his other projects were, as usual, in a state of chaotic disrepair. His day job at the museum was at its winter season lowest ebb. They agreed on Friday at noon, and Brian asked for directions.

"I have never been able to find your Special Heritage Area on any maps," he said. "Is it a recent designation?"

"I am sending you a map," she replied, sidestepping the question. As she spoke, a map popped up on his phone.

"My gosh, you sure are nearby!" Brian exclaimed, gazing at the light-green Special Heritage Area overprinted on the map of a nearby rural area of the county. Her community was near the interstate highway exit a few miles from his apartment. He used that route frequently to get to his favorite hiking area in the hills on the Pennsylvania border. Staring at the handsome little map, he wondered again why he had never seen nor heard of this group.

Brian said, "The inn is in the town of...hmmm...it says here, the name is...Hollymount?"

She replied, "Yes, the inn is at the heart of our village, named after a town in our homeland."

"I don't see a state route number for the road that goes there," he said. "Does the inn have a numbered address, so I'll be sure to find it? I see it's only a few miles from the interstate exit, so I'll plan on a half-hour drive from my apartment – is that about right?"

"Brian," she replied, in that sexy, admonishing tone he thrilled to hear, "you forget that we are a newly formed and inexperienced Special Heritage group. You must forgive us our little failings, such as leaving route numbers off maps." He sputtered an apology, and she continued.

"You will need an hour to reach the inn from our gateway area."

"But the map looks like it's only two miles from the interstate."

"And be sure to wear sturdy walking shoes, please," she said firmly. "I'll see you on the day." She hung up – and he was hung up.

On the day, Brian took the exit, turned left at the top of the ramp, and crossed over the interstate. Ahead were the hills he and his friends knew well, from solitary and group hikes on the hilltops and along the quiet creeks of the New York–Pennsylvania borderlands. The widened two-lane road wound toward them, as he looked for indications of the mysterious Special Heritage Area. Well-informed about local community groups and Native American interests, he wondered how he had missed this one.

Rounding a bend, Brian saw a shiny new sign on the left. Sure enough, it read "Special Heritage Area" with an arrow pointing left down a small side road he had never before noticed, tucked in between old houses and an abandoned grocery store. Turning onto it, he saw that the sign did not conform to standard road-signage, and might get in trouble with the county zoning office. It was wood, and hand-painted. The words were in a beautiful, old-fashioned script, with a stylish runic touch to it. The colors glowed in the cool morning light.

"This group knows what it's doing," he thought, glancing as he passed at the back of the sign, which read "To the interstate" – but the arrow pointed in the wrong direction.

"I take that back," he thought. "These folks need my help." The narrow road trended gently upward toward the hills. Soon a larger sign – again, nonconforming to regulations – announced, "Roundabout ahead – Special Heritage Area Parking ½ mile." Brian slowed and turned right onto the brand-new one-lane roundabout.

Glancing into the woods at the roundabout's center, he saw a small white spire above the trees. Brian was perhaps over-imaginative, having enjoyed fairy tales with his mom and sister. On this day of all days, when he was trying to be a dignified professional, he really did not need to hear from his inner self.

But there he was, whispering, "Going widdershins – counter-clockwise – around a church leads to Fairyland." Shoving away this embarrassingly infantile thought, Brian focused on the roundabout, realizing he had driven the full circle. The exit lane should lead back to the road from which he had entered the roundabout. Yet the hills loomed directly ahead, and a sign pointed to "Special Heritage Area Parking."

Leaving the roundabout for the narrow paved lane, Brian felt disoriented, then queasy as the asphalt paving abruptly ended, replaced by gravel. And what was that small dark thing ahead – was that a cat, a black cat? He stopped the car to get a better look at his surroundings, blinking his eyes to clear them. The air was deeply golden, the way it gets before a thunderstorm, and seemed thicker. Brian shook his head, glancing up at the clear blue sky, and drove slowly forward to the parking area. The golden air deepened the wintry blue color of the hills.

He thought, "The land is full of meaning." This deep thought was interrupted by professional irritation about the abrupt end to the paved road. He grumbled to himself, "Here you are, driving merrily along a nice two-lane highway with a yellow line down the center, and suddenly, no road – no warning signs or anything like what the law requires."

Up a steep slope was a cottage under tall trees, smoke rising from the chimney. A small figure came out the door and walked down a path as he pulled into the "Special Heritage Area" parking lot, his car the only vehicle.

Brian noted with quiet pride that the parking area was paved with the water-permeable concrete pavers he had recommended. Twinkling white flowers grew up through them. At the far side of the parking area – beyond the small black animal – a green footpath headed toward the hills. Covered in short grass, the path was edged with beds of moss. Was that the way to the Inn? Brian could see no other.

The approaching figure resolved itself into a small woman – she came up to the top of the side-mirror of his car – wearing a long dress and white apron. Brian's first impression was of a hippie, then a rural woman with many generations of local residence. She spoke to him through the open car window.

"Hello, Brian Owen," she said. "You should reach the Inn just in time for lunch." She stepped back as he climbed out.

"Hello, ma'am, beautiful day," he said. "Is this the parking area for the Inn – do I walk up that path to the building?"

"Path?" She was confused, but just for a second. "Oh, you be meaning the green road there. The Inn is a nice walk along the road, once you are through the gateway." As she pointed up the path – the green road – a vague feature came into focus, an open doorway in a small hill. Pulling his bag and jacket out of the car, Brian dropped his gaze from the opening to the animal lying between him and the green road – it still did not look quite like a cat.

He asked the lady, "What kind of cat is that?" She was startled. She whirled around and glared at the creature. It rose from its relaxed curled-up repose in the center of the path and moved slowly toward the meadow grasses beyond. It still did not look like a cat, but what else could it be?

"That is – that is a very BAD cat," the little lady shouted, as the animal vanished into the field. Brian felt uneasy about having to walk past it and asked, "Isn't there a road for cars to the Inn? Maybe I missed a turn-off?" She smiled and shook her head.

"Oh, no, honey-lad, they brought the pavement this far and not one foot further. I said we did not need these modern contrivances, but they insisted. Now – I must be back to my baking." She looked up to her cottage. Smaller figures appeared in the doorway and started down toward her and Brian. She waved them back, heading quickly up the steep path. Brian shouldered his small pack and walked forward up the green road toward the door in the hill.

The little lady called down, "Do not dally – be back here before dark." That made sense, with no streetlights in the parking area or along the green road. "They'll need another grant for lighting," he thought, waving goodbye to the little lady, who was shooing children back into the cottage.

Silence fell and the weird "meaningfulness" feeling came back. Brian did not know what to make of it – a deepened intensity of the wintry whites, blues, and browns, the sense that everything had significance. He also seemed to hear sounds – voices? Music? A low murmur, a musical tinnitus. For sure, he did not want to spend the night here. Fairies or what have you, this place was strange.

Approaching the hole in the low, grass-covered hill – what she had called the gateway – Brian admired the beautiful entrance, edged with cut limestone slabs. Inside was a tunnel, lined with stone and ribbed with curved and carved wooden beams. It was about two hundred feet long, with daylight at the far end. One of the project's neon signs hung over the opening above, the red ENTRANCE glowing dimly in the winter sunlight. The neon against the old stone, here in the quiet countryside, was definitely hip. This must have been a dairy, a place to keep milk and cheese cool, maybe a storehouse for ice, he thought.

Brian stepped forward into the tunnel. The low murmuring stopped, and he heard his quiet footfalls – there was a mild echo. The curved ceiling was in darkness. Daylight – that golden daylight – grew brighter, and he emerged from the other end of the tunnel. Glancing up, he saw the dim red neon glow of the EXIT sign against the rock facing above. Brian checked his watch, and found with dismay that its face was blank. He shook it, held it to his ear, and moved faster along the green path. It would not look good to be late to a meeting with someone from whom he wanted further employment – and with whom he was personally intrigued.

Chapter 2

Ten Thousand Secrets National Park Casino & Entertainment District, Kentucky.

The day following the sabertooth incident.

The late night out chasing a sabertooth cat left me dead tired the following day at the Visitors Center desk. At 4:30 p.m. I stood below the security beam, feet aching as I nervously waited for Ada to look up from the security screen and press a button, recording my apparent innocence for another day. Waving bye-bye, I hobbled out into the late afternoon sunshine and sat on a bench to calm down.

I was not yet accustomed to the continuous surveillance by this park's complex security system. The sense of being observed and recorded was intense here, compared to the remote Nevada national park I had been transferred from after the explosion. But the evening setting calmed me as the grey Kentucky day wound down and shadows lengthened. The trash bin at the end of the bench overflowed with fast-food wrappers, the only reminder of the tourist bustle earlier in the day. They had now returned to the big hotels, to play in the entertainment domes, overeat, and lose big at the casino.

Was the heightened security protecting secrets among the park's supposed ten thousand? Maybe the apparent tension was just closer proximity to Washington, D.C. and the high-pressure influence of Kentucky's senior U.S. Senator Harlan Styce. His money-hose flowed freely, and he had pet projects such as the three hydrofracking gas wells – this was the first national park to permit fracked gas wells. This was not controversial locally, as far as I could tell, but it made my blood boil. Being re-assigned here was not the rest cure my supervisors had envisioned following the Nevada park trauma.

At least I was moving up and away from that exhausting job of greeting and advising visitors – the next day I was taking over a people-monitoring position in the main office. Thanks to federal seniority, my position here at Ten Thousand Secrets National Park Casino & Entertainment District would soon equal what I had at Nevada's Historic Red Light District & Jazz Casino National Park. What they did not know was that each new task gave me information needed to complete my mission here. I would not be staying long.

Overhead, the treetops rattled and hummed in the freshening breeze. I heard birds calling, beyond the rumble of tour bus traffic, above the nearby Green, Green River. Buzzards wheeled high and free. Free of what trapped me, anyway. Standing up, I slung my backpack over my shoulder, crossed the road, and crunched along the gravel path into the woods, down the slope toward the employee apartments that sat in a green bowl beneath pine and hickory trees. I liked the old-fashioned two-storey cinderblock buildings. My apartment, with its curtained front window, was up a flight of metal-edged concrete steps. I took out my key – an actual key. The retina-scan level of park security did not reach these crumbling old buildings.

I inserted and turned the key, swinging the heavy door all the way open so that it touched the inside wall. I stood aside and listened. The rooms beyond sounded undisturbed – no scuttling, rustles, or door-closings. I stepped into the semi-darkness, daylight glowing dimly through the curtain on the window to my right. All was still, quiet; private, mine. Turning on the table lamp, I made a quick survey of the small rooms and began to shed my daily vigilance.

There was no reason to think my place was under active surveillance, because suspicion about the Nevada park disaster had never come my way. As a mid-level park resources manager in charge of water quality, my intense nerdiness had been a great alibi. But still I re-checked my Kentucky apartment for bugs every few weeks, using equipment I'd brought out of the ruins of the Nevada park. Gone, burned to the ground there, were the hotels, casino, and meticulously accurate Old West red light district inside the two-mile-long façade of desert town saloons and general stores ("300 beds!" the billboards still screamed, on highways across the Great Plains). And three dead consultants, charred beyond recognition. That burden I had to bear. My fellow resisters were scattered, in hiding or in deep disguise, like me. We each had our next assignment – and mine was here. But tonight it was time for supper and sleep.

Various offices, Washington, D.C.

The day following the sabertooth incident.

**TOP SECRET – CONFIDENTIAL
NOT FOR PUBLICATION
EMBARGOED UNTIL FURTHER NOTICE**
The "Grandfather Paradox":
Results of a Field Study with Defense Applications
Thomas King[1]

Abstract

In the emerging field of temporal transfer, basic principles must be established for researchers to proceed expeditiously toward real-world applications, emphatically the enhancement of past military outcomes for present-day national interests. Of lingering concern is resolution of the "Grandfather Paradox": Can the past be altered without unforeseen outcomes in the present day? Results indicate that it is all in the timing. The principal investigator (p.i.) entered Wichita, KS in February 1902. At that time, p.i.'s grandfather was 35, father to two sons, including the p.i.'s future father. Using approved techniques, p.i's grandfather was harvested. To minimize biomass loss and other essential impacts, the carcass was (hygienically) disposed of in 1902. No unanticipated outcomes of this action have been measured by the p.i. and lab into the present day. Although repugnant to the p.i., this personal sacrifice demonstrates conclusively that, when timing is taken into consideration, targeted past events can be altered without present-day unanticipated outcomes. Implications for defense applications are significant.

Key words: defense applications, harvest, temporal transfer, unanticipated outcomes

Introduction

When temporal transfer was first established 20 years ago as a replicable phenomenon in the laboratory setting (Cadwallader, 2008), the implications for the defense applicability of targeted temporal adjustments were profound and exciting (Tuttle and King, 2008).

However, what then seemed admirable scientific caution, in terms of carrying out necessary basic research in advance of real-world applications, has since degenerated into what can only be called alarmist foot-dragging. The early promise of this revolution in scientific understanding has faltered due to what the present author suggests are roadblocks deliberately set in place by extremists (Zanetti, 2010; Mackey and Terwillegar, 2012; U.N. Review Committee, 2012).

In a nutshell, the original 20-year partnership between the Department of Homeland Security and the Department of Interior for the study of temporal transfer is in shambles, and is due for a shake-up, preferably a complete overhaul.

While this is not the first time that calls have been made for necessary changes (King and Styce, 2020; Styce and Granger, 2022), the present study provides real-world research support that was previously lacking. As a result of the findings detailed below, it is suggested that we can fast-track forward with improved experimental design, and proceed – finally – to reap the real-world benefits of the temporal transfer revolution, for the improved defense of our nation in an uncertain world.

…(report continues)

Conclusions

The success of this apparently "high-risk" study, while it required actions personally repugnant to the present author, calls into question the continued funding of the present "more research needed" approach favored by the Homeland-Interior Liaison Office. A shift in research focus is called for, toward real-world temporal transfer actions in support of our national defense, and away from the woefully outmoded "impact study" approach.

The present focus of temporal transfer research on support of tourism in our national parks (best exemplified at the Ten Thousand Secrets Casino Park) is a shockingly unconscionable misuse of our private and public funds. Our nation's business interests deserve better.

[1]*Professor King holds the Endowed Chair of Business Biology, GOBI (Global Online Business Institute), Dartmouth College. He is the principal investigator (p.i.) of the project detailed in this report.*

TOP SECRET – CONFIDENTIAL
NOT FOR PUBLICATION
EMBARGOED UNTIL FURTHER NOTICE

With King's report in hand, Ed Zanetti called Congresswoman Holm.

When she snapped, "What now, Ed?" he asked, "Anna, have you read Cat King's top-secret research report, came out about three months back?"

She sighed, replying, "That psycho in Ph.D. clothing has gone too far this time, Ed, but he sure has powerful supporters."

Zanetti set down the report and continued, "It was so way out of line that I ignored it," shaking his head ruefully, having underestimated the opposition yet again. "But I've just had a worrisome little visit here from Senator Styce and his creature Sprinkle."

"About?" asked Holm, her internal alarm going off.

"They told me that King's report justifies trashing our research program. Well, that's not what they really said, you know Harlan – he said 'It's time to pull the effing plug.'" Ed heard Holm turn away to speak to her assistant.

"Ed, can you get over here, please," she said. "I am learning that General Granger has been let off the leash to seek immediate emergency funding for a top-secret project. We'll know more by the time you get here, and we'll have to strategize our response."

28

He was already out the door, healthy lunch abandoned on his desk.

Styce and Sprinkle ducked into an empty room as the call connected them to the personnel office.

"Hello, Dan?" barked Senator Styce. "I want to know about Steve Roberts in the Homeland-Interior Liaison office, works with Ed Zanetti." Sprinkle enabled the phone's speaker, and personnel expert Dan Weintraub's dusty drone filled the air.

"...an unusual hire, with top security clearance. With his background I guaran-damn-tee you he wouldn't get hired today."

"What are the irregularities in his file?" asked Styce, giving a thumbs-up to Sprinkle.

"The guy was educated and trained outside our system, and didn't come inside until he was 30. We watched him really close for a long time. But his work record and loyalty indicators and biometrics are flawless." Weintraub paused, scrolling through Steve's record.

Styce said, "I don't give a damn about how good he is, Dan, I want some dirt on the guy."

Weintraub now knew what was wanted, and replied enthusiastically, "Oh sir, sure, in that case, I can say that you got to wonder about a black guy who was an explorer. You know?" He pronounced "explorer" like it smelled bad.

"Right?" said the Senator, encouragingly. Weintraub became downright chatty.

"Sure, he has university degrees and a stable employment record, but he came to us as a wild-eyed nature guy, a lowly park ranger. A lot of eyebrows were raised when Zanetti set him up to be the interagency liaison for park science! Nobody with a big empty spot of five years on his early work record should have the security clearance he's got in the temporal transfer project." Weintraub paused for breath and took a gulp of water. Character assassination is painstaking work, up close and personal with a top Senator like Styce.

The Senator said, "You meant to tell me that before he came to Homeland-Interior, he was *record-free* for five years?" Styce was practiced at injecting synthetic outrage into his public voice.

"Yes sir," said Weintraub, happy at being able to please the man who everyone said would control the country after the coming election.

"Roberts has a five-year gap in his security record from age 20 to 25. Our notes state, "He describes this period as 'devoted to exploration.'" This worried people at the time, sir. Of course," he added with a butt-covering eye for detail, "his record has been flawless since."

"I'd say he is a security risk, for all we know a damn cell-nurtured terrorist mole, waiting for his moment," responded Styce, adding, "Nobody knows where he was for five whole years?"

"Well, said Weintraub, "Not *exactly*. I mean, there's a list of his exploration activities, and a list of grants and publications. "'Cave exploration, mapping,' six months here and there." His voice trailed off as he was drawn into Roberts's youthful adventuring. Styce jerked him back.

"Zanetti hired this guy?" he boomed.

"Yes, his present supervisor, Ed Zanetti, sir." Weintraub scrambled around in Steve's records, and continued.

"He was Zanetti's first big hire. I was new then, but I remember people saying it wasn't smart for him to bring in such an unconventional guy, not trained up in the system. He graduated from Kentucky State University, for heaven's sake." Weintraub drew breath, and injected, "But he's worked out sir, you gotta say that. Not a single negative mark in behavior, attitude, loyalty, or personal biometrics."

"Well, that's unnatural," growled Styce, muting the phone to direct Sprinkle to get the *Daily Media's* security affairs reporter lined up for a quiet chat. He turned back to Weintraub.

"I've heard enough to disgust and shock me, Dan," he intoned, "and I can't thank you enough for helping me set the record straight to unmask this unstable menace in our midst. And to think that Ed Zanetti is behind it." He ended the call at this verbal climax, rose to his feet and in gleeful high spirits slapped Sprinkle hard on the shoulder. Rubbing his shoulder, Sprinkle got the media site's security affairs reporter on the phone.

The Senator filled in this trusted mouthpiece with a subtly poisoned version of Steve's "worryingly unconventional work history...possibility he's unstable, unnaturally well behaved...not at all certain of his loyalty ...wondering about his religious affiliations..." The reporter said she'd call Ed Zanetti right away, and get to the bottom of this potentially disastrous security breach.

"Who knows what damage has already been done," she parroted back at Styce. "They need to get that guy out of top-secret access pronto, and subject him to de-programming immersion." The Senator nodded in satisfaction at this vicious swipe. He decided to throw the reporter a red-meat treat.

"Look," Styce said, lowering his voice to an intimate level, "the reason this is so important is because, well," pausing as if to consider if he really should be saying this.

"Yes?" the reporter bristled with attention.

"Well, once you've helped me get rid of this guy – oh yeah, and while you're at it, you'll need to question Ed Zanetti's trustworthiness – " Styce upped his demand, and the reporter went for the bait.

"No kidding! Zanetti has been harboring a criminal?" gasped the hooked fish.

Styce had what he wanted. He continued in a low, confiding tone.

"OK. Just for your ears. The top-secret program is moving into an aggressively pro-American phase, and I want you to be in on that story, OK?"

"Sir," said the reporter, her voice trembling with excitement, "does this have anything to do with General Granger's meeting today with the President?" For just a moment, a note of annoyance broke through Senator Harlan Styce's synthetically warm, confiding tone.

"Where'd you hear that?" he growled, but calmed down when the reporter stuttered apologies, fearful of losing the story. He ended the call on a high note.

"Well, I can't say anything more at this time, but if you help me clear the decks of these worrisome radicals, I'll be back with you in a day or two about that other thing." Styce handed the phone back to Sprinkle and they headed out for lunch.

Ten Thousand Secrets National Park Casino & Entertainment District, Kentucky.

Two days after the sabertooth incident.

I woke before dawn, alert and listening, lying perfectly still, tracing the irregular scritch-scratch sound to the wall outside my bathroom window. My pulse eased as I pieced together waking to thunder, rain in the gutter, pine branches tapping. The soft glow of the living room night-light showed nothing amiss. Easing out of bed, I made a security round, checking the shower, the pantry, leaning my ear against the front door, listening for intruders. All was quiet, and the storm's rumbles moved away. I fixed coffee and took a cup back to bed, leaning on my pillow to think things over. Even with the excessive security, people here were a lot nicer, compared to the mind-killing Nevada situation.

Sipping my coffee, I looked at the boxes of books and remnants of my long-ago life as a mother and family member. Here were my college textbooks, and cookbooks – and the books my children and I had enjoyed together. I knew which boxes held our favorite fairy tales. Reading fairy tales is a good way to teach children to be careful in a dangerous world. Those old stories provide rules to follow, to remain safe in unsafe places.

But best to leave the boxes alone. I would not be staying here long enough to unpack. In Nevada, after Homeland's terrorism investigators were finished debriefing us, I didn't share much with the PTSD counselors who arrived to help survivors. I was done with emotions. Better to live a light, unexamined life. To float like a leaf down the stream.

There was a waterfall ahead, on that stream. This park's turn was coming, soon. Behind the happy family-fun facade, the place was a citadel of repugnant excess and thrill-seeking. The massive casino and entertainment zones were everything that is worst in America today. Love of nature replaced by money-worship. And this park's remaining natural areas were now open for development by the energy industry. So, the end here was a matter of time, a few months at most. What if I survived this second attack? These boxes, all my stuff, were just memories, easily abandoned if I lived to flee.

I got a second cup of coffee, resting for another five minutes. It was smart, closing off my ties to other human beings. Easier, to let all that go. A year ago I had been full of misery and guilt over how I had parted from my two grown children, without another word or message after letting them know I had survived the blast. Now I was grateful. They had good lives and were better off without me. I sipped coffee as daylight peeked in between the closed curtains. I heard birds sleepily call to one another.

Thanks to the caffeine and sunlight, positivity powered me into the office, smiling, striding past Ada toward my new cubicle in Administration. No more greeting visitors – now I could figure out how this park worked, find its weak points.

Ada called, "Can you go in to see Steve Roberts, in Sonny's office? They need to debrief you about that critter," just as I settled into the visitor-view console chair. Before the headset could wrap its clammy tendrils around my head, I said, "Cancel," and the biomachine backed off. I headed down the hall toward my work supervisor's office.

"Hey, slow down, lookin' eager makes the rest of us look bad," Ada called teasingly. I smiled in her direction while the office access-scanner checked my security level, and the door opened. A camera blinked from the far corner of the room. My movements and mood ebbed as my free will dropped another 5 percent, ensuring the security of my superiors. I had a smile in place and met Steve's gaze as he rose from his seat.

"Hello," he said, shaking my hand (when he let go, my arm fell heavily to my side). I was distracted by the room. Its curving wall of glass, tinted to invisibility, gave me the sensation of being in a treehouse high in the oak forest. A piped-in breeze toppled me into a state of relaxation.

With a shrug and a smile, Steve said, "Sorry, but for this formal process I had to raise the security." I fell into the chair he indicated, trying to marshal my wiliness.

He said, "For this meeting I'm wearing my Region III Administrative office hat. We need to formally review our shared understanding of the cat incident. Could you summarize the situation for me?" The camera twinkled, green leaves moved lazily outside. I replied in Summary Mode, instilled during the new employees training and conditioning.

"The event took place from about 7 p.m. to 2 a.m. on August twentieth and twenty-first." I droned a dry summary, nearly identical to what I had told the security officers. Steve perked up when I mentioned the staircase to the Casino's basement.

"Did you drive the cat toward that doorway?"

"No," I replied, "you and I followed it there."

"Who opened the basement door?"

I replied, "It was open when we arrived. We saw the animal's tail in the lamplight."

"You never saw it again after that?"

"That is correct. It went into the basement ahead of us."

"Well," he sighed, "this is very strange. What's your opinion?"

That final word was a bio-release prompt for my "freely held opinion," (protected, they assured us, by an employee shield law).

I said, "My first point. I think there should be lights in that basement." At this, he smiled. It was a warm, amused smile – as though he knew a lot about the lack of lights in that basement.

"OK," he said, "what else?"

"My second point. I think the animal could easily be trapped and removed, if they take in a team with a diagram of the basement – and lights." His smile widened. He settled back in his seat, apparently looking forward to more of my amusing inanities. We exchanged glances, mine a glare.

He said, encouragingly, raising his eyebrows, "Yes?"

I said, "I am hesitating to express opinion point three, because it is not strictly related to the incident."

"Heck," he said, patting my knee (and violating many regulations), "out with it."

"Point three. I think you are getting undue enjoyment from my opinion points one and two."

He laughed, shaking his head, and said, "Thanks, that's fine. You get out of here and stop talking like a robot. That will be all."

At that release prompt I rose, gave him, the trees, and the camera a willful glance, and left through the opening door. Ada glanced up as I nodded my head toward the bathroom. To its couch. I stretched out to close my eyes and re-order my breathing and heart rate. Much improved after ten minutes, I emerged and accepted the coiled embrace of the visitors view console.

I put in a solid shift of visitor tracking, filing, and follow-up. During the day, Steve passed my cubicle several times in the company of administrative and security personnel. Once, he stopped in the hall to chat to his companion, and when I glanced up he gave me a slow, green-eyed wink. I closed my eyes and sank into the monitoring flow, shutting out him, them, all of it.

At day's end I was weary, but knew that the system was making better use of my strengths and experience. In return, I was learning how this park worked, for my own little project. Pausing for electronic permission, I walked tiredly out the door, past the turnoff to my place, and down the path to the river among towering sycamore trees. The cicadas buzzed, and the odor of cool water and green plants drew me toward the shore.

Walking past the pay benches with their Streams of Time hookups, I leaned against the railing of the plastiwood deck, the closest I could get to the Green, Green River without exceeding safe behaviors limits. I sat on the free bench and closed my eyes, listening to the trees whispering overhead.

Rested, I looked across the river to the far shore. A shimmering mist enveloped the shoreline. It rose fifty feet, and glowed deep below the water's surface. Through the sparkling mist, I could faintly make out trees and other vegetation.

I was looking at Pleistocene Place, the Park's biggest non-casino attraction. Touted as a "100% authentic re-creation of our not-so-distant-past," this amusement park "experience" was another new venture for the Park Service. As I watched, a dark rectangle appeared in the mist on the far bank. Children and adults, led by Pleistocene Place Rangers, filed through the shimmering doorway and down to a ferryboat, deep in the shade of late afternoon. The trailing ranger cast off and the boat crossed to the landing on my side of the river. The passengers were headed back to their Pleasure Dome hotels. The Pleistocene Place Package cost a bundle – it was a special event, to see lifelike woolly mammoths and sabertooth tigers, up close and personal.

Lunch-table gossips maintained that Pleistocene Place was the real past, not a constructed theme park attraction. That was ridiculous. On the other hand, how was it possible that a live sabertooth cat was on the loose? A high, shimmering fence encircled Pleistocene Place, enclosing most of the park's northern section. Sensors and cameras monitored the fenceline for trespassers. I rose and walked uphill toward my apartment, keeping my eyes open for a fast-moving sabertooth cat, relieved when I was safely inside.

Near the Pennsylvania border, south of Corning, New York.

A few months earlier.

Beyond the tunnel, Brian followed the green road along the edge of a small creek. On the other bank lay a clearing, with a cottage and neat gardens. The cottage door opened, and a neatly clothed male figure emerged and walked toward Brian.

Crossing the creek on a small bridge, he called out, "Well met, well met, Brian Owen." The man was no taller than the little lady in her hilltop cottage. He smiled pleasantly. As they shook hands, Brian noticed a flicker of movement behind his legs – and saw the tip of a black furry tail.

Not wanting to be rude, Brian looked into the man's eyes and smiled, saying, "Folks along this road seem to know I'm coming!"

"Oh yes, oh yes," the man replied, nodding. "We are all so grateful for the help you have given us. Did you see the road signs? The roundabout? The parking area? The beautiful glowing red signs, making our old gateway look so modern?"

"Yes, it looks great," Brian replied. "But I have been wondering why there are no indications of construction – you just finished all this, right?" He had seen no newly seeded areas, no naked berms or leafless, newly planted young trees. The brand-new improvements seemed to have been in place forever.

"Oh, Brian Owen, we have our own ways of doing things, you must know that by now!" the old gent replied cheerily. Brian again saw a black tail curling behind him. They walked together on the green road.

"You are making a fine pace, such a fit young man, full of flesh, you will get to the Inn right on time," the man said, waving his hand at the hill ahead. "As Vice President of the Board of Directors, I do have one small request to make of you." They turned to face one another as he continued.

"Please stay on the green road – do not go off it. We have fixed only what you see along the path – we don't want to spoil your visit with unpleasant sights and sensations."

"Fine with me," Brian said. Now aware of the old gentleman's stature, he added, "Maybe I can help you get funding for further improvements."

"Yes, yes," the small man said, standing still as Brian resumed walking. "We are thinking of a loop road, a loop road. But for now, just stay on this road, go straight at the crossroads, and come back exactly this way, before dark." He bowed. Brian bowed back, and began to turn away.

But his imagination spoke up: "Don't turn your back on him." Long-ago advice from his mother's collection of fairy tales reminded him that you don't turn your back on them. On *fairies*. Brian froze between turning away and not wanting to offend this mild, sweet gentleman – Vice President of the group he worked for! The old gent stood still, making shooing gestures, encouraging Brian to turn and go.

The accumulated strangeness of the past half-hour was taking a toll on Brian's common sense. Abandoning rationalism for survival, he remembered from his treasure trove of useless lore that fairies don't like iron. Backing away from the old gentleman, both smiling, Brian dug in his pocket for the miniature iron railroad tie on his keychain. As soon as he grasped it, the old gent bent over as though he had been punched in the stomach – and turned and ran for his cottage. His beautiful black fluffy tail streamed out behind him.

"Yep, he has a tail," Brian thought, as the cottage door slammed. He walked fast along the green road, the creek burbling on the right.

"OK," Brian fumed, "what was that about, you stupid idiot? Offending the locals, trashing your chances for more paid work. So what if they have tails. No wonder they've kept to themselves. Clearly they need the able assistance of someone tolerant and kind, like me."

Inner-Brian piped up, "Look for two more challenges on the way to the Inn. Standard fairy tale rules."

Professional Brian replied: "Shut up with the fairy tales, you immature idiot." Silencing these warring extremes, he focused on the beauty around him, climbing the hill on the unspooling green road, trees ready to burst springtime buds. The purling of the creek washed away the weird murmurs. Brian tamped down a stray worry that Maeve might have a tail…and enjoyed the sunshine on his face.

On this late-winter day, a snow shower sparkled in chilly sunshine. He heard a baby crying as bare branches rattled in the cold breeze. The crying continued, closer now, so Brian stepped up his pace. At the top of the rise, the path curved, the baby-wailing louder. Rounding the curve, he saw a crossroads in the woods. There stood a new sign, reading Hollymount Road & Inn ahead, Apple Island Trace to the left. The right-hand path was unnamed. At the intersection lay a small gleaming white bundle. The wailing was coming from that bundle, lit by passing sunlight for a moment.

Brian slowed down, looking for someone, anyone. How could a baby be lying out here, alone in the cold? Had a parent stepped away for just a moment? He closed in on the wailing, writhing bundle, wondering what to do – carry a screaming baby along with him to the meeting? Surely he would be arrested for kidnapping. Down the unnamed trail on his right, Brian heard a woman's voice calling, wild with fear.

"Baby mine! My baby boy! Where are you?" The voice rose to a panicky scream, "Someone has taken my baby!" This heart-rending racket continued without pause. The gal was losing her mind in fear, and no doubt this bundle was what she sought. Brian stood over the crying baby and looked down the path, but the shouting woman was out of sight. It would be the work of a moment to pick up the baby and walk down the side trail toward her.

"Baby! My only child!" – and so on. She sounded quite close. He kneeled to pick up the baby and carry it to her. Stopping in mid-stoop, Brian remembered the old gent telling him to stay on the green road to Hollymount.

He puzzled it out: "Surely, this is an emergency – an exception? Anyway he didn't mean it seriously – he didn't say that I was 'forbidden' to go off the road – did he? Looked at from a common-sense point of view, what is the problem? What could go wrong if I walked a few hundred feet down the path?"

But – when Brian paused, the baby shut up. The woman's screaming stopped. Brian could not see the baby's face within the blanket bundle, and he decided to take a look. Turning back the blanket, Brian was met by a strange face. Wrinkled and hairy, like a piglet, its small ancient green eyes glared up at him above an upturned piggy nose. The ears – were pointed.

Brian heard running feet and bent down to protect the baby, while glancing up. Running toward him on the side path was an older woman in a bright pink tracksuit, with white sneakers on her feet. A weird sight, in those wintry woods! Brian leaned back. The old gal ran up and in a swoop picked up the now-silent baby and ran down Apple Island Trace, into the woods on the far side of the Hollymount Road.

Brian stood up slowly, grateful for the silence, feeling uneasy – and under observation. The murmurs had started up again. He began to jog, wondering what the heck was going on: "Was that fairyland challenge number two? Would they have trapped me if I had gone off the main path?"

Smelling wood smoke, Brian hoped he was getting close to the Inn. He needed normalcy, felt a little panicky. He fretted, "How have I hiked nearby for three years without encountering these people, with tails and wizened faces? How did this isolated community stay hidden, two miles from an interstate highway?"

The woods ended. Beyond lay winter fields, dotted with small cottages. In one field stood a small horse, a miniature variety. This looked normal – back-to-the-landers, ten acres, cabin, off the grid – though Brian did not see any solar panels. At the foot of a distant wooded hill, buildings lined the road. One was larger – the elusive Inn, he hoped. The beauty of this upland valley scene caught at Brian's senses, the golden light deepening the mild browns and pale blues of winter. The land gleamed with wisdom, speaking a language he did not understand.

"Where are all these wild thoughts coming from," Brian brooded as he walked. "I need to go out more. How can I get my career going, being an introvert? I gotta cut out the fantasy books and games. I'll be useless over lunch with Maeve and they'll never hire me again."

Walking fast, he watched the lazy arc of a crow overhead. It descended to the road, ten feet in front of Brian. The crow was two feet tall. With a strut to its walk and shining black eyes, it approached him, bowed, turned around, and walked alongside. Brian's heart thudded rapidly – this was surely challenge number three. He eyed the giant bird – would it attack him? As the two moved forward, Brian caught the gaze of his silent companion. The crow tilted its head and nodded in what Brian hoped was a friendly way.

Brian said, "Hello, I am Brian Owen, but maybe you already know that." The crow nodded in response, and they proceeded in silence. Nearer, the big wooden building had an Inn-like air about it, romance novel style. Its two storeys had curtained windows along both floors, and it was painted dark blue. Stone chimneys wafted pine-scented wood smoke. Two shapely trees framed wide steps up to a wooden door in the center of the rambling old building. Above the Inn loomed white pines and holly trees – tall, massive, twisted. There was no parking lot.

The crow darted into a nearby cottage garden and returned, in its beak a sprig of the small white flowers that speckled the fields and roadside. Fluttering off the ground, the bird hovered in front of Brian, placing the sprig carefully in his jacket pocket. Then it spiraled upward, cawing loudly in the cold air, and was gone. Brian did not watch, his eyes caught by the sign posted next to the big front door. Written in chalk, it read:

Hollymount Inn

Today's Lunch

Smoky broth

Roast viands

Ambrosia

Today's Special

Serving humans

Something was a bit off there, but Brian was hungry, and climbed the steps. The door swung open inward, and a beautiful woman stood in the doorway. Not red hair – black and soft, curling. Pale white skin, dark blue eyes, long black eyelashes. Wearing jeans, cowboy boots – and a green sweater a little bit unbuttoned at the top – she was smiling at Brian. No tail!

Chapter 3

A Capitol Hill office and nearby sports bar, Washington, D.C.

Two days after the sabertooth incident.

Ed Zanetti walked toward Congresswoman Anna Holm's Capitol Hill office, lunch to follow with Cat King at a sports bar near Union Station. Little had he suspected in their old Ohio State days that Deadhead Anna would end up in such dignified surroundings. Nowadays she was a solid, center-right Democrat representing a central Ohio district. His phone buzzed: a chum in the Homeland Liaison offices, three floors above his own Interior Liaison suite.

"Hey, how's the kids," Zanetti said breezily, but she snapped, "Sprinkle just dropped a job termination order on my desk, for your beloved Steve Roberts. And you're in trouble, too." He heard the echo in the ladies room as she spoke. A pulsing panic started up in his stomach, and he crossed the street against the traffic, ignoring the red flashing hand.

"I'll get back to you later," he replied, stashing his phone as he approached the security field enveloping Capitol Hill. He felt the familiar jolts as his bio-info was reviewed, free-will waiver approved. He strode toward the massive Rayburn Building. Congresswoman Holm was not smiling when her aide ushered Zanetti in, past a departing family of her Ohio constituents.

"Ed," she growled, "you chose a heck of a week to go time traveling."

"Please, Anna! Don't use that totally inaccurate term! 'Temporal transfer' is better. And it's a top-secret H-I project. Hush!"

"Ed, you can dress it up and disguise it, but the *Daily Media* reporter named it just now." She pressed buttons to ensure privacy and swiveled her chair to gaze directly at her greying college buddy. He stared back – she compact, non-glamorous – in silent surprise.

Holm continued, "Yes, they have a copy of King's report. They asked me if it is true that Interior is preventing the Department of Defense from moving forward with a major new superweapon."

Zanetti sank into his chair, his phone buzzing: that same reporter.

He killed the call and said, "What do you recommend that we do, Representative Holm?"

"Looks like they're trying to take your program away, Ed. As far as that reporter is concerned, time travel – "

"Temporal transfer!" Zanetti snapped.

"*What*ever, it now belongs to Senator Styce and General Granger for use in 'developing a new mega-weapon against our nation's enemies,'" Holm repeated, mimicking the reporter's girlish voice.

Zanetti looked at his watch and asked, "At the heart of this situation is Cat King. I'm scheduled to lunch with him – in ten minutes. Should I go?"

Holm's aide leaned in the door, saying, "The delegation from United Farm Companies is here, ma'am." Holm rose, reflexively smoothing her hair, adjusting her suit.

She replied to Zanetti's question, "Meet with him, don't agree to anything."

Zanetti headed out, calling back, "Where's my poison-taster when I need him?" He walked fast, head down, toward a cluster of nearby lunch places. Entering the sports bar, he brooded that jokes and anticipating next moves did not work with a guy like King.

"King cuts the legs out from under you and steps back to watch you fall," he thought as he spotted King watching him from the balcony above. Ed climbed the stairs to join him.

"Hello, my old friend," said Tom "Cat" King silkily, pulling out a chair. Zanetti sat, caught his breath, and gazed at the well-dressed, handsome man. Professor Thomas King, known to all as Cat, exuded the academic respectability that comes with occupying the Endowed Chair of Business Biology at the fabulously wealthy GOBI (Global Online Business Institute, housed at Dartmouth College).

"How do you find the time to look this good, Cat?" asked Zanetti, already in a losing mental battle between what he should eat and what he was going to eat. To the waiter, he pointed wordlessly at a gravy-smothered menu item. "With house salad, no dressing," he added penitently.

King crinkled his eyes in amusement and replied, "I'm in fighting shape, Ed. This – " patting tailored lapels, subtly turquoise tie – "is illusion, camouflage." He paused to sip tea, then continued, "You've been away, Ed – not a wise thing to do when so much is afoot. Others can get the better of you. When you go away like that." He smiled sweetly at his prey as the waiter brought salads.

"I was, if you must know, in 1910 Pasadena, a better time and place than this," Zanetti replied with spirit as he poked at the freshly shaved curls of pure lettuce ("the best vat-cured produce for our nation's leaders," read the trendy menu).

"Oh, Ed, that's just – sad," sighed King. "I don't know why you continue to play in that sandbox, while we pass you by." He finished his salad, but Zanetti could not take another bite of his ("Gorgeous globules of midsummer tomato essence, year-round!" promised the menu).

"About your report – " Zanetti said, trying to retain control of the conversation.

King kicked this aside. "My report, as you call it, has moved ahead to become big-bucks policy, Ed, while you were dreaming your dead dreams in a dead place." He leaned in closer as Ed snagged down forkfuls of gravy-swathed, organic, fat-free, "vat-raised pure beef," fortifying himself with great big calories as the fight arrived.

King whispered, "You'll get official notice this afternoon, Ed. It is my pleasure to tell you personally that your lackluster career is over, buried, gone." He leaned back, a tight smile on his face.

"How's that, exactly?" asked Zanetti, pushing back his plate, wiping his mouth, shooting his cuffs, and placing his feet firmly beneath him, anticipating a fight. King was, to put it nicely, more physical than the average professor.

Braced for action, Zanetti continued, "Murder pays, huh? And you kept it in the family!" That felt good. Even in this isolated corner, their decibel level was rising and the waiters took note worriedly. No D.C. restaurant was ever happy to see Cat King.

"How dare you," hissed King from across the condiment bottles, close enough for Zanetti to feel the heat of the man's rapidly uncorking temper.

King's voice rose to a near-shout, "I have personally and permanently sacrificed my mental serenity in service to my country, unlike you freeloading wackos. You think I'm proud of what I did?" He was standing, face pale, tie askew. Zanetti realized a bit late the pressure the guy must be under, and raised his hands to placate him.

"Shh...calm down, Cat," he said, but rage had overtaken the professor, yet again. King slammed back his chair, stalked around the table and stood over Zanetti, kicking at his chair legs to force him up.

"I killed for my country! We're in a global war! What have you done lately, you pansy-assed snowflake?" he cried, grabbing Zanetti's tie by the knot, dragging him close. The waiters headed over as other diners scattered. King saw them coming and collapsed into his chair, broad shoulders shaking, head in hands. Zanetti almost felt sorry for the guy, while wondering if his distress was fake.

King looked up and spoke, his voice strained but firm.

"Victory has its costs, Ed, you can see the proof here, in me." Shooting Zanetti a malignant glare, King went on, "We're finally getting rid of you assholes, and your do-nothing cowardice that is sapping our country's strength. Thank God for this day." He turned his head aside, saying, "Now get the hell away from me."

Zanetti knew he had better not say another word, got up, and walked away. He waved his phone at the front desk and emerged into the sticky D.C. air.

Time for a private meeting with Steve Roberts, he thought. He had hired Steve, and they were friends. Over the past twenty years, as increasingly vicious right-wing administrations gutted the nation's environmental protection laws, they had come to think of themselves as co-conspirators. Zanetti fought to protect standards and procedures via bureaucratic swordsmanship, and Roberts fought to protect the southeastern federal parks via science. But in the face of continuous, unrelenting political pressure, they were both losing badly.

Ten Thousand Secrets National Park Casino & Entertainment District, Kentucky.

The ancient land-line telephone in my living room was ringing at midnight. Alarmed awake, I listened to the shrilling menace until the voice message took over.

"Janet, please answer, we have a special assignment for you and need to arrange it now." I ran for the phone at the sound of my supervisor's voice.

"Sir!" I said.

"Jeeze, Janet, where were you?" Sonny Scott grumbled.

"Sleeping?" I offered, adding, "How may I help you?"

"A team is headed across the river at dawn to investigate that big cat. We can't have sabertooth cats loose in our park, you know?"

"No sir, not at all," I replied, still shaken by the ringing phone.

"I mean, think if a kid gets eaten. They just filled me in on all this and I gotta say, it scares me. Don't you go out after dark, OK? I guess we ought to notify park staff, but that might scare them worse. I'll have to think about that." Scott tended to ramble. I made a sympathetic noise and he returned to the topic.

"OK, so, our Parks Science guy, Steve Roberts, is headed there with a team, and they want you on it, because you have personal experience and he said you did a good job. With me?"

"Sure," I said glumly.

"Sure, you BET," he said. "Be at the Pleistocene Place check-in at 8 a.m. We'll have everything you need – food, clothes, boots, hat, protective gear."

"I'll be there," I sighed.

"C'mon, this is great, you'll see something people pay big money for. I haven't been over there yet. You're in luck. And bring a heavy coat and gloves. So cheer up! Win-win!" I hung up and crept back to bed, dismayed at having my routine disturbed. But maybe I would learn something useful for completing my mission here.

Come morning, I was buzzed and jolted through multiple bio-reviews on entering the Pleistocene Place building. Unremarkable in appearance, it lay low in the woods, in contrast to the disgusting Casino-Secrets Lifestyle Complex that whooped and hollered and flashed a mile distant.

Steve Roberts stood waiting for me in the lobby, along with a park ranger named Pete, and two burly security guys.

"Here I am, ready or not," I offered, wishing I'd had one more cup of coffee. Steve was professional and crisp in khaki pants, hiking boots and a heavy blue rain and snow jacket, way too heavy for the mild Kentucky weather. He smiled and said, "Sorry if we interfered with your morning routine, but we'll have a good time today."

"I haven't been there before, so I'm excited!" said Pete. He had shed his ranger hat for a wool cap, and was carrying a heavy coat under his arm.

"Well, I'm fucking not," said one of the green-clad security guys to Pete, not caring that we heard him. Steve smiled, and led the way to a covered courtyard where we signed and thumb-printed our lives away on electronic documents at the check-in. Squashed into my heavy winter uniform and wool hat, I followed the others through a germ irradiation room, got personal containers of lunch and water, and walked across a footwear sterilizer. Why this mumbo-jumbo for an amusement park ride? Why no coffee? Yes, I was grumpy.

The boat moved silently across the Green, Green River in the early morning light. Water rippled melodiously, and a heron skimmed the morning river.

"The others went over earlier, and we'll meet them about a mile north," Steve said. "They're seeking the pathway the big cat used to cross the river. We'll contribute our considerable brain-power."

"But it can't cross the river, like by swimming or on a log," said Pete. "The time barrier stops all that. Right?"

"Time barrier." What did he mean? We were halfway across the river when I felt an electric shock, a wave of nausea. I saw that the others were feeling it too, heads down, swallowing hard. No one spoke. The terrible feeling eased as the boat pulled up along the riverbank.

Steve replied, "That's right, Pete. Nothing gets through the barrier except right here, and even then it feels rough."

"I never get used to it," said the youngest security guy, shuddering, as we climbed the bank. We stood on the edge of a grassy plain stretching toward low stony hills. It was bitter cold, and the sky was grey, with an icy drizzle falling. My eyes sought the illusion's edge, finding none. Was it a domed projection? How did they keep it cold? The guards stood watchful as Steve, Pete and I donned packs.

"Somehow the critter is bypassing the river. Maybe it found a hole in the ground," Steve continued.

Pete asked, "You mean – it's going under the time barrier?" Mystified by their exchange and the enormity of the amusement park illusion, I followed the group, walking north toward the hills. Steve shot me a quick look and dropped behind to walk next to me.

"Welcome to ten thousand years ago," he said quietly. I stared around as he nodded slowly.

"She get it now?" asked the guard behind us.

Steve said to me, "The others are acclimated and know what to expect. Stay between the guards at all times. It's the same day every trip, but we have safety procedures. You're under-trained, but you'll be fine. Oh, I almost forgot." He poked around in his pack and handed me an In the Woods Waste Disposal Unit, which I tucked into my pack with a shaky smile.

"I was wondering about that," I managed, over tumultuous thoughts. Although this was marketed to tourists as a fake, theme park experience, we were in the actual, real, Pleistocene Epoch. I stopped to catch my breath, tamping down a swell of panic mixed with excitement.

As Steve moved forward to lead, he said, "This is the Park's second-biggest secret. And, you have security clearance as of now." The cold began to bite – I was shivering, agitated, breathless. Time travel? I looked back the way we had come, but saw only the grey level ground, and rainclouds advancing. Could I run back to the boat and wait for them there? The guard at the back glared at me knowingly. I turned and followed Steve.

We dropped into a shallow valley, slopes covered in long grass. An enormous bird drifted overhead in the grey sky, then another. This was no bird from my world. I thought I might faint from its strangeness. But then wonder took hold of me. A new world! I watched as giant leathery birds descended and disappeared from view below the ridge.

"There's the first teratorns," whispered the guard behind me, "and something for them to eat nearby. Be real quiet." We picked up the pace. I heard unpleasant noises – ripping and tearing, grunting and chomping – beyond willowy shrubs. The sounds died away, and a river came into view.

"That's the Green, Green River," Steve explained as we scrambled down the bank. The water was shallow and we waded across – icy cold through my boots – toward a group of people on the far bank.

"But we just crossed it back there in the boat – " I said.

He smiled, replying, "In our day, yes, but today here, it flows in a channel further north." A limestone cliff rose above the river, and at its base people were gathered.

"OK, watch for teratorns," whispered the guard up front. Suddenly above us were more monstrous birds – two, then four, then six. Small airplanes, they zoomed overhead and vanished over the brow of the cliff. We stopped to watch. I wanted to follow the birds. Where were they going? What lay beyond the cliff?

"Gets me every time," said the guard behind me, as we walked toward the group.

I was confused, and asked him, "How did he know they were coming over, right then?"

The guard asked, "Didn't you get the training?"

"No, I was added to this team at midnight. What am I missing?"

"Well, ask somebody else about it, not me. You shouldn't even be here. I'm not a damn babysitter." He glared, waiting on me so he could bring up the rear. I looked ahead at the people. They were standing around a hole in the base of the cliff, from which a small stream flowed to the river. Above them, a stone roof jutted out from the cliff, providing scant shelter from the bitterly cold rain.

"What's that hole?" I asked Pete.

The grumpy guard heard me and said loudly, "Lady doesn't know a cave when she sees one." OK, a cave. As we walked up, Steve was speaking with a woman wearing a Park uniform and overcoat. Two

Security staff, a man and woman, wore Casino guard outfits and sported weapons – the free-will reduction models, plus semi-automatic rifle capacity. The guards who came with us cradled their weapons.

A man in a wet-weather suit scrambled out of the cave, switching off his headlamp as he emerged. Behind him was a young woman, and I stood frozen in silent shock. The young woman was my – it was Lena.

Wondering again if I could get back to the boat dock before she saw me, I grabbed Pete's arm, gasping, "I'm – " as he looked at me with concern.

The group turned toward me as Steve said to me, "Hey, Janet, our new staffer here says she knows you! Come get introduced!" Lena stared at me anxiously.

"Lena!" I said, "the last time I saw you was – "

"In Denver!" she replied, giving a clue as to how I knew her.

"It's been a long time – you're – older!" I said at random, shaking her hand, looking her over with joy and fear. I had sworn to never again cause trouble for her or her brother. It had been over a year. Yet here she was, smiling, fresh and sturdy, happy to see me.

Steve said to the group, "I brought Janet along today because she helped me chase the cat through the Park. She doesn't scare easily and has years of field experience, so I figured we could use her help." They all smiled, except "my" guard, who looked down, shaking his head.

Lena stood near me. As the others conferred about the cave, I learned a few things, as co-workers getting re-acquainted.

"So," I said, holding back a big smile, happiness welling inside, "you went in there?" I motioned toward the cave entrance. She had liked caves since she was a small girl.

"Yes," she said, looking down to conceal her own smile, squeezing my hand for a moment, "I started this job last Monday. I was in the lab until today."

She rushed on, "I'm living with the other part-time staff in the dorm on the other side of the Casino from where the regular workers live. I guess that's where you are?" I nodded, worried. Had she come to this park seeking me? That would be so unfortunate. She had to go away soon.

"So, what's in there, guys?" asked Steve. He stared into the cave entrance. "Wow," he said, "it is wonderful to escape from D.C. for a couple of days. Think we really need to find this cat any time soon?" We all laughed, and I relaxed a bit.

"It sure smells like cat," said the woman in charge. "We haven't gone in very far – leaving that for you cave experts." She was, I learned later, a top biologist, Hannah Ward. The guy in the wet-weather outfit was the park's cave scientist, Hugh Hynes. Adjusting his helmet, Steve stepped into the cave.

"We can't allow you to go in unarmed, sir," said "my" guard. All four guards stood in a ring around our group.

"I'm just having a glance around," said Steve. "Lena, what did you see in there?"

She replied, "I got video," showing on her phone a stone-lined passageway. "That drops down steeply about fifty feet, then south – under the river. I didn't go far. I felt a good breeze – I bet it goes." Steve was eagerly taking in the screen images.

"Ma'am, you were breaking some serious federal rules by going in that far," said "my" guard to Lena. I realized we had two groups here, the guards watching the rest of us closely. They were armed, we were not. I had assumed the weapons were for use against a sabertooth cat, but began to wonder.

Steve asked the assertive guard, "Lee, what are these rules?" and continued in a mild tone, "I thought I knew the rules, having written them."

"We don't want any trouble here," replied Lee. "We have our own rules and you are breaking them. Can you get away from that hole." Steve stayed where he was.

Hannah Ward said to the guards, "We have to find out if this is where the sabertooth is getting under the river, and into the Park, endangering our park guests."

"That's enough for today," said Lee, evidently the security group's leader.

"Wow, what an asshole," I thought.

"We don't want any trouble," he repeated.

"What do you mean, 'trouble,'" I burst out. "These are top scientists!"

"You, lady, especially, shut the fuck up," he said, and actually pointed the free-will gun at me. Lena stepped toward me, and I put out my arm to stop her.

Steve said, "OK, calm down, that's enough. We'll talk this out when we're back across the river." He backed away, recording images of the river and cave site on his hand-held device.

"This cave hadn't shown up on our maps," he said, as the tension dropped a small amount. "How did you find it?"

Hugh Hynes replied, "Aren't smart young interns great? Lena spotted this area on the map on her second day at work. We had totally overlooked it." Lena smiled at me shyly as we waded back across the river and onto the grassy plain. The guards ambled outside the group, weapons ready.

I whispered to Pete, "What are we, prisoners?"

He kept his head down, replying, "Shhh...this is a new development. Take it easy." I tromped back across the tussocks and soggy grassland next to Lena, feeling the gun at my back. The guard named Lee seemed to take me as a personal insult. Not good to be singled out, noticed.

Steve glanced at his watch and put out his hand to stop us. We stood waiting, the others looking to the left. Into view came wild horses. Small! Twenty or more, brown and grey and black, they ran past, manes flashing in a gleam of sun that appeared late in the afternoon. As their hoofbeats drummed away, we stepped forward toward the shimmering riverbank, now visible ahead. Lena – *Lena!* – was crunching along next to me.

I asked her, "Why did he look at his watch?"

"It's the same day here every day."

"Say again?"

"They control the time settings from the Park headquarters building."

I said, "Lower your voice – I don't think I'm supposed to know that."

She leaned in and went on, "Every morning, they re-set time here to the morning of the same day. That avoids environmental impacts, makes a predictable routine, and the place is fresh every day for visitors."

"So the same things happen here every day?" I asked, with a feeling of delicious horror.

"Creepy, huh?" she whispered, and we broke off to walk through the doorway, Lee at our heels. Once we were on the boat, I looked back through the thickening mist at a cold, rainy afternoon thousands of years in the past.

On the far side of the time barrier, we re-entered Kentucky heat and peeled off our winter clothes. The boat docked and we trudged up the path into Pleistocene Place. Past the decontamination rooms, we put away our gear as Steve spoke to the group.

"We learned a lot today, but not enough." He looked at the Casino guards.

Lee replied, "We'll make a full report about the serious infractions we observed in the field today. It's a new day for this program, and you folks" – he looked at me – "have to clean up your act. No more amateurs and no playin' around." I turned away to hide my anger.

Steve directed his voice, quiet and firm, to our group. "I have to talk to the D.C. office and see if I can sort this out. We'll plan our next steps soon. You did great today, everybody – we've got a good group here. Remember, lips zipped." Outside, Steve walked quickly away, talking on his phone.

Lena planted herself in front of me and said, "It was great to get re-acquainted, Janet," making no move to walk toward the science offices. I had to drive her away; I must not encourage her friendliness or draw attention to the two of us. Her safety depended on it. But I was feeling weak and tired, dazed by the day's revelations.

I said, "You need to get back to work, and so do I. But I'm sure we'll be spending more time together soon." So we parted, with a quick hug, that first day when my daughter found me. I watched her walk jauntily away.

My feet ached and my knees did not want to bend, and I was of little use in the console chair that afternoon. By the time I got back to my apartment my mood was bleak. I did not skimp on the security routine, and knew that I would have to upgrade it because the Casino guards had their eyes on me. But not tonight.

Flooded with hopelessness I stared tiredly at the kitchen table, walls and windows. How could I reach my goal here, with human entanglements wrapping tentacles around me? The child I had left for her own safety had found me. I was being drawn into a friendly work group. I had been singled out as a troublemaker. As for the reality of time travel, I had to sleep on it. Creeping into bed, I hoped that rest would restore my sense of purpose.

I slept well and woke happy. Mental progress had been made, and I got ready for work filled with a strong, weird joy. Lena was here! I would see her today! My plan and goal were re-energized. I had been frittering away time, lured into relaxation and personal career advancement. Now, every moment must advance my personal goals here at Ten Thousand Secrets National Park Casino & Entertainment District.

Brushing my teeth, I stared into the mirror, wondering how to get Lena to leave for her own safety. But not today. I put treats in my bag to share with her, and walked through the woods into the bright morning, suddenly remembering the strangeness of real time travel. Its presence here explained the high security – but why was it a secret? Why didn't they share this wonderful news with everyone on Earth?

The big parking lots surrounding the Casino and Family Secrets Pleasure Dome & Hotel were already crowded. I crossed the road after five golden tour buses rumbled past, and headed into the Administration offices. I settled into the visitor-view console chair for a monitoring session.

After my morning break, Ada said, "Janet, come in here, we're making travel arrangements for you." At these words my heart began to pound. What was this fresh hell? I walked from the dark hallway into Ada's light-filled office.

She said, "You look worn out – sit down at once," so I sat, raising my eyebrows questioningly.

"It's that cat thing, they want you to report to the Midwest office," she said briskly, working the desk screen. "Day after tomorrow, the 7 a.m. flight out of Buchanon Memorial," the airport down on the flats south of the Park.

"Do I have to?" I asked, whining like a child.

"Yes, you have to," Ada whined back at me, smiling. "They have some new gizmo for recovering memories that they want you to sit through. It's no big deal." She poked at her screen, oblivious to my rising terror. "Takes about five minutes, plus some questions. The tickets are on your phone."

I walked back across the hall to my desk, where the tendrils of my chair beckoned. "Memory recovery?" What else might it reveal, about my plans for this park? Best to meet it head on. Best to get some work done now.

Ada leaned around the doorway to add, "Looks like Steve Roberts will be there to meet you. He says," she read from her screen, "'what a waste of taxpayer money and valuable staff time.'" She snorted and went back to work.

I plunged into the embrace of the monitoring chair and spent two hours at the screens, handling the ebb and flow of human movement around the Park's Casino & Pleasure Domes complex. Today I was assigned to the inter-hotel riverboat traffic zone. On my screen at the main Casino landing, a group of grey dots moved onto a yellow boat-shape, forming neat lines as passengers took their seats. One dot, surely a child, roamed briefly before settling. Green dots of Park personnel took position, with purple-dot Guards at bow and stern.

On my screen, the boat-shape moved across the Casino lobby and into the river tunnel, becoming a winking silver-outlined image containing the numbers of passengers, Park personnel, and Guards. As the boat emerged a half-mile downstream at the Top Secrets Pleasure Dome & Spylands Hotel, the passenger numbers on the screen were updated, identical to when it entered the tunnel.

This real-time complexity was a change from my lone-wolf water science work at Nevada. Although I'd worried that my middle-aged brain couldn't handle the multi-tasking, I actually was good at this stuff, the system promoting me to more complex flow management tasks as my skills improved. Across succeeding screens, boats moved along the Styx River loop route linking the Casino with the three Pleasure Domes and hotels, spanning five miles of the wooded Park.

I did not manage the grey dot humans, each with an identification link. Misbehaviors were handled by the Homeland Security end of the operation. If a dot flashed, indicating Aberrant Behavior (AB), I notified the Casino Guard office. On my daytime shift, ABs were rare, usually small children playing too close to the boat landings. Younger staff than

I enjoyed the night shift, when AB action rose. Nighttime ABs were intoxicated, taking swims in the river loop or climbing toward the gleaming domes far overhead. Of course there was no violence, ensured by the 10 percent free-will loss waiver required for all visitors, backed by the rights-reduction beams carried by Casino Guards.

A pink glow alerted me to the potential for delay at the landing farthest out on the loop route, at the Hush-Hush Pleasure Dome & No Name Hotel. A cloud of grey dots spilled out of the hotel toward the landing, as humans from those five golden tour buses entered the system. This crowd should have been anticipated. Seeing no extra boats indicated in the schedule, I called them up. Golden boat-shapes blinked onto the center screen as three empty, auto-piloted Raven Boats emerged from the Hotel's river garage and lined up behind the boat just departing the landing. Purple and green dots emerged from waterside offices.

With one eye ensuring that grey dots took seats, and that green and purple dots were in place, I made the required 15-minute checkup of all the landing areas. They were smoothly absorbing the stream of late-morning arrivals. Another visitor surge would come in late afternoon, not fun when I was tired.

Right now it was time for lunch and to see Lena. I handed off to another observer, grabbed my bag, and stepped into the light of day. But I did not see Lena in the cafeteria, as I waited there for her with my pile of photographs and mementos. I had another cup of coffee and watched people in their laughing groups, feeling my sunny mood drain away.

"Foolish me," I thought. "Thinking she would want to have lunch with her old – with me." I sat out in the courtyard where employee paths met, but no Lena came by.

"Well, she's somewhere nearby, I'll see her soon." I tried that mental tack, but the monsters had returned to the edge of my vision. In the office bathroom I washed my face vigorously, glaring at myself in the mirror, desperate to change the subject of my dark thoughts.

I asked my reflection, "How can I make use of the river landings?" That was an interesting question. Surveillance was slack there. I had discovered other holes in the security system, the biggest being that I was hired fresh from the fireball situation in Nevada, no questions asked. While appreciating the park system's compassion, I was scornful of its stupidity. Feeling better, I walked toward my desk. The monsters receded. I would find Lena's number from the staff listings, have her over for supper, and figure out a way to compel her to leave the Park for a safer location. If someone was going to trash this place, I did not want my daughter nearby.

Back in the monitor chair, I re-entered the landings area, resolving to learn three new things to further my plan.

Near the Pennsylvania border, south of Corning, New York.

A few months earlier.

"Brian Owen – come in! You're right on time!" Maeve said as they entered the old building, finding it warm and comfortable after the chilly walk. Fire crackled in a big fireplace, the food smelled great, the tables shone, and Maeve was breathtaking to look at. They were the only customers.

"Let me take your jacket! Sit down, sit down," she cooed, as they settled at a table near the fire.

Maeve continued, "Did you enjoy the walk? Did you meet some of our strange residents, and stranger Board members?" His unease vanished in the warmth of her cheerful, confident presence. Normalcy was back.

Brian replied lightly, "You have a wonderful, unusual community. I can't believe I've never been here before." Maeve leaned toward him, opened top sweater buttons hinting at her beauty.

He resolutely stared into her blue eyes as she replied, "Yes, the state park borders our Special Heritage Area – some of its creeks flow here as well. Now that you know us, I hope we'll see you here often." Brian sighed, relaxing into the old-fashioned, everyday comfort of the Hollymount Inn. Finally he had this bunch pegged: second-generation back-to-the-land hippies plus long-time rural folks. He ventured a question.

"Maeve, can you tell me about your Special Heritage Group? I specialize in community and ethnicity and tribal interests around here, and have never encountered you before." Maeve lifted a hand to signal the waiter, who was setting tables across the room.

She replied, "We came here a thousand years ago, driven out of our homeland by religious persecution."

This was not what Brian wanted to hear. He wanted to hear that this was an old hippie commune, not "ancient peoples" drivel. He responded politely, "I don't get it. One thousand years ago? Five hundred years before the first European settlers?"

"Oh my dear Brian," she said, with her gurgling laugh, "We were here long before *they* arrived. Oh my, those were the glory days," she sighed, and shook her head, Brian thought, "Like she was remembering it herself!" He decided that she was at best a kook. This was most likely a cult.

The waiter stood at her elbow, eyebrows raised inquiringly.

Maeve said, "I'll have the house lager, please. And you, Brian, what would you like to drink?" She gestured to a list on the wall, "Locally Made – Beers, Intoxicants, and Waters of Great Renown." At her polite question, his fears and fantasies sprang into flame. There was a long pause.

Brian struggled to reply, thinking, "If you eat or drink with the fairies, you become their prisoner." Maeve and the waiter stared at him, leaning close. He thought, "Don't lose your cool in front of these nice people," and finally spoke, stuttering.

"I – I'm not thirsty – thank you." They looked disappointed. Not wanting to hurt their feelings – or curb Maeve's warm welcome – he tried a different approach.

"I had a late breakfast, and brought my own water, thanks." Brian pulled the water bottle out of his pack. The waiter sighed and shook his head as he and Maeve exchanged a look. He placed a drinking glass down hard on the table at Brian's elbow. Maeve sat back, watching Brian. He stole glances at her, she glowing with vitality and youth – a beautiful ripe fruit, she seemed to Brian.

"I'll come back for your food order," said the waiter as he moved away. Grinning over his shoulder, he said, "No humans served today, Maeve, looks like."

Brian whispered to her, "What's the joke? I don't get it." She smiled and shook her head, with a glance at the waiter. Then she looked at Brian and spoke sharply.

"Brian, you were rude today on your way here, to our Board's Vice President!" The suddenness of her attack was startling. He rushed to his own defense.

"What did I do? He was polite and welcoming!" Maeve leaned forward and slid one warm hand over his. She waggled the pretty pink finger of her other hand.

"You remember, I said we came here to escape religious persecution?"

"Well, yes, but I thought that was just an expression – "

"No!" She replied emphatically, slowly turning over Brian's hand, drawing circles in his palm with that pink finger. The sensation was electrifying, and she had his total attention.

"Brian, when you used the cold iron, he had to lie down for an *hour* to recover. I hope to see him here for the Board meeting after our lunch. If you want to continue to work with us," – playing with his hand – "you must overcome your superstitions and stereotypes, and accept us as we are." Releasing Brian's hand, she tilted her head to observe her effect. She was smiling. He smiled back, shakily.

Brian said, "Tails and all, huh?"

She nodded slowly, not taking her eyes off his, and said, "Tails and all."

The waiter drifted over to ask, "What will milady have for lunch?"

Maeve leaned forward. "Brian, may I order for both of us? The local foods used at the Inn are wonderful. We're hoping for a review soon by the newspaper." He started to nod – but stopped – again sensing that Maeve and the waiter were too intent on his reply. Pushing back from the table and looking around, Brian saw the waiter shake his head. Maeve was smiling.

"I know you must think I'm crazy – " he began.

"No, no, Brian, that's all right. Not today," said Maeve, and she was suddenly less pretty: older, tired. She sighed, shook her head, and said to the waiter, "Bring me the regular lunch, won't you darling. The waiter bowed wordlessly and stalked away. Maeve's young glow was gone, her green sweater buttoned up.

"Brian, we loved your work on that proposal," she said in a brisk new tone, "and we'd like your expert help again – you bring us luck!" He did not respond to this good news right away. The room was colder, the overhead lights had a fluorescent office hue. What had he done to deserve Maeve's rejection?

Brian thought, "If I keep up this fairy tale nonsense, I could end up in a locked ward on a steady diet of reality pills." He fumbled for words, wanting her warmth to return.

"I'm sorry, I don't get out much, and unfamiliar food tears up my stomach – " was the awful best Brian could do. His remark fell into dead silence as the waiter brought her a bowl of soup – regular, normal soup. Brian pulled out a packet of trail mix from his pack, to be companionable. The waiter slid a plate under it.

"We cater to humans," said the waiter, setting down Maeve's meat and cup of ambrosia, which smelled like honey. Maeve spooned her soup with a good appetite.

"Brian," she said, "Please take that food packet out with you – we have no way to dispose of it in the Special Heritage Area."

"You don't have recycling here?" he asked. "It's been a county-wide service for years."

She shook her head. "We don't pay taxes to your state, so we don't receive all these interesting services you speak of. We are hoping you can help us." She sipped the ambrosia as Brian stared at her.

Brian said, "What do you mean, you don't pay taxes? That's crazy – illegal!"

Maeve wiped her mouth, pushed the dishes aside, and looked at him. In the harsher light Brian saw lines around her mouth, dark circles under her eyes.

"Oh, we pay taxes all right – very high taxes indeed," she said, reaching across the table for a manila envelope. "They come due on a different date from yours, on the last day in October." She leaned back to watch the effect of her words. The waiter chuckled as he picked up plates and glasses.

Brian said, "Oh. I see," while thinking, "fairies pay a tithe to Hell on Halloween."

"Yes, perhaps you do begin to see, if not understand," she said, pushing the envelope toward him. It was addressed to "Maeve, President SHA" at a post office box address in his nearby town. The return address was the granting agency Brian had successfully wrested funds from, and the sheaf of papers inside was the application for the next round of grants.

"As you head back toward your car," said Maeve, folding her hands in front of her, "we will hold a Board meeting here, to talk about plans for the next round of improvements we want to make. I am authorized by the Board to invite you to prepare the next proposal. Will you accept – that much, anyway?"

As she spoke, the front door of the Inn creaked open, and the Vice President came in, giving Brian a shy smile, his black cat's tail floating behind him. He was followed by the older gal in the pink tracksuit, and a small black-haired man whose upright birdlike bearing and bright eyes seemed familiar. They all nodded and settled into chairs at a nearby table. Brian tore his eyes away from them to look at Maeve.

He said, "Yes – please, yes. I'd love to do this for you – your group. What are your priorities for this next grant?"

"Priorities," she said, and giggled, revealing her hidden beauty. "Is that some of your 'jargon'?" she asked, with a real laugh. Brian laughed too, and the others smiled faintly in puzzled support.

She went on, "We'd like a walking route for the Hollymount Road and Apple Island Trace," (the VP nodded his head enthusiastically) "and to create an eco-tour, for folks to come visit."

"Sounds like you need a welcome center at the parking area," Brian suggested, hoping to sustain the renewed feeling of goodwill.

Maeve nodded. "We cannot abide human – ah, visitor – waste in the Special Heritage Area, so those arrangements would have to be at the gateway," she said, eyebrows raised for his reaction.

"You can't bring in overnight guests without a lot of infrastructural investment," Brian replied, on familiar ground for a moment. She frowned at the unfamiliar "infra" word but must have figured out what it meant.

"We were thinking perhaps a camping-ground – or a festival center."

"Festivals!" he said. "That's great – very popular. You can attract a lot of visitors with a good festival." The Board members smiled at this news.

Maeve said excitedly, "Yes – our Heritage Area has festivals from mid-summer to late fall, and we'd love to have people join us!" She stood up, and lunch was over. Brian pushed back his chair, put the envelope, water bottle, and trail mix packet in his pack, and shook hands. The Board members nodded politely as Maeve walked him to the door. It was a grey winter day outside – late afternoon, dark soon. Walking down the stone steps, Brian felt a nervous urge to get back to his car.

Maeve said, "Go straight back to your car today, and we'll talk next week."

"Sure," he said, "that works for me," and stepped onto the green road. He needed to get out while it was daylight. She stood in the doorway, a sort of shine about her. Brian waved, she waved and closed the door, and he picked up his pace.

Brian's fears rose free: he did not want to get caught here after dark, because fairies keep you a long, long time.

Chapter 4

Homeland-Interior Region 3 Headquarters, central Ohio.

Steve Roberts drove home to central Ohio after the Pleistocene trip. The next morning he kissed his wife and walked to the path leading to the Northeast Entrance of his underground office, determined to find out why the security guards had taken the sabertooth investigation away from him. He would be speaking off the record with his mentor Ed Zanetti, who had arrived the night before to stay at Homeland-Interior's guest house, a rustic lodge built into a hillside in the restoration area.

At the lodge, Zanetti struggled to wake up. Dawn light turned the black window grey, and a golden morning gleamed. Fighting off the dregs of his vacation time-lag, Zanetti sucked down a pot of coffee on the patio. He and Roberts needed to talk, free of surveillance. Magnificent healthy beech trees rustled overhead, crows called to one another as jays quarreled, occasional bursts of blue among the leaves.

Zanetti gazed out at the unnaturally natural setting, Homeland-Interior's first big partnering triumph in its "We Nurture Nature" program. This visionary melding – saturation-monitoring of meticulously restored big woods – was a celebrated product of Homeland's computing strengths and Interior's ecology thinkers. One of Zanetti's early projects, this site was the first in the now-nationwide system of Saturation Monitoring Sites. Based on the popular, highly fundable scientific notion that the least might be the most important, every infant leaf unfurling from within a bud, every breeze rippling through, was a data point. Caffeine intensified Zanetti's sense of unity, immersed in the everlasting modeling and surveilling here.

Showered and dressed, he walked along the EcoPath out of the old woods into the buffer of younger trees and open areas. At the final Filter Point he waited several minutes for a drop in human impact traffic ahead, then headed down the Northeast Entrance escalator.

Roberts's staff had not seen Zanetti "up here" from D.C. for a couple of months. Gathered in their regular meeting room, they asked about his Pasadena time-vacation.

"Unfortunately, the report on that will have to wait," Zanetti said, flanked by Inge Knowles and Steve Roberts. "We need to focus on the survival of our Time Program." Aware of those monitoring the meeting, Zanetti kept the bad news short and formal. "We're facing some powerful folks. Defense has accepted Professor King's report as sufficient proof that they can move forward with temporal military adjustments."

Zanetti paused, and shared King's top-secret report on their screens. He watched their faces as they read its description of "harvesting" his grandfather, and the results section claiming that the past could be altered without harm to the present day. Widened and shocked eyes rose to meet his, one pair at a time.

"This is – legal?" asked Loren Evans, a young ecologist. Homeland rep Stuart Whittaker sat back and watched the others, expressionless. This was not news to him. The Homeland Security half of the Time Program team had already begun shifting focus to using time travel for military purposes. The Interior Department half of the team had some catching up to do.

"Was King's study carried out according to acceptable research standards?" asked another of the younger staff. Zanetti kept his face neutral, awaiting other comments.

"I saw King last week at the Timeline Conference," offered Knowles. "He looked the same as always." She glanced at Zanetti, who nodded encouragingly. "We had lunch, and he was boast – umm, talking about this research, but he didn't say exactly what it was about. He didn't look any different – he wasn't transparent or fading away or anything," she ended, with a small giggle.

"Isn't it scientifically impossible for him to be all right after removing his grandfather's participation in his own existence?" asked Evans.

"Read his report again," said Whittaker, emerging from his silence. "King says it's all in the timing. He 'harvested' " (his voice taking on a "quote-unquote" inflection for this loaded word), "his grandfather *after* his father was born. That's the essential detail. And it has led to a proposal from General Granger's science team." Whittaker looked at Zanetti, a cue that this proposal could be discussed.

"Right," replied Zanetti, bending his head to read from the secret proposal.

"They...hmmm...'seek action points on the far side of an historic event's tipping point.'" He scanned ahead, reading, "'After that point has passed, the military outcome can be altered toward optimum national interest.'" He focused on another sentence, "'Time-related losses would be present, but peripheral, at levels acceptable when compared to the positive overall outcome.'"

"What a – " began a long-time senior staffer, thought better of it, and shook his head. Roberts looked up from his first perusal of the proposal, catching Zanetti's eye for permission to speak.

"This may explain what we encountered in the field yesterday," Roberts began. "As you all know, I was at Ten K" (insider shorthand for Ten Thousand Secrets National Park) "to investigate and seal that sabertooth time-leak." The others nodded, their office-pallid features contrasting with Roberts's vitality.

He continued, "Our science and support team, meticulously following procedures, was overruled by a Casino Guard detachment, and required to depart the field." Roberts spoke carefully for the record, but his stilted words startled the group.

"How do you mean, 'overruled'?" asked Knowles with some heat. "You were the team leader!"

"Four guards, up from the usual two, surrounded our team and displayed rights-reduction arms in a stance I have been conditioned to defer to," Roberts continued. "Members of my team did not respond in a safe manner. So I got us out of there, and came seeking information here. I seem to have found some of it."

Zanetti replied, "Granger's report concludes that 'Defense is positioning for active implementation of King's findings.'" He looked up and said, "We'll need to meet this challenge." Mild, yet nonetheless strong words for the record.

Assessing the range of facial expressions in the room, Zanetti said, "Let's get some lunch." The group lurched to their feet, masking dismay with movement. They departed in thoughtful silence toward the Commons, cameras twinkling from the room's corner behind them.

Roberts and Zanetti got a small table on the sunny Time Terrace near the exit doorway. Under their big umbrella they spoke of families, dogs, and diets. As they ate, they gazed out at the red poppies and daisies strewn across the rolling fields in the sunlight, beyond the velvet rope. A river gleamed in the distance. Their lunch was brief, and they departed one minute apart.

Outside the Commons, first Zanetti and then Roberts turned down an Employees Only hallway, the far end in darkness. Past will-reduction screens set to trap intruders, each walked confidently forward into the "Enhanced Deep Dark" (being tested for commercial uses). They steered by sound to the portal. The brief, intense changeling sensation of the Time Barrier grasped and released each one into the unpolluted sunlight of an 1870s summer afternoon in the Loire Valley.

The warmth and scent hit Roberts in a sensual wave, as he ambled after Zanetti down the footpath toward a bench beneath a horse chestnut tree. In its cool shelter they could speak freely. There was no way yet devised for security-related monitoring and listening to carry across the time divide. Zanetti pulled out a pipe and readied a smoke as Roberts rested in the purple-dark shade.

"You have some wicked habits, buddy," he said comfortably, hitching up his pants legs and rolling up his sleeves to catch the breeze.

"When the going gets tough, the tough start smoking," replied Zanetti between start-up puffs. The sweet aroma of pipe tobacco mingled with the rose-scented air.

"Besides," he added, "that darn sewer is acting up again," as the scent of an open sewer drifted past their bench. These historical realities did not bother Roberts, and he went straight to the heart of their much-needed discussion.

"I heard that you and that dick traded fisticuffs yesterday."

"No – no," Zanetti demurred, puffing happily, gazing at a hawk overhead. "Almost, not quite. He grabbed at my tie, is all. That guy is really stressed, you know? He must be expecting to disappear any second."

"That would be a noble and most welcome sacrifice to our nation's security and honor," said Roberts, pulling a packet of cookies out of his pocket.

"And you say I have bad habits," sneered Zanetti. "Watch the crumbs!" Theoretically, a stray crumb can change the course of history, so Roberts broke big rules by eating cookies straight from the packet without an approved food trap. He let the crumbs fall into his palm, and placed them carefully in his jacket pocket.

"I never could wrap my brain around that time travel rules stuff," Roberts said. "How would we know he was gone? Would it be like he had never been here? Then we wouldn't even know – right? Or would he step sideways into another dimension, so we'd have memories of him from before he left?" Zanetti shook his head, gave up on relaxing, and snuffed out his pipe.

He looked across the fields and whispered, "There he is!" and they gazed at a painter seated at his easel, partially obscured by tall grass and a screen of trees. He sat there every time they visited, because they were always here at the exact same time and date. Zanetti turned the conversation to more pressing topics, because time then and now tick at the same rate, and their working afternoon called them to return.

"What do I do, Stevie? Defense wants our program. I think I've stalled them on having you fired – " This caught Roberts's attention.

He asked, "Senator Styce?"

Closing his eyes in a grimace, Zanetti nodded. "Your home state favorite, yep. They're lining up the big guns for that idiotic project proposed by Granger's anti-science team. King boasted about it, instead of punching me. He said his report is now policy. Big bucks attached. Did you read to the end of Granger's proposal?" Roberts shook his head no.

Zanetti continued, "They want to do two experimental small 'temporal military adjustments' by the end of this calendar year. King is the principal investigator – him and his lab."

"Do they have any particular adjustments in mind? What do you mean by 'small'?" asked Roberts, his enjoyment of the day vaporizing. A dark cloud hove into view; they had to depart ahead of weather changes.

The two stood up, checked for stray crumbs and tobacco shreds, and turned back up the path.

Zanetti spoke rapidly. "You can read it when we get back – they're reviewing a list of 55 proposed adjustments. It's top-secret pork – every Congressperson in the Administration's party has been offered the opportunity to bring home an 'enhanced past event' to their constituents, as long as they ask no questions. Congresswoman Anna Holm is going to see if she can stall or derail this in committee. I talked to her this morning, and she thinks that Granger's science team overreached by offering so many choices – that'll drag it down. She hopes. Kind of a thin hope, when there's big bucks available."

Roberts said, "This may be small potatoes in the bigger scheme you're describing, but they won't let us go underground to locate that sabertooth time leak at Ten K. I really need to find out more, if we're going to plug the time leaks."

"What do you think is going on there?" Zanetti did not like being dragged from the big picture to one small management issue, but was polite to his oldest friend and supporter.

"I think a cave passage has opened up and the cat is going back and forth under the river." Roberts looked at Zanetti to make sure he was heard and understood.

"How do you reckon that?" asked Zanetti, appalled and fascinated.

"In the Pleistocene, the riverbed was further north. I suggest that a cave ran beneath it back then, but was filled in as the river shifted to its present course." The dark cloud was overhead, and they were almost at the shimmering curtain.

Roberts went on, "I think that the cave passage under the river re-opened when we set the north side of the park in the Pleistocene. It's an impact we did not anticipate, because we only considered surface impacts."

"Oh right, I remember now," said Zanetti as he stepped toward the curtain. "Those caves are under there. So, why not track the cat from the Park end?"

"Ed has good ideas," thought Roberts, pausing to let Zanetti step through the portal. Across the fields, the painter shook his head and rubbed his eyes, then went back to his painting.

Ten Thousand Secrets National Park Casino & Entertainment District, Kentucky.

Janet has another late night.

I closed the apartment door behind me and tiptoed down the stairs onto the pine woods path. At 1 a.m., Park activity ebbs; visitors are carousing or sleeping, and guards are napping. Solar glows lined the pathways, and perimeter lights high above bathed the surrounding woodlands in artificial daylight – no rest for the trees.

"Or for me," I thought, craving real darkness. Be careful what you wish for, they say. I walked quietly past sleeping tour buses. Tree shadows fell across my path, but no shadow did I cast. Clipped inside my jacket was a non-detect device, removed from its hiding place in my apartment. An outdated model, it worked fine for my uses, deleting personal shadows, fading out my image on screens and in most bio-detect situations. These small devices were easy to lose from office inventory, if forgetfully stored while set on maintenance level non-detect.

Avoiding the cameras mounted on light poles and in less obvious places, I neared the rear of the Casino complex. As I moved into the shadow of parked buses, dissolving into darkness along the back wall, I saw the glowing streetlight at the back door. The door was open, allowing cool air to spill out into the warmer Kentucky night.

On the pavement near the door sat a metal cage, eight feet long and five feet tall, open at one end. In it, flies buzzed on a heap of squalid meat – a giant cat trap. Just in time, I saw blue light beams criss-crossing the doorway and trap. I stepped carefully over them, easing through the revolving door into the darkness of that giant basement.

My goal for the night was to find a light switch, and walk through the Casino basement to the River Styx – a back route to the tourist zone. I needed to map it in my mind to finalize my plan. I walked to the staircase, flicked off the flashlight and looked down. The red EXIT light gleamed below. Maybe the switch was there. Suppressing sabertooth fears, I shined the light at the ceiling and cinderblock walls as I descended. A cool breeze flowed up the stairwell, carrying the scent of mud and water on cold stone.

At the EXIT sign I put my ear to the elevator door and could hear the hum of machinery. No light through the crack. No light switches. Maybe there were at the foot of the staircase? I leaned over the railing and shined my flashlight down. I could not see the floor – just the staircase, descending. I looked up and saw a faint glow from the outside streetlight reflected onto the ceiling, far overhead. Nothing for it but to keep going. This was the necessary next step in my plan. Fear begone!

I counted the landings as I descended, the sounds of dripping water increasing around me. The walls closed in, and the stairs dropped steeply. Ferns grew out of the rough rock wall. Ten flights down, I shined my light over the railing. Below – far below – was a concrete floor, and a doorway.

Finally, at the bottom, my flashlight revealed a metal door propped open with a rock, and on the wall, a light switch! I flicked it on, illuminating a narrow cinderblock-lined corridor ahead, curving out of sight. I figured it was a quarter mile to the Styx River Casino and hotels zone, straight ahead by my trusty compass. Turning off flashlight and non-detect device to save power, I walked down the narrow hallway. The light was on a timer, clicking rapidly, so I watched for the next one.

The corridor twisted and turned, cinderblocks replaced with stone. This began to look like a cave passage, not a built hallway. The walls glistened with moisture, and large brown crickets skittered across the ceiling. I spotted a light switch, just as total darkness hit. The timer behind me had run out. I stood still listening, enjoying the deep darkness, a warm, comfortable blanket. Switching on the light, tripping the timer, I stepped forward into a higher, wider passage. Along it were – bathroom doors! One with man and child symbols, one with skirted woman and child. They creeped me out, and I hastened forward.

The breeze picked up at the intersection of two passages. I stepped into the center and shined my flashlight down the cross-passage – on both sides, stone ledges rose to the cave ceiling twenty feet overhead. A stream meandered along the floor and through a culvert under the paved path I stood on. Same vista in the other direction. The breeze blew strongly from the electric-lit hallway that continued straight ahead, headed toward the River Styx. As I stepped across the tinkling stream, I felt the whisper of a big cave out there. This park had been celebrated for its caves, the longest in the world, until the Casino and Entertainment Domes were built. Now the caves were forgotten.

From switch to switch I pattered along, compass aimed at the Styx River with the hotels, boats and Casino glitz. I was relying on there being a doorway, or gap in the cave wall to let me sneak into the tourism zone without being seen, so that I could find good sites for the explosive charges.

As I paced forward, the silence and darkness of the cave grew deeper. Crossing another large passage, I saw three locked doors in the wall. I rattled the knob on one – sounded big inside, empty. With a squirt of panic I skipped forward, skin crawling. Surely I had come a quarter mile, even with twists and turns? As I reached for the next switch, the light went out. The darkness now felt edgy, *not* comfortable.

Ahead, my dark-adapted eyes saw a dim glow. Not daylight or Casino glare, but something brighter than the solid dark around me. I walked toward it, emerging from the narrow passage into a larger, unseen space. Above, a glowing EXIT sign pointed back the way I had come. I felt a large cave chamber around me; the air was still. No Casino noises or lights. My watch showed I had been out an hour, one hour before I should turn back. Deep stillness. The flashlight illuminated a stony path, winding across dark space in the direction I wanted to go. Should I stop now, go back, and try again another night?

The flashlight illuminated dusty bootprints on the path. They could be a hundred years old – no wind or rain would touch them here. I liked their look. The path still called me forward. I wondered where it went, and decided to go just a little way. Maybe there was a straight shot around the next bend, to the river and Casino. But around that next bend, the path went on, straight and flat. My flashlight revealed empty electric light fixtures set into the walls; the path seemed groomed for easy walking.

Around the next bend, I walked into an even larger cave room. Ahead were wooden benches set in rows. Beyond them, the path headed up a slope, steps cut into the rock. I sat down and looked around. The room was as large as the Casino spaces above, graced with calm and serene darkness. I relaxed, turning off my light to listen and look. My hand in front of my face was invisible.

A streak of light passed across the room. Then it was gone. I saw another streak – a flashlight, moving at the top of the slope. I heard the murmur of voices. Two figures came into view, limned by their lights, descending the slope. I heard the deep tones of a man's voice, the lighter notes of a woman's. Two more people appeared behind them, following down the steps. Headlamps and flashlights bobbled beautifully as the group approached.

The leaders settled onto a bench. I hunkered down in the bottom row, unseen, listening as they chatted. There was something familiar about the woman's voice. I realized that it was Lena. I almost called out, but stopped. She heard something, turning in my direction. Their lights picked me out.

"Lena!" I called.

She replied, "Mom – I mean Janet – what!" She moved toward me.

"Who's there?" called the man, so I walked toward their lights. I must admit, I was happy to see them. I could use a little company, down here.

"Hello, honey," I said quietly as she got close, "I'm very glad to see you," and patted her cheek in the darkness. We joined the group and she introduced me to the others – Dr. Hugh Hynes, the Park's cave ecologist, and two members of his Science team, of which Lena was the newest. I had met Hugh and Lena on the time trip, but that was not mentioned.

"Were you sent here to join us?" asked Damaris, about Lena's age.

"That's a kind of mystical question," I replied, garrulous with gratitude at finding them in this "really big basement." Steve Roberts's words came back to me with new understanding.

I laughed, "I went out for a midnight stroll across the parking lots, and here I am."

Hugh Hynes said, "Ron, give her a couple sample bottles to carry. She can help with the other two sites, and we can all go out together."

Handing me two plastic bottles, Ron said, "You caught up with us halfway along our sampling route – we're headed to the Styx River, then out via the staircase you came down. We sample at night to prevent tourists seeing us."

"Where did you enter?" I asked, hoping to learn a shortcut.

Hugh replied, "That's for us to know" – and for me to find out.

Lena gentled his remark, adding, "Dr. Hynes is very protective of his cave."

"What's left of it," he said tartly. From the big room he led us into a hidden opening in the wall, along a passageway that sloped deeper into the cave.

"We just sampled at an injection well casing," Hugh said, justifying his crustiness. "Even wearing our masks" – by the collective flashlight I saw breathing masks around their necks – "we had to get in and out fast. It's leaking like a sieve and the fumes are getting worse. They're spreading into the passageways around the well pipe."

"That's where the Park disposes of its liquefied garbage, right?" I asked. This "eco-disposal innovation" had been touted in the most recent employee newsletter. Hynes turned to look at me, his eyes bright in the headlamps.

"No. The liquid garbage goes into a *new* injection well, number 8. It's exempt from our monitoring because garbage is classified as 'ninety-nine percent harmless.' What we just sampled," (he shook his backpack, and bottles gurgled), "is the *other*, deeper injection well, permitted by EPA for Homeland to dispose of 'certified non-toxic waste.'"

"What are they pumping into it?" I asked, feeling familiar stirrings of alarm. We popped out of the narrow, sloping corridor to walk along a stream – an underground river. The water was low and musical, trickling in its rocky creek bed. Lights and eyes flickered, reflecting the beauty of the subterranean scene.

Hugh shook his head, laughing: this time the joke was on him. He said, "What they inject into that well is for *them* to know. We take the samples, and hand them off to a lab guy in the parking lot" – he looked at his watch – "but they never tell us what they find when they do the lab analysis."

"Next stop is frack well pipe #3," said young Ron in a cheerful voice. "I bet it's a mess, too." Hugh snorted and shook his head in disgust. I had heard about this one. The three fracking gas wells in Ten Thousand Secrets National Park were touted as an "intergovernmental eco-innovation" between Interior and Homeland. The Park sold the gas to pay for road repair and nature enhancement. Win-win!

"Another hundred feet," said Damaris, "and we need to put on our masks again – this time it's methane gas leakage from the frack well casing." She handed me a spare mask. Down a side passage to the right, I heard a roaring noise – and the toot of a Styx River boat. Finally!

"Please extinguish all cigarettes," joked Hugh. Entering the passage, he added, "Carbide headlamps" – with their open flames – "not allowed." Lena helped me put on their spare mask as we walked down the passage, the roaring louder and the breeze rising. Around a corner, the source of the noise was revealed – a floor-to-ceiling wall of giant fans, blasting air nonstop. Through gaps in the whirling fans, I saw bright lights – and there was my long-sought opening in the cave wall to the River Styx and Casino area.

We walked past the intense noise into a dark corridor. As the sound and breeze lessened, my daughter bent her head to mine and said, "The fans prevent ninety-nine point zero-zero five percent of methane fumes from reaching the tourism corridor. And they are solar-powered!"

"What can I say but 'win-win'!" I replied. Our lights converged on a slim shaft rising through the open space ahead. Hugh walked up to the well casing, which gleamed with a wet, oily sheen. The shaft extended into the ceiling fifteen feet above, and disappeared through the cave floor at our feet.

He turned to us, held up two fingers, and mouthed, "Two minutes." The team nodded, and Lena took samples. Wearing plastic gloves, she scooped moisture off the casing in several places, capping them into separate bottles that she handed to Hugh for labeling. Ron took air samples with a small electronic device. I watched Lena, proud of her competence, my mind swirling with new information. My task here at Ten Thousand Secrets National Park had just gotten easier.

We walked back through the fan room and were soon in the river passage, where we turned left and trekked quickly upstream along the trickling river. Hugh stopped to look at the water. We adjusted our packs and waited.

He said, "Why is the water down? It should be a pool, part of the cave lake downstream." He looked in that direction, then at his watch, shook his head, and continued upstream.

"Next trip?" asked Ron.

"Yeah, we'll figure that out next time." Soon we were back in the big room with the benches. As we walked in silence, we removed face masks. Maybe the others were mulling over the mess and danger we had seen. I was planning my project's next steps.

"We'll be on time for the lab guy in the parking lot," said Hugh, entering the passage below the EXIT sign, scorning the light switches. As the mood lightened, I began to think about the long climb ahead, and fresh air. I reached into my pocket to turn on the non-detect device.

Ron rattled doorknobs on the locked rooms and hammered loudly with his fist, causing the hair to rise on the back of my neck and the young women to giggle.

Passing the men's bathroom door, he stopped and shouted into the rusty keyhole, "Hey, Floyd, hurry it up, will ya?"

Hugh snapped, "Stop that right now," and began to jog. We picked up the pace and in a few minutes were at the staircase – the distance back seemed shorter than on the way in. The youngsters scampered easily up the hundreds of steps. Older and slower, Hugh and I walked steadily upward, the cave falling behind and below us, the outdoors calling. We breathed woodland-scented warmer air as we neared the top.

I heard Ron calling, "Here, kitty kitty," as they encountered the empty cage. At the door, I stepped carefully over the blue beams, and edged against the wall of the Casino complex. Layers of clothing and helmets came off in the cool Kentucky night. Bats and bugs buzzed and swooped in the bright perimeter lights around the parking lot. It was 3 a.m.

Across the parking lot an engine started, headlights shooting from a pickup truck. I stepped outside the beams as the team pulled sample bottles from their backpacks. When the truck approached, it was time for me to go. I patted Lena's arm as she cradled her samples for collection.

I said, "Let's do lunch!" – at which she laughed and nodded. I stepped away from the headlights toward the tour buses (some already idling).

Hugh called to me, "You enjoyed that, right?"

I said, "Yes."

He replied, "You're a caving natural – we'll see about getting you on the team. I read your resume – we could use a water quality professional."

"No need to mention meeting me, right?" I said. "I don't have the security clearance to see what I saw."

He said, "There's a lot more than ten thousand secrets around here – no worries." We nodded in agreement, and I stepped into the shadows, creeping along the wooded edges of the vast pavement, dodging cameras.

I was thinking, "'A natural,' huh. Takes years of training to get good at sneaking around in the dark." A person has her pride, no matter how perverse. I reviewed the night's work for flaws, planning ahead. The time spent with Lena had been great. In my apartment I did a basic security check and slept well until the alarm woke me for work.

Senator Styce's Capitol Hill office, Washington, D.C.

Senator Harlan Styce's outer office in Washington, D.C. was heavy with drapes and swags of powder blue, flanking the fireplace mantel and bullet-proof tall windows covered in sheer curtains. Ceramic eagles punctuated walls crowded with photos of Styce's career. These captured the early years in Louisville, a ball game with nephews, the embrace of Ronald Reagan. In one corner, a cluster of flags hung ready for visitor photos.

Styce's office manager sat midway between the outer door to the Russell Senate Office Building's vast hallways and a handsome door in the far wall. Beyond this inner door the Senator, his assistant Ard Sprinkle, and Professor Tom "Cat" King sat comfortably in armchairs around a gas-fueled fire crackling in an historic fireplace. Cat savored the bourbon in a heavy glass cupped in his hands, and raised his restless eyes to look at Styce.

"Zanetti is out?" he asked. They were done with the chatty preliminaries, niceties he could barely tolerate. The whiskey slowed him down to the fast lane.

Styce met his glance and replied, "They're all history, pardon the pun." Sprinkle chuckled appreciatively.

King asked, "How, exactly?" Realizing this was too abrupt for his illustrious company, he shifted his head and shoulders humbly forward. The Senator glanced at Sprinkle, who picked up a sheet of the Senator's letterhead from beside his untouched glass of spring water and read aloud.

"'From: Office of Coordination, Departments of Interior and Homeland Security Shared Programs Planning' – "

The Senator slammed down his glass and snarled, "Skip that shit, Ard. Get to the meat." King smirked as Sprinkle recoiled, moving his eyes down the page.

"'Effective two months from today's date,'" he read, "'the illustrious long-standing shared programs between the Departments of Interior and Homeland Security will end.'" Sprinkle glanced nervously at the Senator, but Styce was leaning back, enjoying a long pull on his drink, and every syllable; so he continued, "'They are being upgraded to an Action Task Force between Homeland and the Department of Defense.'" King nodded in satisfaction.

Sprinkle read, "'This change signals the fruition of decades of research that has produced powerful new tools to strengthen our country's outer defenses and inner security.'"

He paused, sipped his water, and continued, "'The Action Task Force will be led by Thomas King, Professor of Business Biology at Dartmouth's GOBI Institute. King begins work immediately, to shepherd us through a complex transition period. We take this opportunity to thank outgoing Interior-Homeland Liaison Edward Zanetti for his outstanding years of service – '" Sprinkle stole a glance at the Senator, who was glaring at him, and stopped.

King said, "This is a done deal?" He mistrusted formalities.

The Senator set down his glass and shrugged, "Will be soon. We gotta get out in front and point the way. Needs a few more meetings and signatures." He saw that King was upset by these vague phrases.

"For heaven's sake, man," Styce said, "there's a fucking process to follow. But we got it!"

King yanked his impatience back under control, staring toward the big windows.

He said tightly, "Of all those asshole scientists, the one I most want to see the back of is that damn Hugh Hynes."

Styce's mind was on his next meeting. But King deserved another minute. He asked, "Who is he?" Sprinkle opened his mouth to explain, but King cut him off.

"Hynes is the ecologist at your home state's national park. He's a nature-nut extremist who has stalled us for years, saying things like 'gotta go slow' and 'needs more research.' What a time-waster. When I take over, my first task will be to fire his ass." King suddenly realized with whom he was sharing revenge fantasies.

He said, "Sorry, sir. My excitement for the task ahead sometimes overwhelms me."

"Finish your whiskey, boy, I got a delegation coming in," replied the Senator as he stood up, smiling fondly at his science henchman's small indiscretion. King set his half-empty glass on the table, shook hands and departed. Sprinkle cleaned away the glasses and napkins and made the room nice for the incoming group.

Janet heads to Homeland-Interior Region 3 Headquarters, Ohio.

As the plane rose off the runway at Buchanon Memorial Airport, I gazed over the Park below. The Casino and Pleasure Domes gleamed in the sunlight, as did Wilcher Drive, a new six-lane highway connecting airport and interstates across the Park. The drill rigs and pads at the scattered fracking and injection wells caught the rising sun. On the north side of the Green, Green River, the Pleistocene was faintly visible through the shimmering time mist. I quit looking, and leaned back with eyes closed until we landed in Ohio an hour later.

Following signs from the Day Visitors arrival area, I approached the Northeast Entrance to Interior-Homeland Midwest HQ. The famous ecosystem restoration was underwhelming, mostly native grasses lining solar-heated walkways. It looked natural, was merely naturalistic. The monorail link to the airport accentuated the theme park feel, and camera eyes glittered everywhere. I trudged along the crunchy path to meet Steve Roberts, me nervous and brooding. The activated non-detect device was in my pocket.

"Hi there," called Steve, walking forward to shake my hand. "This won't take long, and maybe we can have a late lunch afterwards on the Time Terrace. You been here before?" He knew I hadn't, but the courtesy was appreciated.

"I'm kind of nervous," I admitted, as we approached the entrance. The low roof of the underground building mimicked a limestone ledge, topped with trees and native grasses. We walked under the feigned rock-shelter coolness of the entryway onto the escalator. I turned to look up at dangling ferns and dripping water as we descended. Below were lights, walls, doorways, people.

"Don't be nervous, this will only take a minute," said Steve. His suit and tie blended well with his workplace habitat. I had on my one dress-up outfit, with sturdy boots in case I needed to move fast. We reached the first landing and continued down the next escalator.

Steve turned to explain, "You sit in a chair, they focus this new device on your eyes and head, you stay still, and then it's done. Homeland and Defense co-developed it as a tool for helping people recall forgotten details."

"Uh-oh," was my unspoken reaction to his words. "This will not end well." I struggled to keep my voice light as we approached our step-off point. "Do they keep it set at legal limits?"

"Of course," said Steve, guiding me past a bank of shiny camera eyes toward a well-lit open space through which a stream gurgled. We crossed it on a small bridge toward a wall of multi-toned blue tiles. In the center was a handsome dark wooden door set with glass panes, flanked by flowering native milkweed and purple coneflower in big purple pots.

He opened the door, smilingly adding, "Except for the standard ten to thirty percent employee reduction in free will, of course." His wink might have reassured an innocent.

Inside, a holo-sign glowed green above a hand-hewn wooden desk: "Office of Questions Asked & Answered." A young woman rose to meet us, smiling.

"Hello," she said. "You must be Janet Harper. Thanks for coming to help!" She led us down a central corridor between work areas, dappled in a green, shifting light.

"That's real daylight," said Steve behind me. "Very healthy." People glanced up smiling from screens and desks, as we walked a green-tinted path toward a glass door. We were burrowing deep, and I reviewed the path back out. I had seen no human guards, and the cameras and sensors had flickered unseeing past my eyes as we descended. I would not even show up as an extra shadow.

As the final door opened into a low-lit, dusky rose room, I halted on the threshold. I could not take this test. My non-detect device did not protect against brainreading – they might learn about my plan, or be able to detect its presence. I turned to go, but Steve's arm was across the doorway.

"The hard part's over – we're almost ready for lunch," he said. I turned, seeing four comfortable mossy-green chairs set around a low wooden table. Time slowed as I regarded the rear wall, set with big mirrors. A spherical hand-held device lay on the table, and a smiling young man stood waiting, wearing a forest-green outfit. Cookies and cups sat on the table next to a cut-glass water pitcher. Flowers grew in raised beds encircling the chairs, all bathed in morning sunshine.

Only the one door out, and everyone smiling at me. I sat in the chair nearest to the door. The woman, young man, and Steve settled in. Refreshments were served as the young man, whose green holo-tag read Rupert, recited the standard government phrase.

"Your legal, God-given USA rights are protected here." He went on, "This device is set to screen solely for memories pertaining to the dates and times of your encounter with the subject of study. The records will be stored. After five years you may personally access them via gov.gov."

As Rupert thumb-activated the small sphere and held it in front of my face, I stood up, panic taking over. I could not get a full breath. Rupert leaned back, protecting his damn device from my movements.

"I got it," he said. "Done."

"Let me out of here now!" I shouted, unable to breathe.

Steve said, moving forward, "Let's skip lunch, Janet, and go outdoors." We emerged into the big room. Steve and the young woman held my arms, steering me to a door in the wall with a blinking green light next to it. Inside was an elevator, light blue, white holo clouds playing across the ceiling.

I did not feel upward movement, but the door opened to real daylight – we were back at the top of the escalators. Ferns and flowers moved gently in the breeze. I stepped out, Steve on one side, the young woman on the other. She let go of me, leaving a reddened wet patch on the inside of my wrist.

She said to Steve, "Have her sit in the sun for five minutes, and then she'll be fine." She smiled at me and said, "Being down there takes some people the wrong way. We're really sorry for your discomfort and you should feel better soon." The elevator door closed behind her, and we sat on a sunny bench surrounded by flowering plants.

I said, "I can catch the next monorail train, OK?" and started to rise.

Steve said, "Give it a few minutes – she gave you a mini-sedative, and you need to wait."

"But I didn't ask – " I said, feeling both outrage and a creeping lassitude.

"It's in the small print of your contract," Steve replied. "You know all that." He looked away, at a bird high overhead. "You kind of over-reacted down there, Janet," he said. "Got something on your mind?"

"I get that way sometimes," I replied. "Especially after what happened in Nevada."

Steve gazed down the path and continued, "Just between us, I hate what my park has become."

In my relaxed state I almost said, "That makes two of us." Instead I replied, "I'm grateful for this second chance." We sat companionably together, faces lifted to the sun, the buzz of insects and distant traffic the only sounds.

Steve saw Janet off at the monorail station and walked back to the escalator, wondering why she had not triggered the standard New Visitor check-in. Two Visitor Vector points had silently let her through, unchallenged.

He stepped onto the escalator, thinking, "I need to check that out, but right now, let's see if her readout gives us new information about that sabertooth."

Brian heads back to his car.

Intent on getting back to his car before dark, Brian jogged past the cottages and fields into the woods. The sky was grey, darkening into dusk. The new sign gleamed at the wooded crossroads. It pointed to "Gateway" straight ahead, so he quickened his pace toward the cottage where the old gent with the tail lived.

Brian soon heard the reassuring sound of the creek – but it was on the wrong side of the green road, which sloped more steeply downhill than he remembered. Late afternoon sunlight gleamed through bare beeches to reveal a waterfall on his right. This was not the route back to the car. Somehow he had turned right, onto Apple Island Trace. Brian stopped, glanced ahead – and stood staring, as the afternoon light drained away.

The waterfall skipped and glistened into a lake. The sun was low, but he discerned steep pine-covered slopes rising beyond the lake. Before him a fallen tree trunk extended from the lakeshore, forming a bridge to a small island. There, around a bonfire surrounded by pine trees, two figures were sitting. They were looking his way. One walked in Brian's direction, stopping at the bridge.

"Hello, Brian Owen!" came his pleasant, amused voice. "We hoped to have you here for lunch, but no doubt Maeve's comely company was preferable."

Brian peered at him and replied, "Hi! I made a wrong turn at the crossroads. I'm in a bit of a hurry, I'll just go back – "

"Not to worry, directions often go amiss there, especially at this time of day," the man replied, continuing, "Won't you join us on Apple Island?" There was laughter in his voice as he gestured toward the bonfire.

The man seated there shouted, "Yes! Come on over! Best beer in the land!" Brian finally realized what was strange about the island.

He asked them, "Are those trees – in bloom?" Brian was gazing at a cloud of pink-blossomed trees, shining in bright sunlight. Their springtime beauty crowned a slope above the bonfire clearing.

"Why yes, those are apple trees at the top of their blossom," the first man replied, as his companion approached the bridge.

"It's mid-May over here, you see," said the large, indistinct figure as he stepped onto the bridge. Brian stepped back.

"There's lots of daylight over here, Brian Owen," he said, taking another step.

"I – not today, I'll just – go back to my car," Brian gasped, trying to be polite in his haste to leave. The man laughed lightly as Brian turned back up the path.

He called, "Next time then! You're safer here than with Maeve!"

Brian heard them chuckling as he dashed up the slope and, breasting the hill, came to the crossroads sign in the gathering dusk. It read "Gateway" to the right. Hoping for the best, Brian ran downhill and soon was passing the old gentleman's cottage. Smoke trailed out the chimney and light glowed through the curtained window.

The day was nearly done, and Brian looked for the EXIT sign above the gateway tunnel. Walking fast, he could not see it. Around the remembered bend, the green road stopped dead in the woods. Brian fought off panic, running back to see if he had missed his way again. There was the old gent's cottage. He went back to the dead end, where a high stone and brick wall extended into the darkening woods in both directions.

Brian wondered if he had come at the tunnel from the side. He walked along the wall through the trees – but it did not end, and the day was nearly gone. That incessant murmuring was louder, and it wasn't spring peepers! Something crashed through the trees, nearby.

Beyond the leafless beech trees Brian could see the familiar hills of the state park, wintry blue at dusk. The sun sent day-end gleams across the fields into the woods, illuminating the sprig of flowers placed in his pocket by the crow. Brian tossed it on the ground – and the glowing red EXIT sign appeared, away to his left. He ran toward it.

Here was the green road, here was the tunnel. Brian ran panting along the passage, footfalls echoing, with just enough daylight to see the far end. Emerging, he ran toward his car, alone in the parking area. The cottage atop the hill was silent and shut tight, chimney smoke the only sign of life. Beeping the car door open he jumped in, turned on the engine, and got into gear.

The car bumped back onto the narrow paved road and sped toward the roundabout. Brian drove it clockwise. Ignoring the sign pointing in the wrong direction, he aimed toward the interstate highway, humming with cars, as nighttime arrived. Brian's watch glowed to life on his wrist.

Chapter 5

Janet returns to work at the Park.

I accepted the embrace of the monitoring chair and immersed myself in the riverboat traffic zone, tracking boat movements and stealing glances along the Styx River for that gap in the cave wall. At the required ten-minute, thirty-second eye rest I closed my eyes, then stared directly at the screen where the gap, backed with those massive fans, had to be. I saw an indentation in the wall near the Family Secrets boat landing. A hand rested lightly on my shoulder, and I jumped guiltily.

Ada whispered in my ear, "Hand off to number two and go see Sonny boy, OK?" Heart pounding, I headed to Scott's office, to be met with his beaming grin and the mild gaze of Hugh Hynes.

"Janet!" cried Sonny, like I was his long-lost sister. "Here's Dr. Hynes! He says he liked the way you worked with Steve in that cat caper, and wants you on his team." Hugh beamed blandly at me: our underground meeting would not be mentioned.

Hugh said, "Steve Roberts reports that you performed well across the river, and your D.C. brain scan came back '99.95% accurate to your verbal description.' Whatever that means."

"It means she's sharp!" enthused Sonny. They waited for my response.

I offered, "I have experience for this type of work, you know. I did a lot of back-country water monitoring work at my last posting." Their eyes fell, respectful of my traumatic experiences during the Nevada park conflagration. Scott bounced to his feet and leaned on the front of his desk.

He said, "We'll get Ada to adjust your chair time – we're reassigning some of your hours to the great outdoors. Congrats!" He shook my hand. I could not completely dislike this enthusiastic people-person, and shook firmly back.

Hugh smiled and said, winking at me, "Last time I was doing the water testing, I saw a clue to the whereabouts of that cat. We need you to help us, Janet." He too stood up, signaling an end to the meeting.

"We'll have your new schedule ready by tomorrow," said Scott, waving me out the door. I trotted back to my cubicle.

Ada wiggled her eyebrows, said, "Hey, big shot!" and gave me a big smile. "Congrats!"

I replied with a question, "This is a good thing, right?"

She snorted, "Duh!" – the answer obviously "Yes." I was not joking, though I dared not tell her why. Increasingly entrusted with protecting the park, drawn in to collegial fellowship, and seeing my daughter daily, I worried that I would lose the outsider edge that kept me focused on completing my personal task here.

Conservation and defense interests collide at the Park.

The Parklands Casino Enterprises building was tucked away from taxpayer eyes, built into the side of a steep sinkhole below the park's science and management offices. The gleaming glass cube faced tall oak trees, their leaves rich with the yellow and bronze of autumn. Light rain spattered the windows of the conference room where Steve Roberts and Ed Zanetti sat with Park Superintendent Bogler, Professor Thomas King, and Ard Sprinkle.

The woods and sinkhole were calling Roberts. On the way up from Buchanon Memorial Airport to the park he had cracked the car window, smelling the muggy air as the thunderstorm approached. Trapped in this room with his fellow suits, he was thinking about the sixty-foot dome and cave passage that opened up under the sinkhole's stony drain, directly below this building. He glanced at Sprinkle, wondering at the man's long pallid face and famed loyalty to Senator Styce. Roberts was uneasy about this meeting, and Zanetti's unsmiling face suggested trouble. They were both expecting to be fired.

Sprinkle was on a mission for the Senator. This was the day that Roberts and Zanetti were to be taken down. He loved doing Styce's dirty work, anticipating the great man's compliments later.

Zanetti sagged with wariness and dread. He had fought today's decisions with every procedure at his disposal, failing in the face of Styce's dark persuasive powers and powerful allies. This would be an afternoon of deep regret. He avoided Roberts's questioning glance, thinking calming thoughts of his children and wife.

Sonny Scott came in, whispered to Tom "Cat" King, and sat down.

Roberts thought about the trio of cavers, underground on an official Park trip. Janet, Lena, and Hugh were documenting the sabertooth cat's underground pathway starting from the south side of the river. Roberts had seen them off earlier that afternoon, and pined to be with them. He was amused at how quickly Janet had taken to caving. She and Lena were probably mother and daughter – why did they hide that? He had a fun cave trip in mind for them – ah, that unpleasant man King was speaking.

An hour earlier – Janet, Lena, and Hugh go underground.

Our cave trip started in the science office with a review of underground water monitoring. Lena handed me a bag containing helmet, lights, coveralls, and boots.

"We carry this stuff in bags until we get to the cave," explained Hugh, "to keep the trip private. We'll suit up there." With water sampling bottles and test kits added to the load, we emerged into the overcast autumn day, and turned down the path toward my apartment.

"Now we'll show you that cave entrance you were trying to weasel out of us," said Hugh. Lena was grinning.

"Hey," I said, lightly, "no problem." A helicopter roared overhead, sullying the morning in this quiet corner of the busy park. Hugh took the side path downhill to my apartment building. Skirting the steps, he walked along the wall past an old couch and opened the basement door to the laundry room.

"Hey," I said again, "why are we going in there – " but they were already inside. I followed them into the small room. Lena looked at me, as I looked at Hugh – talking to Steve Roberts.

"When did Steve get here?" I whispered to Lena. She shrugged. As we clambered into our cave suits I went on, "He meant it when he said there's a lot more than ten thousand secrets around here."

"The cave is in there," Lena offered, nodding at a locked cupboard in the rear wall. I, self-styled surveillance expert, had missed a giant hole in the ground? We tuned in on Steve and Hugh's conversation.

"I wish I could come," said Steve, "but I have a meeting in the Casino Enterprises building at 1 p.m."

Patting his suit to indicate unfitness for caving, he continued, "Did you hear the helicopter? It was delivering Senator Styce's assistant, Ed Zanetti from our D.C. office, and Hugh's favorite guy, Professor Tom King."

Hugh, inserting his second leg into the cave suit, began growling.

"That monster is here in our park?" He looked sharply at Steve. "Can't be good news," he said. "Do you know what the meeting is about?"

"'A major new program' is all Bogler would tell me," replied Steve. "They're eating a fancy lunch, and then I'm allowed to join them." He shook his head.

Hugh unlocked the cupboard door. Inside was a dark space with limestone walls. Set into the floor was a manhole cover, also locked. Lena squatted to unlock it, and the cover sprang up to reveal a metal ladder descending into darkness.

Hugh swung onto the ladder and descended several steps. His shoulders, pack, and helmeted head still visible, he addressed Steve.

"Just close it up behind us, OK?" Steve nodded, putting the keys in his pocket.

"It'll be easier, later on, if we don't have to unlock the manhole and the cupboard, when we're tired and carrying samples," Hugh continued, voice fading as he descended. Lena pointed for me to go next – new person in the middle. I stepped across the opening and onto the ladder, squeezing my cave pack past the rim, clambering down rung by rung. Cool, moist air rose up around me. Lena's feet appeared on the ladder above, and Steve's voice echoed down the shaft to us from the receding circle of daylight.

"Find out where that big cat went, and stay safe."

Hugh's light beamed up at me, and after a long step, my feet landed on solid rock. Eyes adjusting to the dark, I moved aside as Lena dropped down. We heard the laundry room door close, and stillness enveloped us.

"Ah," said Hugh, "listen," and we stood entranced by the deep silence. My shoulder muscles loosened as I took deep breaths.

"This way," he said, and we followed, lights revealing a gradual descent along a cave corridor, wide enough to walk side by side, about eight feet high.

"You two are a lot alike," said Hugh unexpectedly. I stiffened, vigilant. "You look alike, you talk alike, and you're both comfortable underground. What's it all about?" We rounded a bend, lights outlining the end of the passage, with a bigger space beyond.

I replied with an evasive bad joke, "I've been in the dark all my life."

He snorted and said, "Well, it's none of my business, I suppose. Just another damn secret." Lena patted my arm invisibly in the darkness. We emerged from the side passage into the larger space – on the path next to the underground river, which burbled and chuckled, downstream to the right. The water was low, the river more rocks than water. I shined my light up and down the path and spoke with irritation.

"We must have walked right past this on our way out the other night. How come you didn't tell me – "

"Secrets," said Hugh. He was intent on our mission: "Something has changed, downstream. This water should be backed up and pooled. Maybe it has something to do with the cat getting under the river to our time."

He walked rapidly down the path, and we followed. Wind blasted us from the side passage that led to the fans, frack well and gap in the wall to the River Styx. Rounding the next bend on the main path, I felt a big space opening around us. Hugh pulled a powerful light from his pack, and illuminated the scene.

A round room lay before us, oval stone ceiling arching thirty feet above. The path continued to a stone landing. Two ropes were tied to its metal posts and extended across the mud-coated floor of the room toward a hole in the center. At the end of one rope was an inflated rubber dinghy; nothing was attached to the other. Water from the cave stream flowed across the floor to the hole and poured noisily over the edge. Hugh swung around, in his excitement shining the power light into our eyes, bathing us in super-brightness. The scene behind him vanished into darkness.

"Whups sorry," he said, switching off the light and returning us to deep dark punctuated by our headlamps. Hugh spoke invisibly.

"Like I suspected, the plug is gone. This was a lake, and that hole in the center was glued shut with old debris – rocks and rock-hard mud. Let's go look. Watch out – the mud is slippery." He turned the big light back on and jumped off the low stone landing onto the muddy lake floor.

"We need to be looking for cat spoor," called Lena, gently reminding him of our official mission. Hugh walked over to the hole in the floor as she and I shined our lights around the empty lake bed.

"Yep – look," she said. Dried cat tracks were visible along the lake floor, leading from a small opening in the wall of the big cave room. Scraped mud covered a scat pile. Paw prints headed to the path we had come in on.

"I bet it went out to the Park from here," I said. "We'll need a tracker to find paw prints on the gravel and stone paths."

"The good news for me," said Lena, "is that the tracks are old. I don't want to meet the cat in here." We turned toward Hugh, who was on his stomach next to the hole in the floor, shining the big light down. We crept up carefully, peering into the round hole. About ten feet across, it fell away below us, straight-sided like an elevator shaft.

"How deep?" asked Lena.

"Thirty feet," said Hugh. "Guesstimate." The cave stream poured over the edge next to him and plummeted noisily to the bottom, where it flowed across the stony floor and vanished into a crevice.

"That drain," Hugh shined his big light at the crevice, "must head toward the Green, Green River, which is only about two hundred feet that way" – he pointed toward the far wall – "north." He got up and we backed away from the hole, stepping carefully in the slick mud.

"We shouldn't be so close without a safety rope," Lena said, but Hugh was shining the superlight at the opening in the wall of the room.

"That has always been full of water," he said, striding over and bending to look inside.

"Let's go," he called, climbing in.

"Wait," said Lena, leaning after him into the small opening. Her light shined down a narrow passageway that sloped steeply downward, parallel to the hole in the floor of the cave room. "What are you planning to do?"

"We're here, we have the time, let's see if this goes," Hugh called back, his voice muffled by the tight space.

Lena leaned out and turned to me. "Can you manage this?" she asked.

"Only one way to find out," I said, and climbed into the steep passage, feet first.

"Go Mom," she said, scrambling in behind me. The tight walls supported my shoulders as I scooted down, feet seeking the way, Lena close above, both of us accumulating a mud coating. I soon heard Hugh's voice below me. His light was shining on my feet.

He called, "Just lie down and scoot out on your butt and back," and I slid out onto the bottom of the hole we had been peering into from above. Lena popped out after me. I dodged the waterfall and saw Hugh shining the superlight at the crevice in the floor. Water was pouring into it from the lake room far above.

"It goes!" he cried excitedly, and slid into the crevice, looking around for us to follow.

"Can you just wait a minute," I said. Lena shined her headlamp at the sides of the hole and up to the top thirty feet above us, where the tourist trail and stone landing were.

"What's the plan, Stan?" she called to Hugh over the racket of the waterfall, loud in the confined space. Removing a chocolate bar from a pocket, she broke off a chunk and handed it to me.

"Water break," she said, deliberately slowing the pace. Hugh stood up and joined us. We had a long cool drink from our canteens and relished our candy bars.

"It's only another two hundred feet to the river," repeated Hugh, wolfing down his snack. "Based on what we already know, this crevice here opens up, drops ten feet, and goes right under the river." He adjusted his pack, put the superlight away, and turned toward the crevice.

"You're saying that this little hole here goes underneath the Green, Green River?" I asked. This situation was beyond my comfort zone. "Is this safe?"

"I think," said Hugh, visibly impatient, "and Steve Roberts thinks, along with our entire science team – "

Lena raised her eyebrows to interject, "A whole five people," as he continued.

" – that setting the river's north shore into the Pleistocene re-opened a passage under the river during that ancient era. Water pressure pushed open a plug. We can now get under the Green, Green River and into the Pleistocene via this drain hole. It's the path the cat used."

He said, "We've been in here only an hour. Let's give it one more hour. OK?" We nodded.

"C'mon," he said, scrambling into the crevice. I followed, Lena behind, climbing down, leaning away from the water. I slid down a slick rock face. We scrambled downward on ledges, back and forth across a widening canyon. Hugh's light shone up from below and he shouted something I could not hear above the noise of the waterfall.

"What'd he say, did you hear?" I called up to Lena.

She puffed, "This is deeper than he said it would be. Damn it."

I heard Hugh again, and reported to Lena, "He said, 'hand-line.'"

"Oh, shit," she said, "Wait a minute, OK?" I leaned into the wall as she opened her pack, removed a short rope, and tied it off on a projecting rock. The line dangled toward Hugh's light, fifteen feet below.

"OK," she instructed, "hold onto the line the rest of the way down. You may have to drop." I edged carefully down, one hand and arm wrapped around the slender line. Next step, my left foot met empty space.

Hugh called, "It's only a three-foot drop. Use the line to brace yourself – straighten out – " He was right there as I dropped and landed. I let go of the line as Lena landed lightly behind me. We were in a small bowl-shaped room.

Water flowed across the flat floor into a side passage, about five feet high and narrow. Something shiny on the floor –

"Is this cool or what," said Hugh, walking over to an inflated dinghy. He spoke loudly over the racket of the water. "This was sucked all the way down here when the lake emptied." He lifted and dropped it. "You saw there was only one up there, at the landing, right?"

"Why did it stop here?" asked Lena. She shined her light at the small passageway ahead.

"Maybe the suction dropped, at this point," said Hugh, "like, you know, the giant toilet bowl flush was complete." I envisioned the rubber raft being yanked from its rope, circling the hole in the lake room, plummeting as the water dropped, then squeezing through the canyon we had just scrambled down. I'm mentally tough – have to be – but with the distance piling up between us and the blue sky above, I was feeling a little bit uneasy.

"Not much use here, is it?" I said, masking my discomfort with a kick at the poor lonely thing, stranded down here. Lena, knowing me well, shot me a look.

Hugh laughed and said, "We're about ten feet below the bed of the Green, Green River – and that passage there will take us underneath it to the Pleistocene." He added, "I hope you understand how important this is," and led the way. The three of us hunched over to fit into the narrow passage and headed north, splashing in the stream.

Meanwhile, back in the conference room.

In the glass-walled conference room hundreds of feet above the caving team, daylight diminished as the rain came down, whipping torrents against the windows. The beautiful building gleamed bright in the darkening woods.

"Gentlemen, this is a great day for Homeland-Parkland cooperation. Once the General joins us, we'll finalize the details," said King, sprawling in his chair. His hooded eyes were ciphers; he smiled a small insider smile. His words sounded strange to Roberts – maybe it was just King's intolerable smugness grating on him.

He pushed back, "Since when do we need a general at a monthly science update meeting?" King and Superintendent Bogler exchanged glances.

King said, "This is not a routine science meeting, Stevie!" Distant outdoor noises resolved into a helicopter landing above. Roberts was stricken with apprehension and looked at Zanetti, who lowered his eyes and shook his head.

Eager to defuse tension, Scott made nice conversation while they waited for the General.

"There's a science expedition underground, right now," he enthused.

King said encouragingly, "I heard a rumor – are they tracking a sabertooth?" Roberts gestured to Scott to head him off, but the effusive man continued.

"You heard about that? Hugh Hynes and the park science team found out that all the water drained out of the lake room. They think maybe the sabertooth found a pathway under the Green, Green River and got out to our time that way."

"A path opened up under the river?" said King, eyes gleaming with interest.

Scott chattered on, "Yeah! So Hynes and a crack team of expert cavers are down there now, on the trail of the cat." Turning to Roberts for backup, Scott received a blank stare, realized he had stepped in it, did not know what, and shut up. King's eyes wandered toward a locked door in the corner. Behind it was the time controls room. Roberts noted the direction of King's gaze.

Noise of the rising storm entered with the distinguished retired General Granger, who shook off raindrops and said to the group, "Brings back good times, flying through a storm. Probably broke some rules, but I was not going to miss this meeting!" His old eyes gleamed as he sat down. The rumble of thunder dropped when the door closed.

"So," said Granger, looking at Sprinkle, "please proceed." Sprinkle began to read from a sheet of Senator Styce's embossed letterhead paper, extracted from a manila envelope.

"Dateline Ten Thousand Secrets National Park Casino & Entertainment District, Kentucky: Today marks the welcome implementation of the new Action Force between the Department of

Homeland Security and Department of Defense. Effective immediately, the Action Force replaces the venerable Office of Homeland-Interior. We thank outgoing Interior Liaison Edward Zanetti for his service. His office is replaced by the Defense-driven Action Force, headed by Thomas King, distinguished Professor of – "

Sprinkle paused, sensing he had lost his audience's attention. He took a sip of spring water. Zanetti was standing, staring at the smiling King. Superintendent Bogler sat wooden-faced. Scott's face showed surprise and confusion as he stared at the two glaring men.

Roberts paid no attention to the human drama. He was watching the rain, which was really coming down, slapping in sheets at the windows, plastering golden leaves onto the glass.

"Well," thought Sprinkle, "he'll pay attention, when I get to paragraph three." He resumed reading, but King stopped him.

"Really," he said sweetly, "reading words off a page is a little cold. After all, these men's lives, and the entire Park's reason for being, are undergoing big changes. Let me tell them about the grand transformation." He walked to the head of the table and eased into a chair next to the General, taking charge. Zanetti sat down, his face drained of color.

They leaned in as King spoke quietly, "Ed Zanetti, we're transferring you to the Science section, but it's undergoing a big re-organization to gear up for military operations, so we'll give you a few months to see if you want to stay."

"Steve Roberts," said King, looking at Steve, who was paying attention now. "You're working for me, as we reshape the Park Service's Time Science program in cooperation with Defense. This is a real-world, applied science position, and I hope you can adapt." General Granger grinned at these long-awaited words, like water in the desert to his parched warrior soul. No more "research and study." Zanetti was out!

Granger said warmly, "If I could have a moment, Cat, to announce changes here at the Park." He smiled at Bogler and Scott, the former impassive, the latter pinned back in his chair, eyes wide.

"Let's take a five-minute break first, General," replied King. "These folks," he smiled around the table, "need a few minutes to process the good news. After twenty years of hard work, they have finally reached their objectives!" Beaming, he stood and stretched. The group rose with the General, staring dumbly at one another. Zanetti left the room, his phone out. Roberts watched King walk toward the locked door, taking Superintendent Bogler with him.

King said, "Finally, I can learn how this operation works. Get the door open – please." His new authority suited him just fine. Bogler summoned a technician and introduced her to "the distinguished Professor King, our new boss. Please show him the control room," and turned away. The young woman shook King's hand and carried out the arcane security steps of opening the door. King ushered her, hand on the small of her back, into the room beyond. Roberts moved toward them but was slowed by the anxious Scott.

"Steve, he said you keep your job, right? Is that what you heard? Sounds like the Super and I will too, you think? Oh gawd why did they have to take a break – " he jabbered.

Roberts stepped around him toward the open control room door. The Time Controls for the Park were in there, with access only for top techies, who had to pass through several I.D. checkpoints and the Superintendent's office to get there.

"That door 'must be locked at all times,'" Roberts mentally recited from the Park regulations, stepping into the small, windowless room for the first time. On the walls, an array of digital tools included visitor management and surveillance, next to a panel and keyboard. The words "Time Standards & Practices Staff Only" were emblazoned under a glowing skull and crossbones, wall-mounted next to hand and iris biometrics identification devices that the techie was demonstrating for King.

Set apart, a hand-sized red metal cage protected a small keyboard with a red power button. The room was cold. An emergency back-up server hummed behind a partition; generators were set on continual stand-by, and massive hunks of wires vanished into the walls. Lights, sensors, and cameras twinkled from the room's upper corners.

The technician explained the devices and their uses to the perfectly charming Professor King, who touched each item as he asked questions.

"That's the daily visitor management array," she said, as Roberts edged in behind them. Her breath puffed white in the refrigerated air.

She noticed him with a nod, saying, "Mr. Roberts here is our boss for those operations."

King smiled tightly, saying, "Yes. We are adjusting his access," moving his hands lightly above the keyboard. He pointed at the small array under the cage.

"Is that a fake?" he asked. The techie laughed at her new boss's little jest.

"That's Time Re-Set. I am not supposed to talk about it," she said, and shut her mouth firmly.

"Very good, proud of you, young lady," purred King. Pointing left-handed at the far side of the array, he asked, "What's that do?" while swiftly pulling the cage off the array and pressing the power button with his right hand. Roberts gasped and jumped forward, but was too late, as King pressed the button again at the prompt CONFIRM REVERT TO PRESENT DAY on the main screen.

Roberts's new boss turned to face him, saying, "Get the fuck back, or you won't last another day here." They froze eye-to-eye for five long seconds. The technician stood staring. Roberts turned and left the control room, headed out the door, down the hall. Zanetti, on his phone near the stairs, tried to intercept him.

"Steve, Holm wants confirmation – " but Roberts was already down a flight, out the glass door into the heavy rain.

The cave trip continues.

"This is nuts," I said, inching along the narrow passageway. The ceiling had risen, so we walked upright. The stream underfoot was a few inches deep. In the tight space the water made a lot of noise. I did not like the water seeping through the ceiling, dripping onto my helmet and under my collar. This had started about twenty feet back.

"We'll be out from under the river in another minute," Lena reassured me.

I said, "Must go faster." Ahead, Hugh was proceeding slowly, excited by the ancient passageway.

He said, "Unprecedented in the history of science," his light on fossils and undulations in the walls. I was still trying to understand this cave passage, both old and new at the same time.

"Look, I am clueless," I said to Lena during a scientific pause. "Can you just go over it one more time, and why it's so important for us to do this scary thing?" She turned to lean against the wall. Hugh was taking photos and scraping small bits of wall into plastic containers.

As she spoke, Lena's headlight illuminated rivulets running down the walls, joining the stream underfoot. "Under a cooperative research agreement with Homeland, the Park set the land on the north side of the river into the Pleistocene. So that visitors could see the ancient animals and have adventures, while thinking it was a safe fake experience. And meanwhile Homeland-Interior could conduct research to determine the safety and usefulness of time travel. You know all that." She dug out another chocolate bar and gave me a chunk, which I tried to eat slowly. The chocolate was strangely soothing.

Lena continued, "In our modern time, there is no cave passage that goes under the river. But our science team, all five of us, think there *was* a passage, during the Pleistocene. By our time it had filled in with soft sedimentary rock layers." Hugh moved ahead and we shuffled forward into the ancient past.

As we moved out from under the river, the ceiling dried out and the passage dropped steeply. My sense of terror receded and I looked around with renewed interest. Hugh took up the tale, his voice filtering back through the noise of the stream underfoot.

"We think that setting back the north side of the park on the surface re-opened a Pleistocene cave room underground. Today's Green, Green River seeped down through cracks in the river floor to erode the sediment and rocks that blocked the ancient passage. This passage under the river opened up, spilling into the big cave room. And here it is."

"Did all those changes take a while?" My voice was muffled by the big space we had emerged into. Hugh shined the superlight around the giant room. We were high up on the wall, a steep climb to the floor below. He smiled as he turned to face us, and began climbing down.

Hugh replied, "Yeah, it took a couple of years, from the time change to when the passage cleared out. Then the sabertooth strolled through the under-river passage, up and out of the cave, and you and Steve saw it."

I focused on climbing down the wall. Lena went first, reaching up to nudge my boots to foot-holds. The ceiling rose as we clambered down. We soon stood on the floor of the giant cave room that soared to a height of one hundred feet, revealed in the superlight and measured with Hugh's laser-mapper. Its green pin-point bounced back and forth across the walls and ceiling, accumulating geo-data. Across the room's vast floor spread a pool of water, mud, clay, and shattered rocks.

Hugh shined the light across the debris.

"That's the contents of the cave passage – dumped there when the water pushed out the plug." We edged around the room, scrambling over rocks fallen long ago from the ceiling. I liked this big gloomy room. I felt less tense, and refused to think about the trip back. Hugh swept the ceiling with the superlight. In his other hand I saw a small tool.

"What you got there?" I asked.

"It's a stun gun from Park security," he replied. "I can dial it up to kill if I need to." This mystified me, so I waited for more.

"For the sabertooths, you know?" Hugh added. "And the woolly mammoths that are outside, if we find the entrance to the out-of-doors."

Two can play the tough guy game, so I sniffed the air. Stepping away from our pooled light into the surrounding dark, I scanned the big room from edge to edge with my flashlight. I wanted to tease Hugh, scare him in return.

"Oh, whatever are you doing!" said Lena breathlessly, trying not to giggle.

"Can't you smell it!" I barked. Hugh had been playing his fancy light over the pool, but he whipped round and came over, anxiety in his eyes.

"Smell what!" he whispered sharply.

"I smell a wild animal," I replied, but then found what I had been joking about.

"Look!" My light illuminated a fresh pile of cat scat, just ahead. I instinctively stepped closer to Lena, hand out to her. We froze in place, straining our ears into the darkness. We became aware of the stream cascading from the hole back where we had entered the big room. Hugh played the light on the climb back up. The stream seemed louder than before.

"You thinking what I'm thinking?" I said, sensing that the sabertooth might be watching us. In silent reply, Hugh made a small gesture suggesting that we might want to mosey back to that climb. We crept quietly across the rocks, past the pool, and started up. Hugh covered us as we clambered swiftly and silently up the wall through the cascading stream, and into the small passage under the river. He shined his light back down the climb, and around the big room. Nothing down there was moving. I turned to Lena, she turned around, and we all crept back through the passage.

"Feels like home!" I called to Lena, eager to get back under the river. The stream seemed deeper.

"This wasn't ankle-deep when we came in, was it?" I asked anxiously.

Hugh answered, "Maybe there's a rainstorm up top. It was in the forecast. We better hurry."

We splashed along, faster. The ceiling began to drip.

Hugh said to my back, "We'll need to install a gate to keep the animals on that side."

"Whatever!" I hissed, moving fast, intent on getting out from under the river.

Steve heads into the cave.

Roberts ran along the wet path, slick dress shoes skidding in the matted leaves. The rain was slowing, but he was soaked by the time he reached the path to staff housing and laundry room. He called the Science office.

Ron's young voice said, "Hello, you have reached the – " Roberts cut him off.

"Ron. Emergency. Damaris there?"

Ron replied according to his training: "Emergency. Copy. What do you need, where?" He was climbing into coveralls, grabbing an emergency kit bag, as Damaris did the same. They knew where the caving action was that day.

Roberts replied, "Join me at the Staff Entrance. I need a helmet and coveralls and boots, and we need first aid and ropes."

"OK," said Ron as he and Damaris gathered the needed items and emerged from the building at a run, dashing under the monorail line and across the road, toward staff housing. Roberts ran up the walkway, along the building wall to the laundry room. Inside, he kicked out the off-duty staffer who had been peacefully immersed in the first Harry Potter book as he waited on the washing machine.

"You know what 'Emergency' means," Roberts said, letting Damaris and Ron in before locking the outside door on the guy, who grumbled about his wet clothes and wondered what the emergency was inside a small basement laundry room. Roberts opened the cupboard door to the manhole.

"Head to the lake room," he said to Ron and Damaris, who were already climbing down the ladder. He pulled on coveralls, boots, and helmet, pausing to toss down the two coiled ropes Ron had brought, calling "Rope!" after them.

Roberts closed the wall door behind him, the washing machine churning away, and slid down the ladder, throwing a first aid bundle ahead as he dropped. He touched down, picked up the bundle, and ran. Headlamps raked the ceiling and walls as the three pelted down the path along the now-roaring cave river, swollen with runoff from the rainstorm. They came around the bend into the big lake room, dark and deserted. Roberts caught up at the landing.

Ron shouted, "Where'd the lake go?" The river roared noisily next to them, pouring across the lake room floor, cascading into the hole at its center. Roberts set down the first aid bundle and handed them each a rope coil.

He gestured at the hole, saying, "The lake drained out under the Green, Green River – but a madman just reset the time button to the present and plugged the hole under the river. So this rainwater is refilling the passages below us. Our friends are down there somewhere and may get trapped by the rising water." Ron and Damaris carefully stepped through the slick mud to the edge of the hole, peering down. Roberts untied the rubber raft from the landing.

The climb out.

Lena and I stepped out of the river passage into the bowl-shaped room, the waterfall shimmering in our lights, louder than before. The inflatable boat and dangling hand-line were reassuring links to the outside, far above. I adjusted my cave pack for the canyon climb. Lena turned toward me, on her face a startled expression.

"Did you notice that?" she asked.

"What?" I said. I was intent on the three of us clambering back up that canyon, through that nasty crevice, and then the thirty-foot climb up to the lake room, and was not "noticing" anything else.

"The air changed," she whispered. She was staring at the river passage we had just emerged from. It was jammed shut with rocks and mud. The waterfall was pooling on the floor of the little room. Water no longer drained toward the big room beyond the Green, Green River.

"Where is Hugh?" Lena asked. We played our helmet lights and flashlights along the wall, but the passage we had emerged from was gone. And so was Hugh, trapped in the rocks and mud. Unknown to us, King, in the office far above, had just reset Pleistocene Place into the present.

"They *knew* we were down here," Lena said, staring around, her headlight bouncing wildly off the small chamber's wet walls. Wondering if Hugh had somehow slipped past us, I shined my light up the canyon climb. No one was ahead of us.

"Hugh told me that a decision to change the time back to the present would be made *after* this trip was completed and reported on," Lena went on, standing in the now knee-deep water, motionless with shock. The rubber raft was afloat on the rising water, its natural habitat restored as ours deteriorated.

"Decision to do what, now?" I asked. I did not understand what she was talking about, but I knew we were in trouble if we did not get moving soon.

Lena replied, "The science team said that if we found a passage under the river, they would consider getting rid of Pleistocene Place – reset it to the present. But that would have been a long decision-making process, and it looks like they did it just now! The time change controls are in the Superintendent's office."

Her words bounced off me as the round low-ceilinged chamber filled up with rainfall pouring down from outside the cave. It could flow no further, the passage under the river blocked. The water grew deeper, up to our thighs and rising. I took Lena by the elbow, and moved her toward the canyon. Her breathing was uneven.

I said, "Get in the boat. We gotta go." We climbed in, fending off the ledges as the raft rose into the canyon. The water bubbled up fast, the round room now submerged. The thundering waterfall crowded the raft as the canyon narrowed.

"It's another thirty feet up this canyon and then another thirty up to the lake room with the tourist trail, which is probably where the water will rise to," Lena said, holding onto the raft's ropes to steady herself. "But – what if they re-set time again to the Pleistocene? We'd be dead ducks." She nodded her head upward toward the Park office.

"What do you mean?" I shouted over the noise of the pounding waterfall. We grabbed at the stone ledges that closed in around us as the raft rose in the narrowing canyon.

Lena shouted, "Someone up there just pushed the button to set the north side of the Park back into the present. They trapped Hugh in the rock when the passageway refilled. If they decided to reverse that and re-set to the Pleistocene, the passage would instantly re-open under the Green, Green River."

She turned to look at me, continuing, "We'd flush down out of here, through the river passage, and into the big cave room we were just in. You saw the rocks and debris in there. That would be us, busted up and drowned, along with whatever remains of Hugh." Lena wrapped her arms around herself to keep from shaking. She was frozen with fear, so I took charge.

The ledges around and above us suddenly looked solid and friendly. If what she said was right, the raft could drop from under us at any moment. I pulled the raft to a wide ledge and scrambled out onto it, holding the raft steady for Lena to follow.

I said, "We can climb faster than the water can rise. And this inflatable might not fit through the tight spot up there." We began to climb the wall of the canyon, from ledge to ledge. We got several feet above the water, but it was gaining, getting closer to the bottom of our boots. The canyon narrowed, and we had to climb up through the waterfall, heavy as a blasting fire-hose.

Lena huffed, "Canyon is narrower – space fills faster," and we tried to put on speed. I was not enjoying the idea that we were climbing out of a giant toilet bowl that might flush at any second.

I shined my headlamp upward, whining, "Are we getting close to the top?"

Lena, re-energized, flashed a sporting grin, saying, "Oh, yeah, I can see the lip of the waterfall." Past the squeeze through the crevice was the hole at the center of the lake room. We could climb up the narrow side passage to the tourist trail.

The inflatable shot up between us.

"Killer whale!" laughed Lena shakily. We were at the crevice, and Lena waved me to go first. I turned off my brain and jammed into the tight climb on the slick, smooth rock. Huffing and puffing and swearing, I wormed upward and rolled out onto the floor of the hole. Now we were just thirty feet below the lake room.

I shouted, "Go!" Lena started the climb. My light showed her knee-deep in water, the raft wedging her into the waterfall. I extended my hand, but she surged up and rolled out of the crevice next to me and was on her feet in a second, shining her light upward. The pounding waterfall was plummeting down from the lake room above and pouring into the crevice we had just climbed out of.

"It must be raining hard out there," Lena shouted over the din. The raft made horrific squealing noises as it was expelled from the drain. It popped out, flipped, and plopped onto the floor next to me, noisily losing air as it deflated, from a hole torn during the final squeeze.

Water spread out across the floor – the drain below was full. Thirty feet above us was the tourist trail to the surface. But with the raft dead, how could we get up the straight-sided hole? We ran over to the narrow passage that we had come down following Hugh, but it was already inches full of water and rising rapidly.

"We can't stay ahead of the water in that tight climb," said Lena. Playing our lights around, we saw a steep slope of rocks rising up the wall, maybe ten feet high. Lena moved to the rock pile, and began to climb.

"What's the point?" I shouted, adding, "The tourist trail is still way above us."

She called, "I guess we'll just float up as the water rises," and moved closer to me, so that we could speak without shouting over the waterfall's tumult.

"That will be a long, cold float," I said. "We don't have any choice. But, if they turn the time back – "

"We'll flush down and out and join Hugh in the distant past," said Lena, beginning to shiver, water over the top of her boots.

Above, a helmeted head and shoulders appeared at the top of the hole, headlamp shining into our eyes.

A young voice shouted, "Raft!" as the other inflatable raft sailed into view and landed next to us in the rising water, now over our knees. We fell into it.

It was Damaris's voice, calling, "Rope!"

First one, then two ropes snaked down the side of the hole. The raft was pushed away by the force of the waterfall, but we held onto ledges as the water rose under us, and pulled the raft over to the ropes. Lena grabbed them, handing one to me. We both glanced up, eyes following the ropes. Three headlamps shone down.

Steve's voice bellowed above the din of the waterfall, "Where's Hugh?" We shook our heads.

Ron shouted, "Get those loops around your waists and tighten them." I looked down, dazed, to see that my rope ended in a slip-knot loop. Lena and I fumbled the loops over our heads. Hands numb, we helped one another tighten the ropes around our sodden waists, and looked back up. The water had risen rapidly and we were only six feet below the lake room floor. Damaris and Ron's faces were intent and watchful, Steve behind them pulling in and securing the loose rope.

"Hold onto those ropes with both hands, as far up as you can reach," shouted Steve. The lake room floor came into view. Ron leaned down to pull the raft over to the edge of the hole, Damaris holding onto him.

After the button is pushed.

A high-pitched tone was beeping. It filled the conference room, the outer office, and the handsome hallways of the Parklands Casino Enterprises building. Bogler and Scott stared as King emerged from the Time Controls room with the technician.

"Time for a change!" King announced to the astonished faces. The beep sounded across the Park. In every hotel room; on the Styx River boats; in each of the Ten Thousand Secrets; on phones and devices. Down at the Green, Green River, the north bank emerged from its Pleistocene haze. Revealed were U.S. EPA signs and fences, notifying the public of a fracked gas well "Recovery Area and Wildlife Refuge." At the boat landing, Park rangers and passengers readying for the afternoon trip to the Pleistocene stared across the Green, Green River at this unappealing sight.

King sat down at the conference table next to Sprinkle, gesturing for the others to join him.

"Let's finish this meeting," he said, raising his voice over the beeping, which changed to a low sonic wail. Granger and Scott sat down. Zanetti stood next to Bogler, who was talking to the techie and listening for the sound of approaching feet.

Holding up his hand for silence, Bogler stepped forward as three Park Security guys came in. Two flanked the control room door and turned to face the group. The third man was Lee Turner, the security guard who had clashed with Steve and Janet on the field trip to Pleistocene Place.

He stepped up to Bogler and said, "Sir, was that change authorized?"

Bogler shook his head and said, "No."

"Is there an emergency reason for the change?" asked Turner, as the three guards pulled out their free-will irons and thumbed the power to "full." Their eyes never left the group at the table.

Bogler shook his head and again said, "No."

"Excuse me," said King. "I am in charge here. I am fully authorized to make changes in the system. What seems to be the problem?"

"What authority is that, sir?" asked Turner in an icy tone.

"I am Superintendent Bogler's new boss, effective ten minutes ago," said King, coming around the table toward Turner, who stayed put, free-will aimed at the floor. King held out the paper Sprinkle had read from.

"I am 'Head of the new Action Task Force between Homeland Security and the Department of Defense. Effective immediately. The Task Force is headed by Thomas King.'"

He loomed over Turner, pushing his I.D. holo into the guard's face, continuing, "That's me. If I want to change the system here, I can. Defense is in charge now. You should be delighted." Turner did not budge, eyes on the Superintendent.

King said to the techie, "Go in there and make the system changes permanent and turn off that damn siren. We're ending the Pleistocene gimmick. All those resources – " his gesture included generators, servers, distant power plant – "are now in service to our country's strategic interests."

"But someone might be stranded – " the techie said shakily.

"Or dead," said Zanetti, mind running through the implications of shutting off the past. "Isn't there a Science team down in the cave right now?" he asked, looking around for Steve Roberts.

King brushed them off. "There's minimal impact this time of day. You think I haven't researched the program, Ed?" he said. "You suggesting that I am irresponsible with human life and safety?" He too looked around the silent group for Roberts, now his subordinate.

He said, "Roberts is not going to work here much longer if he is absent in the first minutes of his new appointment. His job is to dissolve the research and monitoring programs, so we have a clean slate in the service of our country. This park is a jewel in the crown of Defense's research-for-action installations."

Zanetti slumped in despair, his beautiful research world ground to dust under this man's heel. King's eyes moved to the wall clock, and he drew a slow, deep breath.

"Probably enough time," he said quietly, and addressed Turner, who had not budged.

"Why are you still here? You men need to go, so we can complete the program transition. Scott here" – King gestured at Sonny Scott, sunk in his seat, hoping to survive the purge – "wants to get going on his new duties." Scott's face brightened, then faded as he began to worry if his upcoming vacation would be canceled.

Behind King, Superintendent Bogler locked eyes with Turner, and shook his head tightly.

Turner said to King, "I have standing orders from the Superintendent. They are 'Status remains unchanged until and unless specifically authorized and approved.'"

Turner spoke to Bogler. "Please re-set, sir. Everyone else, stay where you are," he added, gesturing with his free-will to the technician to go into the control room.

King pushed up against Turner's chest and grabbed at the free-will. "You are fired," he said, turning to shout at Bogler, "My authority supersedes this trailer low-life." The two other guards raised their free-wills toward King, who froze in place.

Bogler strode after the techie into the control room, waiting as she authorized access. He pushed the power button twice, resetting the north side of the river into the Pleistocene Epoch. The young woman replaced the cage over the small array, hands shaking. Bogler patted her shoulder, eased them both back into the conference room, the control room door shutting and locking with an audible snap.

"Sorry for the inconvenience," Bogler said to King, who stood white-faced, trembling with rage. Bogler continued quietly, "We have procedures here. There's a reason for them. We'll need new orders to supersede them." He walked out the door with the technician, Turner, and his guys close behind.

Park-wide, the sonic moan faded, and guests returned to their entertainments.

"Was that a drill?" employees and sub-contractors whispered to one another. Heads shook "No" as word spread, spiced with the dire insult leveled at Lee by the new boss.

Water falls.

Two hundred feet below the Park office, our raft was level with the floor of the lake room, and I reached out to grab Damaris's hand. Ron pulled us toward him. Steve was tying off the ropes on the landing. The waterfall made a satisfied gurgling sound. The hole was filled to the brim, and water slopped out onto the lake floor.

Steve walked back to stare down at the water. He shouted, "Hold on, everyone brace – " as the raft dropped out from under us. A massive roar filled the lake room. The ropes gripped us as Lena and I fell and smacked against the side of the hole, five feet below the lip. Instantly we were both being dragged upward. I looked down to see the hole emptying, water swirling in a tight whirlpool toward the drain below, waterfall pounding into the falling, spiraling water. Then Lena and I were yanked by ropes and hands over the edge and onto the lake room floor.

We were sodden lumps, boots full of water, clothes saturated. My helmet was gone. Lena's backpack was gone. I could not feel my hands or feet. The ropes were tight, constricting – but then our friends were loosening them, freeing us, helping us up and over to the stone landing. Steve stepped away and went back to look down the hole, where we could hear a final fading roar.

He turned to look at our huddled group and said, "The drain is open again." I began to be conscious of my surroundings. The cave stream next to us was a torrent, flowing across the lake room floor to the hole.

"We kinda had a major rainstorm up here," explained Ron, as he and Damaris untied and removed our boots, peeled off our sodden cave suits and wrapped us in blankets.

"Drink," said Damaris sternly, handing us each a metal cup filled with warm liquid. Sitting next to me on the landing, Lena was shivering. She closed her eyes and tears swelled down her cheeks. Steve stood in front of us, his eyes full of worry.

Lena looked up at him and said, "The passage under the river snapped shut with Hugh in it," and began to weep. I put my arms around her, as did Damaris and Ron.

Steve, who (I took the time to notice) looked a lot better in a cave outfit than in a suit and tie, swung his head sharply away from us and stared up the passage along the roaring river toward the way out. He told us later that he was thinking about the chaotic meeting he had left behind, and that Cat King had murdered Hugh Hynes.

Across the park, the siren wail faded. Today's problems vanished from the north bank of the river as the sparkling mist returned. Faux-rustic signs at the Pleistocene Place entrance read: "Gone Fishin' – Back Tomorrow." Dejected families argued with rangers, and full refunds were promised. Security guards stood by, hands on their free-wills.

Outside the laundry room, huddled away from the rain on the old couch propped against the building's wall, the off-duty staffer glanced up foggily from his fifteenth reading of Harry, Hermione, and Ron in the life-sized game of wizard's chess.

"Was that the Time Alarm?" he wondered. No, he must have imagined it, and went back into the world where he felt most alive.

Next to him, the laundry door swung open. Out staggered the rude people who had ruined his perfect day off.

"My turn, finally?" he asked indignantly, but they swept past without a word, up the stairs. All were soaking wet, and there were two more of them than he remembered – must have been his day-off morning toke. Those two looked worse for wear, the older woman who worked in the main office and that cute young Science gal. The group squelched up the concrete steps; a door opened and shut. Solitude returned, and the staffer moved his clothes into the dryer. The laundry room floor was soaking wet, equipment piled up along the rear wall.

Not at all curious – "This is my day off, dammit" – he sat down, pulled out a candy bar, and sank back into his book.

Part II
The Highway Men

Chapter 6

Brian's reluctance is overcome.

Following that first, memorable visit to Hollymount, Brian sent a list of ideas to Maeve and her community board for the next round of funding, due in the fall. He didn't hear back; was busy with the software day job at the museum. On a golden September day, he and his friends went out that way for a hike at the state forest.

"Can you find room for my pack?" Rita asked Harris, who was in the back seat. She sat beside Brian.

"Last winter I worked on a community heritage project out here," Brian said, heading southwest from town toward the park.

"What kind of heritage?" asked Harris.

"I'm still not sure," Brian said. "It was pretty strange, helping a community get a grant without knowing why they deserved it or who they are."

"What are they like?" asked Rita, as Harris handed around a bag of salted nuts.

"One of them – has a tail," Brian replied, getting to the point faster than he had intended.

Harris said, "Tails. Like, what kind?"

"They don't have TAILS, Brian," said Rita. "What kind of outrageous racism is that? You jerk."

Brian fired back, "I stand corrected. Maeve does not have a tail." Rita would not like the sound of that.

"Maeve!" said Harris. "Women named Maeve are trouble."

"You got that right," Brian said.

Rita was thinking. She was a good thinker, working on a grad degree in economics. She said, "So Maeve is the community leader, and some of the locals have tails. Are the tails a secret?"

Brian replied, "I only saw one tail, but that was on the Vice President of their heritage board, so it can't be a secret. He was, like, you know, wearing it outside his clothes."

"It swished around?" asked Rita. Brian nodded, as they left the interstate for the small local road that led uphill to the forest and trails. He decided to show them the roundabout, on the way.

"OK, here it is," Brian said, slowing down and signaling for a left turn.

"Here what is?" asked Harris, as Brian pulled the car over at a field by a tree stump.

"Ahh..." he said, "it should be right here. Maybe a bit further, I only went there once." He knew the stump was where the turnoff should be.

"You sure this is the place? It's a nature preserve back in there," said Harris. They stepped out into the sunshine. Crows cawed above a field dotted with purple asters and goldenrod.

"This is the place, and real money was paid into my account and I spent it on rent and groceries," Brian said, eyes seeking the side road and the roundabout.

"What's that white thing?" asked Rita, and they looked at the white spire above the trees, a mile distant.

"It's the church at the center of the roundabout," Brian said excitedly, stepping forward.

Harris broke in. "Look, we're going to miss the hike, they'll leave without us, you know how they are," he grumbled. They jumped back in the car and headed off.

On the hike, the group climbed out of a hemlock-shaded gorge into the beech and oak woods near the top of one of the steep hills that march east-west along the New York-Pennsylvania border.

Brian was walking with Harris and asked him, "You ever hear of a place called Hollymount, in these hills?"

"Kind of place?" Harris asked, scrambling to stay in front, needing to lead. They had left Rita and the others resting in the shade of a big oak tree.

"It's a village with old homes, big white pines, and holly trees, over there," Brian said, gesturing eastward. "But no roads or cars," he added, as Harris yanked him onto a boulder for a wider view. Brian looked down on the creek, across autumn woods to the surrounding hilltops. Harris stared at him.

"You are very weird today," he said. He poured salty nuts into Brian's hands.

Through a mouthful he continued, "Is Maeve on your mind? What's this about?"

"What?" Brian said defensively. "All I asked was had you ever heard of Hollymount over there."

"There is no Hollymount over there, dude," said Harris. "There are no old homes, no village."

Brian replied firmly, "There's an inn, and farms, and hiking trails, and parking, and an island on the creek, with apple trees – " The look in Harris's eye stopped him.

"That's near-wilderness over there," Harris said firmly. "I know the place. It's the Cherry Wildlife Preserve. Federal, state, and private. The only inhabitants after the Native Americans were pushed out was a small free black community established right after the Civil War, and they got kicked out for an airport that was never built. No one lives there now." They scrambled to stay ahead of the approaching group.

Brian asked, "Are there trails?"

"It's rough country – they don't want crowds. You have to get permission to hike or stay overnight."

"So let's go," Brian said.

"I guess you're up to it," Harris said generously. "Let's do a hike before the days get too short." When Rita caught up, the three agreed to go there together as soon as Harris could wrangle permission.

That Monday, Brian was exhausted at the end of the workday and opened the fridge, hoping to find dinnertime delight. None there. He looked through the kitchen, workroom, and living room at the front door, and was soon treading the sidewalk, its stone slabs uneven with big tree roots. The full September moon hung above the neighborhood. At the end of the block Brian gazed at the silent elementary school, its bilingual sign announcing teacher-parent meetings and a games day.

Where to go? Ah – yes. A twenty-minute walk brought him to Romney's, for a beer and burger. He sought calm in a bath of voices and kitchen noise, to help him sleep soundly that night. Food and drink ordered, Brian looked around at the hubbub. The tables were filled, the bar area packed, televisions blaring. He saw no familiar faces – except – his eyes drifted back to a woman at the bar talking to her companion. Yes, it was Maeve. The guy was big, well dressed, flashy. Her gaze slewed toward Brian, causing the guy also to look at him. Brian wanted to duck, but focused on his fries, selecting among them for the very best. He ate slowly, not looking in their direction.

"Really, you know," Brian said to himself, "I am not up for big events tonight. I just want a quiet evening and sound sleep." His heart went whama-whama, belying the mental pep talk.

"Brian!" Maeve called. Uh-oh.

"Come meet your colleague Gregg!" She was standing next to Brian, and the guy was back at the bar. She was smiling at Brian, him alone, so it seemed.

Brian stood up and said shakily, "Well met, fair stranger!"

Maeve ignored this idiot remark and said, "I want the two of you to work well together! Join us!" She carried Brian's plate toward the bar, so he grabbed his beer and followed, noting admiring glances. Her beauty was evident, and it was he she had fetched. Brian set down his glass to shake the hand of Gregg.

Gregg was no more delighted than Brian, and if looks could kill – but Brian was all amiability, grinning into his irritation, saying, "Colleague?" with a glance at Maeve. She was smiling at Gregg. Brian was transfixed – such a perfect, tiny woman, so nice to gaze upon – and then came back to earth in the noisy bar.

Gregg boomed, "We'll be working together on the highway project, Brian! Glad to meet you ahead of time." He sipped his short dark drink and patted his breast pocket – looked like he needed a smoke. Brian stood silent, surprised at his words.

Maeve said, "That next grant, Brian, is for the – hmm, they call it 'support for landscape and community enhancements' – to go with the new interchange and – um, regional highway." She stumbled through unfamiliar words.

Gregg added, "My company designs the whole deal, and gets it built."

"Interchange and spur road?" Brian asked, not even trying to look pleased for Maeve. "I thought your board wanted a hiking trail and day-festival site. A *highway interchange*?" he repeated. His voice got louder as he remembered the wildness of the area. The already-built nearby highway interchange was not heavily used. "There's no need for that!"

Gregg smiled into his drink, pleased by Brian's distress. Maeve rushed to support Gregg's words.

"Oh, Brian! Really, yes! We can have it all, you know. The interchange is just what we need to bring our old-fashioned area into the modern world, and the money you get for us will buy the pretty things my Board desires." Gregg put his arm around her shoulders for a quick hug of agreement. Maeve broke away but smiled, leaning toward him.

Gregg said, "This great project will give easier interstate access to business in both Pennsylvania and New York, and help out Maeve's community. It's that old expression, 'win-win.' Good for everybody!"

Brian took a long look at Gregg – wide shoulders, blue shirt, khaki pants – the consultant outfit. Gregg in turn saw a medium-sized guy, scruffy, mismatched clothes, worn-down hiking boots, not shaved – a snowflake liberal.

"So," said Maeve, "Do you live near here, Brian?" Her pale face glowed in the bar spotlights, black hair gleaming.

Brian sidestepped replying by asking an insider's question, "How is your Board? What was the lunch special today at the Inn?"

Gregg topped this with ease. "Irish stew and their local beer, really powerful stuff," he said, winking at Maeve, whose eyes had not moved from Brian's face.

She said, "Brian, why would you deny us the chance to better ourselves? With an interchange and big road, we can draw in visitors for short and longer stays. We want what the rest of the world has. And we need humans." Gregg nodded.

Brian ate a bite of burger and took a pull on his beer before replying, "Your community is great just the way it is. You can draw visitors without destroying the area with concrete and lights and cars – "

Gregg cut him off. "Maeve, we went over this today. The highway will exit your cute little roundabout and run down along the creek, off the ridge where most folks live. You'll never know it's there."

Brian stared at him in horror. "What the hell crazy project is this, anyway?" he asked, pushing away the rest of his meal. His voice was loud, and people stared, as did Maeve, her expression one of gentle puzzlement.

"Now, boys," she said, as Gregg smirked into his beer, "our Congressman contacted me about this special opportunity. He said this highway project would be 'locally and regionally beneficial.' Whatever is wrong with that?"

"And your Board's on board with it," added Gregg.

"How about those guys down on Apple Island?" Brian shot back. "A highway would decimate that timeless place. I bet your Congressman wants to turn it into a scenic overlook. With flush toilets and vending machines."

"Oh," Maeve said, "we need you, Brian, to make sure we don't make any mistakes in dealing with these ruthless highway men," and she glanced flirtatiously at Gregg.

Brian decided to man up and meet this challenge.

"OK, Maeve," he said. "What is it that you want from me, exactly?" Brian crossed his arms and leaned against the bar, staring at them. Calm and cool.

Gregg nodded in recognition of his new attitude and said, "Maeve's Congressman has gotten us waivers on the review and approval process, so we're good to go with design. In fact we're already behind, which is great news for getting the job done quickly. Maeve didn't fill me in on the details, but I think she wants you for – "

Maeve cut in, "Brian, you will bring us the money for the Visitors Center and Festival site, as we discussed last spring. My Board has numerous other charming devices and blandishments they would like to see." She glanced watchfully from Brian to Gregg – as though she were trying to figure out how to manage an unusual life form.

Brian kept his mouth shut, and she smiled at the apparent cooperation. The three agreed to meet in a week at the highway turn-off, 9 a.m. That gave Brian time to do some advance exploration with his friends, and figure out what was going on.

When Brian, Rita, and Harris returned to the site early Saturday morning, the old stump had been bulldozed aside for a graveled driveway and parking area. Neon orange survey flags marched in two parallel rows across the field toward the church spire. Brian parked next to a port-a-potty.

"Definitely not a figment of your imagination, Brian," said Rita, as they scrambled out and pulled on their backpacks.

Harris was staring at the neon flags and said, "This isn't right. The Cherry Preserve boundary starts here. That's all protected land." He spun to look at Brian. "They said an *interchange and highway?*"

"Didn't believe me, huh?" Brian replied, fishing his water bottle out of the trunk. "I looked Gregg up. He works for Walden 2, a big engineering and road building company around here."

The three followed the neon flags toward the white spire. White and yellow butterflies danced among the asters, and bees bumbled on the heavy goldenrod blossoms.

"That's a family company, founded by Old Man Greer," Harris said.

"How come you know that?" asked Rita.

"I interviewed with them," he said, "when I graduated. Not my cup of tea. They also provide gas field services. Their regional headquarters is over there, through the hills, in Horseheads." He gestured east across the rural small-town landscape.

Brian replied, "That makes sense. Gregg said the highway would make it easier to get to their headquarters." Harris showed them the map on his phone: they had crossed a boundary marked Cherry Nature Preserve. Ahead, the survey flags marched left and right in a big circle around the spire.

"Shall we hike around the church?" asked Rita gaily, gesturing counter-clockwise.

"No," Brian said, "let's go straight. I want to see that spire up close." They crunched through the autumn field, tangling with buckthorn and head-high invasive honeysuckle. Past shagbark hickory and oak trees, they entered an open mowed space around a small white church.

"This is nice," said Rita. The church was well tended and freshly painted. A historic marker stood next to a small graveyard. Brian walked over to read it.

Harris explained, "There was a town here. Developers kicked out the residents, and tore the homes down for an airport that never got built. The state bought it and made it into a protected area."

He smiled. "We won that one."

The plaque read: "Freeport, NY: Early settlement by freed slaves in New York State. This thriving community boasted 300 homes, a school, businesses, orchards, and productive farms. RIP."

Rita rested her darker hand on Harris's paler shoulder and said gently, "Who's 'we,' white boy?"

"Aww, darn it, sorry," said Harris. He looked at Rita. "Folks come back to mow and tend the graves, twice a year." The trio stood in the quiet space, listening to the wind in the trees, falling leaves spiraling to earth.

Brian looked at his watch. "We're two miles from the creek. Let's go see what Gregg and the family business have planned." They walked out of the clearing, through brambles and trees, and crossed the far side of the encircling orange survey markers. The parallel neon rows continued forward, at an angle to their route toward a wooded hill.

Based on Brian's previous visit, they should have been seeing a cottage with smoke curling up from the chimney, and should have been crossing a paved parking area to walk along a wide green path toward a tunnel with a gleaming neon ENTRANCE sign. But all they saw were the fields and rising hills, until Harris pointed out a faint trail.

"It's been a while since I was here," he said. Little more than a deer path, the narrow trail wound through purple asters toward the hill. But no tunnel, Brian thought to himself, wondering if he was crazy, not for the first time.

"What's these rocks?" asked Rita, as the trail led them between piles of rocks – carved and shaped. Harris stroked one of the rocks – just right for the keystone in an arch.

"The local historical society think it's an old dairy," he explained. "There was an entrance at both ends. It was in ruins long before the preserve was established. I went to a talk about it last winter at the library." Crossing the creek via stepping-stones, they followed the trail along a fern-covered cliff, just the same as on Brian's last visit. Rounding a familiar bend, Brian remembered the cottage ahead.

He grabbed his pals, whispering, "The guy with the tail lives over there in a little clearing." They saw his intensity and crept forward together. Thanks to their kindness, Brian was not too mortified when they saw only an open, empty grassy dell, cottonwoods, and golden sycamores whispering high overhead.

"Well," Brian said, attempting to save face, "that would be a great place for a little cottage home."

Rita asked, "Why did you know that clearing was coming up?"

"Bear with me," Brian said. "This is weirder than any of us knows. I am not crazy. I did not imagine the whole thing. I paid the real rent with the real money they really sent me." They stopped for water and a snack, Harris studying the map on his phone.

"OK," Brian said, "I'm going to make a prediction about what comes next. I have not seen that map."

"Challenge accepted," Harris replied. "What comes next?"

Brian closed his eyes and said, "We go a few hundred yards on the flat, then up a steep slope, into the woods, around a bend, and come to a trail crossing in the woods. If we go straight at the crossing, we come out into a wide valley with a wooded slope beyond." Harris's fascinated gaze toggled between Brian and the map on his phone.

He said, "One hundred percent correct so far. What else?"

"If we go left at the trail crossing," Brian continued, "The path drops down along a small stream with a waterfall – " Harris stared at Brian – "and at the foot of the slope you step across the stream to – "

They said together, "Apple Island," as Harris read the words on the phone map. The three looked at the faint path ahead, winding through a wooded wetland, thick with ferns and old tree stumps. Crows cawed and flew high overhead, surprised by humans.

"Let's go to Apple Island," said Harris. They walked together in the waning warmth of the year, up the far slope, and into the woodlands toward the trail crossing.

"I kind of hate to mention it," said Rita, "but I see survey flags." The trio crossed a line of orange markers and found themselves between two rows, flanking the trail, two hundred feet apart.

"Oh, no, not here," Brian breathed, moving faster toward the crossing. He had run toward a crying baby last time he'd come this way.

At the crossing marked on Harris's phone map, two faint paths crossed in the woods. No sign, no groomed green walkways. The trails ahead and to Apple Island on the left were deer paths, nothing more. To the right and left, orange flags marched through the trees.

"The nature preserve management plan calls for 'support of wilderness values,'" said Harris. "They discourage visitors, and the trails are undeveloped." He kicked an orange flag. Brian smelled wood smoke.

Rita sniffed, said, "Someone's here," and they turned onto the Apple Island trail, walking toward the sweet woodsy odor.

"Maybe there's coffee," said Rita hopefully. They crossed the line of survey markers and the slope dropped into the valley holding Apple Island. On their right, the small stream flowed with clear notes of falling water, the bonfire scent strengthening as they walked downhill under big hemlock trees to the water's edge.

Unchanged from Brian's previous visit and hasty departure, a tree trunk served as a bridge to Apple Island where, around a bright bonfire backed by white pines, two figures sat. Just as before. Beyond, gleaming in spring sunlight, the apple trees were glorious in full bloom – just as before. Brian glanced at his watch – it read 11:00 a.m. on that late September date. A figure stood up from the bonfire to walk toward them.

Brian said to Harris: "Your phone work?"

"Yes, of course," he replied, gazing from the autumn woodlands to the springtime finery on the island.

Brian said, "Let me know if it still works over there," as Rita crossed the tree trunk bridge to the island and the person waiting there. The lithe bearded fellow offered a gentlemanly hand, which she did not need, and the other two followed.

The tall man said, "Brian, you return, bringing fair and handsome warriors."

"Warriors?" asked Rita, eyes only for the apple trees. Their fragrance wafted down to where they stood in new springtime grass, blue sky above. Lilies of the valley and small purple violets grew at the foot of the tall pines.

"Maybe you do not like Maeve's new plan?" the man said to Brian, bowing them to the fire, introducing himself as Greenwood, and his ginger-bearded companion as Acton, as they shared names.

"You were following the ugly path they marked in the woods up there," added Acton, gesturing the way they had come. Brian turned to look at the hemlocks and beeches crowding the steep slope above.

"Yes," he replied. "They're not supposed to do that without public scrutiny and government review."

"But they are doing it anyway," said Greenwood, eyebrows arching, with a faint smile. Brian remembered to look at his watch – the face was blank. Harris shot him a puzzled look, pocketing his own dead phone.

Harris asked the two hosts, "What and where is Apple Island?"

At the same time, Rita said plaintively, "I don't suppose you have coffee in that pot?" eyeing a battered metal kettle resting on the coals. Acton and Greenwood nodded in unspoken agreement to one another. Ignoring Harris's question, Greenwood turned to tend the fire. Acton headed up the slope to the nearest apple tree, where he broke off three twigs, a pink blossom on each one.

"I'm afraid all we have is tea," Greenwood said to Rita, lifting small chipped cups out of the grass and pouring a warm fragrant liquid into them. Acton handed each of the visitors a flowering twig, and tucked them firmly into pockets or buttonholes.

"We don't want any problems for you today," he said. "Not for our fellow warriors. Please hold onto these until you are on the return trail beyond the church. Apple blossoms protect you from harm." They patted their flowers into place as Greenwood handed round the full cups.

He smiled at Brian and said, "It is safe for you to drink." Brian had to trust. Today did not feel like a fairy tale, but again, how would he know if one hit him over the head? The drink tasted of tea, honey-sweetened.

"Oh, ambrosial," breathed Rita, her eyes closed as she inhaled the cup's warmth.

Greenwood laughed, "We don't go in for ambrosia here. That's Maeve's idea, up at the Inn. This is just good old Irish tea. I buy it at the grocery store down by the highway."

Harris looked at Brian, then at Greenwood.

He said, "There is an Inn? How is that, hmmm, possible? Ummm, no offense?"

"There is no Inn today," said Acton, "because Brian here," he grinned, "did not take the correct route. He cut across the circle."

Greenwood said, "You humans!"...at which there was a short silence. He continued, "Brian, you know some of the rules here. But I am worried, because you may not know enough."

Just when Brian thought that things were getting informative, Greenwood stopped, saying only, "We are bad hosts. You are safe here today. We will show you Apple Island, untouched by the world around us. Then we will cross the bridge and see what the highway men are doing downstream."

Acton set their empty cups by the fire as Greenwood started up the green slope to the flowering orchard. The grass twinkled with the same tiny white flowers as in the parking area out beyond the tunnel – along with bright yellow dandelions. Brian grinned, seeing these cheerful flowers, invasive plants in what was *maybe* becoming a fairy story. Best to take it as it comes, he thought, these men mean us no harm. And – no tails!

Greenwood said, "I hope you can help us stop Maeve's plans for what she calls 'our betterment.'"

Then they were among the apple trees, and dark thoughts fled. The blossoming orchard spread out before them across the island to the lakeshore a quarter mile distant. Old grey trees, pink-crowned, ranged across the green meadow. Branches and twigs carried newborn leaves, pink buds and wide-open white blossoms. Yellow and white daffodils and nodding narcissus stood along the margins of the orchard and the shoreline. The group trod a green path down the center of the orchard between low stone walls, dotted with bluebells.

Rita saw violets and snowdrops. "Look, crocuses," she whispered, pointing to the scatters of purple and orange beneath the trees. They walked below the pink clouds of blossom, breathing the warm, scented sunlight, hearing birdsong, seeing blue sky above. Reaching the end of the orchard path far too soon, they stood on the edge of the island next to a row of woven baskets. Water rippled and lapped on the lake's pebbled shore.

Turning, they gazed back at the rows of trees, the pink array rising up the gentle slope to where they had first glimpsed this wonder. Beyond were grey bluffs with the trail they had followed down to Apple Island. That steep slope was covered in dark green hemlock trees, burnished with the autumn bronze of beech leaves. The scene was certainly spellbinding. Was it a *spell*? Was it real? Brian's fretful human mind asserted itself.

Rita asked, "Is it like this every day?"

Greenwood replied, "It is today."

"What could that possibly mean?" muttered Harris, turning around to look at it all, trying to understand. "It's late September, back where we parked the car. Is this some kind of micro-climate?"

Acton bent over one of the baskets, asking, "Would you care for a fresh-picked apple?" He pulled ripe red apples from the woven basket and handed them around. Brian hesitated – apples, you know? They have a *history* – but Greenwood grinned at him knowingly and shrugged, driving away doubt. Brian joined the others crunching into the refreshing, normal apples.

"If it's always springtime here, Acton," said Harris between bites, "where'd these come from?" Acton dropped his apple core into an empty basket.

"The orchard continues," he said, as they looked across the lake to the far shore. Yes, the orchard continued there. Grey trees bent with ripe red fruit marched in rows across a narrow meadow, hemmed in by autumn woods. More baskets stood under the trees, some filled with apples. They heard the splash of falling water.

"There's a waterfall over there, to the left of the ripe orchard, where the creek departs the lake for the gorge below," said Greenwood. "Let's go see what Maeve's highway men are doing down there." Their return walk re-immersed them in the perfect springtime day, but Brian was no longer part of it, his mind returned to the world beyond. He admired the trees and flowers, but as they walked up the slope and past the small fire to the creek and bridge, worries filled his mind. The visitors' faces were troubled as they readied to cross the bridge. They turned to stare back at springtime.

"Can a person stay here?" asked Rita.

"With a little bit of luck, you can return," said Acton gently. "You may come back again."

"Any time we want to?" asked Rita.

"No," said Acton. "Only sometimes. But this day is here. You can take comfort in that."

Harris rubbed his eyes as he stepped onto the log.

"I feel sad," he said. "And I don't know why."

Across the bridge, Greenwood led them down to a path along the water, Acton last.

"I can come with you as far as the ripe orchard," he said, "and Greenwood will lead you from there. We have to keep an eye on this place, and tend the fire." They walked silently in single file, the steep slope on their right rising under hemlocks and golden beeches. Beyond the small stream on their left, they could discern the shoreline of Apple Island and its blossoming trees. But the view was obscured, blurry.

"What's that sparkly haze?" asked Harris.

"I can't explain right now," said Greenwood over his shoulder. "It will take several beers in a warm, comfortable room, and your willingness to hear me out," he finished. They stepped from the wooded streambank into the old orchard, and walked under the trees, bent with fruit, in the long green grass of autumn.

"Fill your pockets," urged Acton. They each picked an assortment of apples – red, pink, yellow, green, some with blemishes, all tasty, distending their pockets. Harris stuffed a handful into his backpack.

He whispered to Brian, "Check your watch?"

"It's on," Brian whispered back, "and an hour has gone by since we stepped onto the island."

"Yeah," Harris said, as they came out of the orchard onto the bank of the creek beyond, "my phone, too. And it's the same date and year," he added, smiling broadly at Brian.

Wherever they had been, it was on the same schedule as the daily world. No fairyland shenanigans, no returning to find a century had gone by. The three looked around to wave at Acton, back in the orchard. He waved, piling apples into a basket. Behind him was the lake; across it, Apple Island, obscured by the sparkling haze. Greenwood led them past a low dam to where the lake's waters poured down a stony slope into a steep-walled shale gorge. The gorge dropped deep, water flowing along a narrow, flat creekbed thirty feet below. Greenwood pointed downstream into the woods.

He said, "I'm not sure you can hear it, but they are working right now."

"You mean that bulldozer?" asked Rita. "I've been hearing it since we got on this trail." She turned to Harris. "I don't understand," she went on, "you said this was a fully protected nature preserve." They all heard it: a roaring engine, along with snapping and crackling. The noise came through the trees, not far downstream of where they were standing.

"Maybe it's far away," said Brian, without much hope. "Sound carries."

"Holy effing heck, let's go stop them," said Harris, already ahead of the group.

Greenwood took his arm, saying, "Careful. I'll show you. We don't want them to see us." He led them into the trees, the sound growing louder. They crossed a line of orange flags, which descended the slope toward the grinding, roaring noise.

"We're back in the proposed highway corridor," said Harris, speaking loudly over the racket. "But how could they be working on the project when it has not gone through the public review and approval process?"

As the trees thinned, Greenwood gestured for them to slow down, a finger to his lips. They crept forward, following suit when he dropped to his knees and crawled. Another ten feet, and they were lined up atop a cliff, which they peeked over, heads down.

The creek lay far below – "sixty feet down," whispered Harris, reading from his phone map. A series of bluffs and cliffs descended to the water. Downstream to their right, fifty feet distant and twenty feet below, a yellow bulldozer was clearing a ledge. Brian watched the operator in his cab, as the machine's claw raked a patch of trees and shrubs, uprooting and pushing them over the cliff. They crackled and snapped, crashing noisily into the gorge, bouncing and tumbling. The creek below was jammed with trees and rock debris.

Greenwood pulled them back into the woods. Wordless, they walked downstream along the clifftop. Again peering over the edge, they saw a busy scene where the gorge widened. A steep graveled road was carved into the slope across the gorge. Down at the creek, yellow-helmeted figures were directing a smaller vehicle as it shoved debris out of the creek, piling it on the stony shoreline.

"They burn it," said Greenwood.

"Everything we're seeing here is illegal," said Harris. He was pale, intense, beyond emotion. The two lines of orange flags stair-stepped down the cliff into the gorge, delineating a route along the creek, which bent out of sight downstream. The stony shoreline between the flag rows was smashed and broken, small trees and rocks bulldozed into piles along the route.

"We'd better not stay here much longer," said Greenwood. "We are visible, across from that road. But let me show you where that highway goes to." Before they could move, they heard steps crunching leaves in the woods behind them.

Maeve's voice said, "I saw someone, more than one person." The group dropped and lay still. Rita's eyes were squeezed shut. The crunching continued as the walkers passed by.

More distantly, Gregg spoke, "If they're just hikers, they won't stay long." The trio lay quietly, watching Greenwood.

"Time for you to go home," he whispered, rising into a low crouch. He patted his breast pocket, checking to make sure they still had their apple twigs. They followed him into the woods, away from the cliff's edge, loping and bent over. Greenwood kept the group between the two lines of flags, heading away from Apple Island. Within a few minutes they were back at the Apple Island trail crossing, huddled low in a tight group.

"That was Maeve," Brian observed to Greenwood.

"Yes," he replied, "and the highway man Gregg."

"What are they – " began Rita, but Brian stopped her.

"We'll talk back at the car," he said, and to Greenwood, "What are our next steps?" Greenwood smiled when Brian said "our."

Brian said, "I'm coming back here next week, to go over the project on the ground with those two."

"And I'm his assistant," chimed in Harris.

Greenwood's smile broadened. He replied, "I have to go now, because they are walking near the Island, and Acton may need my helpful persuasion to keep them off it. Not everyone is welcome there," he continued, his head cocked for sounds from the Apple Island trail.

He rose, speaking as he looked at each of them, "So glad to have you as allies, our human liaison team." He walked away down the trail, calling back, "I will be in touch, Brian. You all stay on the trail, cross the meadow straight past the church, get in your car, and go."

Greenwood vanished down the trail. The three friends walked silently along the pathway, stepped across the line of orange flags, and were outside the proposed highway corridor.

Harris whispered, "I want to tear out the flags, but I don't want anyone to know we were here." Oblivious, Brian brooded on why they had been called "human," as if Greenwood and Acton were not, and on his growing pizza hunger. He ate an apple from the supply in his pockets.

"You know what," Harris said as they crunched across the fields on the far side of the church, "I think I have Apple Island figured out."

"I could use some help with that," said Rita, "I don't believe in parallel universes and that stuff, so how does it stay the same every day?"

"Time travel! From an article I read last week about Ten Thousand Secrets National Park, in Kentucky," Harris began.

Rita said, "I saw that! You can visit secret places, take underground boat rides, gamble in the casino, and sleep in fancy hotels. Eat barbecue."

"The new, improved National Parks," sneered Harris in a sour tone. "That's one of the parks where they've thrown out nature for mass entertainment. It's a sacrifice park."

"Hey, don't be a snob," said Rita. "Some of the really popular parks are being converted to entertainment and casinos, to bring in more money for the rest of the parks. Makes good sense."

Harris whirled on her, "'*Makes sense*'? Are you crazy? How can you say that? Trashing a natural wonder for *money*?"

"Calm down, man," Brian said as they neared his car. "My mom works at Ten Thousand Secrets. Why is it like Apple Island?"

"Your mom works there?" Harris said. "Wooo...." he chanted the Twilight Zone theme.

Parked close to Brian's car was a giant white pickup truck. Brian's little car barely rose to its windows. "Walden 2 Engineering & Consultants – Creating a Better World" read a sign on the truck door.

"Yeah," Brian said, unlocking his car. "Mom survived that big blast at the Nevada park last year, and they reassigned her to Ten Thousand Secrets."

Rita went off to use the port-a-potty, saying, "Just in case that was fairyland or whatever, I did not want to pee there." (The guys felt guilty.)

Harris said, "What was that like? Is she OK? How come you never mentioned it before?" He stared at Brian. Everyone knew about the blast that destroyed the casino and attractions at the Nevada national park and killed three people, consultants to the company that built the place.

But Brian's mom had been way too close to the action, leaving him and his sister uneasy about her possible involvement. He did not want to talk about it, saying only, "Learned about it from her afterward. My mom is OK, but she was weird enough already. I figure she's safe enough in quiet old Kentucky. Not much goes on there."

Harris helped shift the topic away from Brian's mom, observing only, "The Kentucky park has a pretend time travel attraction. But some people think it's real. That could get interesting."

Returning, Rita said, "There's a research buzz about time travel, but at a national park?"

"You can spend a day there, in the Pleistocene," said Harris.

Rita continued, "It's a theme park experience, like Jurassic Park," as she climbed into the car.

Thoughts of pizza loomed in their hungry young heads and rumbling bellies. Rita opened the car window. "Visitors pay big bucks to see holograms of giant birds and robot woolly mammoths and fake ancient horsies. Can we go get food *please*?"

"Well, but, I'm saying, maybe it is real time travel, to the Pleistocene," said Harris, settling in next to Brian.

"'Real,' huh, what's that supposed to mean, *human*?" Brian snorted, pulling onto the highway toward their beloved Mushroomy Fields Forever. He was glad they were no longer talking about his mom. He loved her, and she worried him.

"The article said, and maybe our starving passenger remembers," Harris replied, grinning at Rita, "'There is a sparkly haze around the Pleistocene.'" Rita nodded, distractedly staring out the window toward the pizza.

"Visitors can see the Pleistocene theme park across a river, but it's hazy – like when we were across from Apple Island," Harris concluded.

"So you are putting two and nothing together," said Rita severely, "to get time travel?"

"Yeah, well, Homeland Security and the Federal Park Service have been in cahoots for years with secret projects, and that ain't healthy," said Harris. "It's reasonable to wonder, don't you think?" he said as Brian parked, and pizza fumes filled the car. Rita was out the door, heading for the entrance.

She called, "See you at the table. I'll order the usual."

Brian said to Harris, "Maybe we'll know more after we meet with the highway man and Maeve next week. You really coming with me, Harris?"

"I wouldn't miss it for the world. We have to stop that highway," Harris replied, as they followed Rita inside.

Chapter 7

Janet gets promoted.

The morning after the disastrous cave trip, I woke and sat up – carefully. My body was covered in bruises, and my hands and arms ached. I placed my feet on the floor, but my legs did not cooperate, thighs rubbery. Lurching upright, I tottered out to make coffee, suddenly reliving the shock of Hugh's death. I remembered Steve saying it was intentional, caused by a bad guy in the Park's control room. But I could not get that far, stuck with trying to understand that a vital, generous man was gone from us.

The first cup restored brain-mind-muscle links, as I sat on a hard chair at the table and looked around. The apartment smelled and felt different. People had been here! All my dishes had been used, washed, and dried, piled up in the basket by the sink. Someone had made chili! Who did that, and where did they get the ingredients? How could all this have happened, in my fortress of solitude?

I did remember parts of it. Steve and the two youngsters shoved me and Lena up the stairs, unlocking the door because my hands were too numb to use the key. Lena had a long hot shower, then I did, and everyone talked. In a haze of exhaustion, I sat on the couch with Lena. We were piled high with blankets and plied with water, soup, the mysterious chili, cornbread, coffee, and aspirin. People were on their phones.

Park authority figures came to the door and were told to leave. The Park's paramedic team had been allowed in to give us brief checkups, but my friends were angry and forceful. The team did not linger, reporting into their phones as they walked down the stairs. I remember sitting on my bed, to rest for a moment – someone must have put a blanket over me and closed the door.

I thought about my secrets and stashes, and my lone wolf plan. Fun and companionship weaken a person. I had to get a grip, had to scare myself into the reality of my situation. Thinking about Hugh, and the near-death of Lena, shook me fully awake.

"What if...?" I began, seeing again her head rising out of the surging waterfall, me reaching down to pull her up – but I knew this was a bad mental path to travel, and cut it off. I was now back in myself, body not fully cooperative. The clock on the wall said 10:00. I glanced out the window at bright daylight. The phone rang and I answered, wincing from pain in my shoulder.

"Hello, Janet?" said Sonny Scott. "I hope I didn't wake you," he said with hushed concern. "I just want you to know you have the day off, with pay."

"Thank you," I replied, remembering Steve saying that the Park was responsible for what had happened to me and Lena and – Hugh. Steve had also said, "Keep your mouth shut and don't tell them anything, until I talk to you again." He repeated this later, to make sure we heard him.

I said no more, waiting for Scott to continue.

"You still there, Janet?" asked good ol' Sonny, voice oozing with concern.

"Yes, sir," I said, coolly, "drinking my morning coffee. Beautiful day out there."

"Yeah," he said, enthusiasm returning, "After that big rainstorm yesterday, the world looks new-washed and – " he stopped abruptly, muting the line. I imagined the hand-signals from whoever was in the office with him, stage-managing this call: *"We told you not to mention yesterday!"* I waited, sipping coffee.

"Hey, Janet, still there, ha-ha?" Scott resumed. Maybe he had his part memorized now.

I said, "Yup, sitting still. It hurts to move, you know."

"Oh my God – ah – well, Janet, you rest up today and we'll see you when you report in tomorrow. There's been some management changes, and we are promoting you, OK?" I did not reply.

"Sound good to you?" he pleaded. I cut the call.

That afternoon, Lena and I drove to a distant park trailhead, beyond the noise and hustle of the entertainment district. We wandered far in the autumnal oak and hickory woods, dark tree trunks, and rustling branches providing privacy for family talk. Her brother, my son Brian, was doing all right as a consultant in New York State. We talked about having Thanksgiving together. She hoped I was healing from the Nevada catastrophe. I was proud of her new science job here.

We walked past an old graveyard with a faded brown sign, Mammoth Cave Cemetery. Lena placed a small stone atop the gravestone of a cave explorer who meant a lot to her. In the years since the Park had been changed to promote entertainment and gambling, few remembered the caves – and now their expert was gone.

That evening we shared supper quietly in the Park hotel restaurant, with Damaris and Ron. We traded memories about Hugh and made plans for a memorial event for the Park staff. People left us alone, smiling gently and patting our aching shoulders. That was a good day with my daughter.

Still sore the following morning, I looked in at the Science office before heading up to see Sonny Scott. Steve rose to shake my hand, gesturing for us to go outdoors.

"Beautiful day for a walk," he said, staring around the room and hallway to suggest surveillance.

Outdoors, he said, "Forgive me if I talk fast, but they may send someone for you." I did not see anyone, but we were walking below the Admin office windows. He went on, "They want two things from you. They want you to do the brain scan again – " I recoiled in alarm, and he smiled, continuing, "and they will offer you a promotion to a new planning position." The door to the Admin offices opened, and Sonny came strolling toward us, head down. I had never seen him outdoors before.

Steve spoke quickly. "Take the job. Sign the paper. You'll be working for me. We have a new boss. He is an evil man – he murdered Hugh." As

Sonny puffed over to us, Steve added quickly, "Once the promotion protects you, they can't require you to take the scan." I stared, startled at his support.

Smiling, Steve turned to Sonny. "She looks pretty good, considering what she went through," and turned back toward the Science office.

"Hi, Janet!" said Sonny, glowing with synthetic happiness. "C'mon in, we've got lots to talk about!" He took my arm in that manly, helpful way. I pulled free, and we walked indoors shoulder to shoulder, me shoving my way through the glass door, letting it close on him. I was barely keeping a lid on my contempt for these fools. All of this had to go. He huffed along the hallway behind me.

I said, "You'll make me late for my monitoring shift."

"Oh, no, no!" he said, catching up and gesturing me into his office.

"We've got a new position for you, with your skills and experience. C'mon in," he added. We crossed the foyer into his deep-carpeted, cool office and I fell stiffly into the soft chair he offered. Cameras twinkled from the corners. Sonny sat at his desk. I watched his fingers playing with the console buttons, and dreaded the drain on my free will. He saw my glance, and moved his hand away.

"No more of that for you, Ms. Harper," he said cheerfully. "You're climbing the ladder of opportunity today!"

"Wow," I thought, "this dismal bastard is playing to whoever is watching."

He continued, "As of two days ago, we have a new program administrator, Professor Thomas King. Do you know his work?" I shook my head, feigning ignorance of the man who had killed Hugh.

"Well," Sonny Scott went on, "he's a great innovator who is taking our Time Trips program in a new direction. Twenty years of painstaking research has paid off. Our long-time Homeland research partner has just handed over the Park's time programs to Professor King at the Department of Defense." Sonny spoke like a written report. He offered me a bowl of candy corn. I glared, and he hunched down.

"No, thank you," I replied. "What's this got to do with me? What are you doing to investigate Hugh Hynes's death?"

Sonny's expressive doggy eyes bulged at my unhandsome words, both of us aware that we were being heard elsewhere. "For the time being," said Sonny, "Steve Roberts is working for King, to dismantle and transition the time travel program from civilian to military uses. Ten Thousand is becoming a DoD Center for Action Excellence." I let go of the question about Hugh, because this was alarming news – I would have to move faster to complete my mission here.

"But we're also expanding the visitor time-tripping program. Talk about your win-win!" Sonny smiled. "We're franchising the time travel trips at parks nationwide. You're gonna help us develop that."

He went on, "Steve recommended you for a new Exploration Management position in the time-tripping marketing – uh, research program. We're promoting you over the heads of others" – rueful face – "but considering what you've been through" – first mention of the disaster – "and the tragic loss of Hugh" – wow, outright frankness – "it's the least we can do," he finished, with a pleading look from the amiable huckster behind the curtain.

"Sure," I said, "where do you want my retinal John Hancock?" Sonny relaxed visibly, and leaned back.

"So glad you're joining this great new initiative," he said, handing me a pen and a single piece of paper and continuing, "You're above all that low-level security stuff now. We just need you to sign here." Once my actual signature was committed to real paper, the office manager came in carrying cups of coffee and wearing a big smile.

"We're prepping a space for you in the old liaison office," the office manager said. "Congrats! And – how ya doin'?" he asked, staring at me.

Sonny said, "Bo, don't – "

Bo said "Whups," and backed smiling out of the room, saying to me, as the door closed, "Can I hide in your suitcase for your next time travel trip?"

I turned to Sonny. He was no longer my boss, but I did not know what we were to one another now. I struck a neutral tone.

"Good coffee," I said. "Where do I report?"

"You're kind of in charge," Sonny replied, uneasily. "The liaison office is closed effective immediately, so Ed Zanetti has gone back to D.C., and taken Steve Roberts with him." Ah yes – another helicopter had just buzzed overhead.

He said, "We need for you to take over the Venice project, asap. You know about it already?" I shook my head.

Sonny continued, "I'm gonna hand you over to your research staff in a minute, but briefly, we are about to greenlight Park trips to Fifties Venice. Customers will embark here at a new river dock, pop out onto the lagoon and dock at St. Mark's Square in 1959."

"Why that date?" I asked. "That's not very long ago." I had to admit, I was fascinated.

"That's the point," said Sonny, standing up to welcome and introduce a woman I'd seen around but did not have a name for. Tall, dark, and dignified, Sally Drew sat down, cradling her coffee cup. As head time researcher, she took over the meeting, Sonny sitting back to listen.

She had heard my question about 1959 and replied, "That was a golden age of tourism, with near-modern health standards and a lot fewer people. Also, we won't stand out as an alien species, like we did when we visited New Amsterdam in 1660." She shook her head, recalling a bad day at the time travel office.

Sonny's breathing or posture must have reminded her that cameras and new bosses were watching, and she continued briskly, "Also, the pre-1960s period is really popular right now. People love the clothes, the style. They think it was a more innocent time." She rolled her eyes.

"Not a lot of that, through human history," I replied.

"May I show you to your office, and introduce our staff?" Sally said, leading the way. People gawked from their office desks as we walked down the handsome hallway into a big office with a window onto the oak-hickory woodlands. A pal of mine from the cleaning staff was just leaving with a box of papers and books and stuff from the top drawer of the costly desk. I sat gingerly, nauseated, and a chill swept down my back. There was danger here – complacency and comfort. The illusion of power. A deal with the devil. I stared at the meager pile of items delivered from my monitoring cubicle.

Sally said gently, "I'll give you a few minutes, Ms. Harper – "

"Oh, please, call me Janet," I gasped, staring out at the trees, nearly leafless after the big storm. I was feeling my age, shocked and overwhelmed. Sally placed a fresh cup of coffee in front of me, smiled warmly, and walked into her office next door.

She called back, "We've completed two test trips to 1959 – we need you for the dress rehearsal. Your new eyes and real-world management experience will help us find any remaining safety flaws." The door shut behind her and I put my head down on the desk to get my breathing under control. I hoped the cameras were pointed away from me.

Ed Zanetti goes to a holiday party just outside Washington, D.C.

Ed Zanetti sat back for the drive from Capitol Hill into the Virginia suburbs. Early cold weather had iced the region, but the *Daily Media* had no information about it, phone headline blaring, "Experts Seek Consensus on Warming Earth, Cold Weather Paradox." He stared out at the traffic and darkening horizon as the smartcar driver aced the VIP lanes.

The car's transparency had taken getting used to, but he now enjoyed the sense of naked speed, a harmless illusion as he rode safely in his tinted bubble. The human driver was an accessory, a high-income status marker. The car's smart plates and info-beams provided wide access to private places, and privileged travel on restricted roadways.

"As if any of this matters to me anymore," Zanetti sighed, trying to avoid self-pity. He thought about the other headline on his phone, "Zanetti Out, King In: Secret Program Revelations Promised." He cringed with humiliation, a feeling he'd known well since his outsider days in middle school. It was not as though he were off the payroll – people at Zanetti's level never experience direct economic shock – but his power was gone. More than that – and here he felt authentic civic outrage, not just personal feelings – the time travel research project was gone. He stared at red taillights as the car inched forward, Congresswoman Holm's election season bash his destination.

He brooded, "All that work. Careful science. Twenty years, thrown out. Obliterated! To be replaced by extremist patriots led by that...no words...maniac, Cat King. That lying sicko is going to misuse a precious, dangerous tool. What historical trainwrecks will he cause, and how fast?"

The car picked up speed and Zanetti readied himself for the evening ahead. Friends and foes would be there, and he hoped to recoup lost ground with quietly influential conversations. He wondered whom King would be seen with. The car turned in to a hushed, esteemed neighborhood, moving without pause past the electronic gatekeepers.

Zanetti thought back to his lunchtime chat with a genteel horse farm lobbyist. The old gent was shaking a newspaper as he sat down at Ed's table.

"You have to admit, Ed, it's all for the best!" crowed Mr. Bradshaw. "I saw Senator Styce this morning, and they are fast-tracking for military action!"

Zanetti glanced at the animated gentleman farmer, swallowed his bite of organic brine-cured tilapia patty, and replied, "Action plans have to wait until after the election, and after Congress settles down in the new year. Don't get your hopes up just yet, Mr. Bradshaw." Zanetti was instantly ashamed of his sharp tone.

Bradshaw didn't notice, replying gleefully, "Styce promised my district the first Time Action Project. Our battlefield and graveyard, sacred ground, have sat in ignominy since 1862, so a few months more won't hurt any." He reached for the hot sauce. "Heck, when they go back and change history – " at this public revelation of what was still nominally top secret, Zanetti looked around for listening ears, but the din of noontime dining drowned out Bradshaw's indiscretions.

"...If I understand it right, it will be like we always won that battle. But first, that smart Professor King told me, they're doing the research to make sure a small change doesn't cause too much collateral damage to history." Digging happily into the day's grilled RedMeat© special, Bradshaw chattered on as Zanetti's appetite ebbed.

"Extrapolation. Scenarios. Statistics. That's what King is doing. It's too bad," Bradshaw pointed a fork for emphasis, "they can't just bite the bullet" – he winked at Zanetti, whose stiff upper lip was trembling – "and just fix it so we won that war, like we should of." Zanetti shoved back his chair with a screech and stood up, deeply alarmed at the possibility that, any minute now, the South had won the Civil War.

"Gotta go," he said, fleeing as Bradshaw shouted after him, "Those damn Yankee liberals will have to bring back all those statues they got rid of."

As the smartcar glided into the lineup at the pillar-lined portico entrance, Zanetti shrugged off the memory by imaging his young sons, a trick the therapist had taught him.

Emerging from the car ahead was Cat King, a glittering younger woman on his arm. They were followed by General Granger, and the lickspittle – thought Zanetti – Ard Sprinkle, who spoke to the driver before following his crowd indoors.

Climbing out of the car, Zanetti summoned up his nerd-based powers for an evening of political knife fights. Inside,

Congresswoman Holm was greeting her guests, looking over King's shoulder to smile at Zanetti. With her, at least, he felt safe.

"Ed, you need to talk to the staffer from my Massachusetts Senatorial colleague's office," she whispered, delivering a faux kiss accurately past his ear. "Her committee has been confidentially briefed about you-know-what being moved to Defense, and she is outraged." Zanetti sighed inwardly: the esteemed Senator was great on the issues and a peerless public speaker, but did not have clout where he needed it.

"Anybody else?" he asked plaintively, as the pressure of new arrivals moved him toward the big room ahead.

"Just start there, for courtesy. Big states are worried, too – environmental impacts and spending cuts on their minds. I'll do introductions later." Zanetti plunged into the ballroom, abuzz with hundreds of people under gleaming chandeliers, and wormed his way to the bar. Armed with a glass of club soda, he turned to survey the crowd, a star-studded Congressional cast in a sea of operatives and lobbyists.

Zanetti did not like parties, but these were his people, this was his native habitat. Everyone here knew that headlines announce career adjustments, not failure. He took a sip while eyeing the food tables. He and his wife had been through this upheaval before. He would find a better job, as she had. If only, he thought, isolated in the chattering uproar, the loss of that program was not so *important*, and the new bosses not so unstable, so *dangerous*.

Zanetti looked around for the Massachusetts Senator's staffer, but caught the eye of that guy from the Smithsonian, for whom these events were the lifeblood of fundraising. Unable to remember his name, Ed shook hands.

"Ed! Just the man!" enthused the guy. "Come work for us! Take a rest from the fast lane. We need you. I can put in a word." They fell into a short burst of party chat as Zanetti relaxed. His world was not about to end. But here came Cat King, tall, shouldering his way through the sea of partygoers toward Zanetti, who set his glass down on a passing tray and readied himself. Maybe he was not going to get any supper, darn it.

King had augmented his pre-party drinks with whisky neat, twice. Standing next to his date, he had scanned the battlefield for prey, lusting to inflict lasting damage.

He saw Zanetti and thought, "Time to finish him off in public."

Professor King's signature bullying move was to plow into a person's private space belly-to-belly, eye-to-eye. Few in polite society could withstand this. He had tired of the hushed brutality of academia, where professorial gladiators fight for the death of their colleagues' programs and careers via committees, publications, and tenure, always smiling and collegial.

King brought physical intimidation and violence into the university coliseum. He used these weapons carefully, lacing aggression with charm and synthetic warmth, catching opponents off guard. And now, his new position made him unassailable, even terrifying. As he shoved through the crowd to get at Zanetti, people turned in irritation, falling back when they recognized him. The Smithsonian guy felt the force approaching.

Looking up, he saw King, said to Zanetti, "Oh, shit, well, come see us when the dust settles, a quiet life is what you need," and vanished.

King addressed Zanetti loudly, playing to the crowd.

"Go home, Zanetti. You're out of the game." His animal nature smelled out the weak spots where his victim's vitals rode near the surface. He could hurt Zanetti quickly. "This party is for winners and players. You need to be sitting in the bleachers at Kevin's ball game. At least *he* misses you. You're wasting your time here."

King's public naming of Zanetti's child was a threat. Zanetti was suddenly on fire, as King intended. But a quick retort was unwise, so he stood quiet, pale. A hand patted his shoulder – a warning to keep it cool. Who was that? Zanetti broke stares with King to glance at the Massachusetts Senator's young chief of staff, smiling at him supportively.

King took advantage of the distraction to step forward and push Zanetti against the wall.

Zanetti smelled the whisky as King stage-whispered for all to hear, "Your liberal-assed science is dead, and I killed it. My science is *hard* – and mean – and takes no prisoners." He pressed Zanetti into the wall with each word. Even for King, this was excessive use of force in public, and a little gross. A voice called out the big man dominating the smaller man.

"Hey, King! Get a room!" This drew shocked laughter from the group, which scattered as King swung around, looking for the heckler. Zanetti moved away, sucking in cold air from an open window. Up came the Massachusetts Senator's staffer, mighty pleased with himself over his anonymous act.

"Do I need a drink after that?" Zanetti asked him, shaking his head to deny the impulse. "What I need is dessert first, dinner later. I am starving." They walked to the buffet and Zanetti piled up all the sweet stuff he wanted, thinking how he would describe the fancy array to his kids.

Through the crowd they heard King boasting, "New science, action-focused, restoring our nation's pre-eminence after decades of waste," but the words failed to sting. The two took their plates to a quiet nook and Zanetti began to eat, soon feeling a rush of relief and calm.

"My name is Ravi Sen-Ellis, by the way," the staffer said. "We met at the Parks Science conference last month."

"Right," Zanetti replied. "I was trying to hint to you, around the top-secret elephant in the room, that time travel is emerging as an excellent tool for ecosystem management and recovery." Sen-Ellis's eyes flew open, and he stopped munching on a fancy morsel to think about what he had just heard.

He said, "Suddenly I have a million questions, but why don't you keep going for a minute or two." He took a couple of bites as Zanetti continued.

"It won't be a secret much longer, with that asshole in control," Zanetti said, shrugging a shoulder in the direction of King's voice. On the other side of the room, Sprinkle was having a heck of a time convincing the boss that it was time to go home. He had one of King's arms into his coat and was walking him slowly, begrudgingly, toward the door.

Anna Holm waved bye-bye, shutting her ears to King's exhortations: "We can finally optimize our country's military heritage. George Bush is gonna thank me big time when we go back and clean up his messes. Congresswoman – Ohio's bases are going to benefit big time." Out the door, his voice trailed off, "Better get onboard while you can."

Cat's date was waiting in the car, fuming. General Granger stood clear of the uproar, lobbying on behalf of King's interests with a Ukrainian arms dealer while they nipped at martinis, the door closing behind King and Sprinkle.

Granger shrugged, "Hey, he just won the biggest fight of his career. Has to let off a little steam, you know?"

In the quiet nook, Zanetti told Sen-Ellis, "The Homeland-Interior program I just lost was researching the environmental and societal impacts of time travel."

"OK, so I *didn't* imagine you said that," replied Sen-Ellis. His voice trailed off; he was dumbstruck with wonder. And desire. "Oh my goodness," he said. "That Kentucky Pleistocene theme park. That's real?"

Zanetti nodded, smiling. "Each day there is the same day, re-set every twenty-four hours. That way we can – *could* – entertain visitors safely, and do research, without long-term impacts." He scraped the last bit of ganache off his plate and looked at the dessert buffet. He would snag some of those almond cakes for his sons. They loved the silly stories about his big nights out, his wife giggling, relaxing after her own hard day.

Sen-Ellis was staring at him. "Can you come give me and the Senator a briefing? I can barely believe this, but I guess I have to."

"Sure," said Zanetti. "I'd love to tell you the science. I'd love to talk to someone who appreciates what we've achieved. The secrecy has been a real bummer."

"I don't get that part," said Sen-Ellis. He asked, "How could they keep a discovery like that under wraps for twenty years?"

"Back in the day, the development team at Cornell Tech was Homeland funded, with proprietary protections in the contract. When they hit paydirt, a bunch of profs quit their day jobs to work for Homeland under tight security." Zanetti swept a pile of neon-frosted almond cakes into a napkin, and the two walked toward the door.

Putting on his coat, Zanetti bent close to Sen-Ellis's ear. "You may be too young to remember that we had a brief window of liberalism in the White House back then, so Homeland was forced to go halfsies on the program with the Department of Interior. They gave it to the Federal Parks Program, where it landed in my lap. It was my top-secret baby until they gave it to King." Out on the steps they breathed cool air, momentarily alone as Zanetti's car approached.

He summed up: "Twenty years of top-secret time travel research, serving the Park Program's twin goals, protection and enjoyment. While fending off Homeland, which pushed us to develop 'military applications.'" Zanetti spared Sen-Ellis the "quotes" gesture.

"So," Sen-Ellis said, "the Senator and I regard King as a kook. His teaching colleagues say he is disruptive, and they suspect his science is fake. Why is he running this show? What's he planning to do with..." he sighed and shook his head in awe, "...time travel?"

As Zanetti stepped into the car he said, "They call it fake science, huh? That could be very useful. He's running the show because he says what some in the military want to hear. What's he wanna do? He wants to go back and change history, so the USA comes out on top. I mean, to coin a phrase, *duh*."

Sen-Ellis watched the car depart. The muted nighttime roar of our nation's capital region hummed outside the enclave of big houses. He was aflame, his life's dream of time travel come true, in a casual party conversation. Wherever this led, he was already there. In a state of bliss, he walked to his car in a distant lot.

Professor Tom "Cat" King goes global.

Hung over and hard-hitting Professor King strode down the hallway toward his afternoon class, talking via his implant; students nudged one another as he passed. The midnight flight and drive from D.C. to New Hampshire had been rough, but here he was, negotiating a generous leave of absence with the deans on his way to the final lecture for his star-struck students and global audience.

The gabble stilled as he walked to the classroom lectern and said, "Internships. The lifeblood of our nation's new intellectual muscle. Who wants an internship?" A sea of hands rose from the packed classroom. Tens of thousands of Hands-Up buttons clicked across the Internet, as fervent followers leaned into their screens. Outside the classroom window, fat flakes of snow whirled earthward, the season's first storm.

King roared, "I am departing this cold paradise, 'where the snow drifts deep along the road,' and I am taking you all with me into the heart of power. Our dreams are coming true. Out of the shadows, scorned and denied, we step forward to take the reins!" He paused for a long, restorative chug of water, emptied the plastic bottle, crushed it, tossed it aside, and resumed at top volume.

He called out, "What lessons have you learned, class?" His enthusiasts, perhaps twenty percent of the class, chanted the responses.

"Science is hard. Science is not for softies. Science is fact – throw out the fiction! Science is dangerous! Science is walking boldly up to the cliff of facts and jumping off. You might not come back!"

These aphorisms came from readings and lectures focused on King defying the establishment with research results that stood accepted science on its head. He self-promoted as a contrarian regarding climate change ("We make our own climate"), energy production ("Frack till it hurts!"), human nature ("What humans want, humans get"), and future global prospects ("All we need is greed").

Non-enthusiasts stared ahead during the mass recital. They debated the professor's fascism over evening beers, but were reluctant to speak out, because tattle-tales were listening and cameras ubiquitous. It was best to be careful – a person might need a job someday.

Today King would speak about time travel, the grand finale topic on the course syllabus.

"Very good, class," he said, flashing a smile for the swooning screen watchers, a.k.a. his "Cat's Whiskers."

"Today I present a long-promised topic. Time travel! Not fiction. Fact! Revealed to you, exclusively, at," – he looked at his watch – "2:32 p.m. Eastern time, today's date worldwide." He gripped the sides of the lectern, staring at class and cameras.

"Yes. Unbeknownst to the trusting tax-paying American public, over the past twenty years, 'temporal transfer' – that's what the word-nerds call it – has been developed by our stalwart Department of Homeland Security and its pioneering scientists. But a controlling cabal of liberal extremists has kept this earth-shattering development a secret for their exclusive use!"

Around the world, heads of governments were called to their screens. The White House was scrambling, last to learn what the other hand was doing.

"'Temporal transfer' means what?" King went on, sucking a swig of water from the next bottle. "Until this week, it meant that a small group of privileged elites have been taking expensive vacations in Athens, Greece, 450 B.C.; France in the 1880s; the Hawaiian Islands in 1962; and Manhattan Island in 1660."

He paused, then roared, "But were *you* invited? Did *you* get to see our planet's ancient glories, drink at famous watering holes, sail the wine-dark seas of the ancients? No! These pansy scientists kept it secret, a boondoggle for themselves and their cronies. And that's not all!" Afire, King's glare swept the room.

"During this time only one man, one stalwart patriot, stood up for the rights of all Americans to enjoy this new world, this new dimension of experience, if you will. Yes, only Kentucky Senator Harlan Styce demanded, and got, public access to the past. The past is open to the public at Ten Thousand Secrets National Park. And only there!"

King built to the kill. "To satisfy the mincing liberal overlords of this secret program, Pleistocene Place has been advertised as a mere theme-park experience. Visitors have been guinea pigs in the science experiments of the bureaucrats. No one told them they were visiting the past!"

King dropped his voice thrillingly: "It's time for a change! And I am that change." He stared around, lordly, hangover extinguished by feel-good chemicals flooding body and brain.

"I have warned you repeatedly that scientists stand in the way of progress, and this project has been the Big Daddy of their mindless control. But! Their era has now ended."

King leaned forward, intent. "Battling behind the scenes, with allies like Senator Styce" – who was, at that moment, experiencing a small quiver of alarm about the good professor – "I have fought ceaselessly for the American public's right to the past. I even put my life on the line to disprove an establishment lie about time travel."

World-weary, wise, sexy, he sighed: "They were using that lie to bring progress to a halt."

King stood tall. "Cutting to the chase. Effective immediately, I am director of a Defense-Homeland program to usher temporal transfer – time travel! – into the public arena. Mistakes and defeats will be corrected." A copy of his now de-classified report, *The "Grandfather Paradox": Results of a Field Study with Defense Applications*, appeared on all screens. King shot a big fat wink at the transfixed planet. "America is back on top – great again. The American public will be time traveling as soon as we fast-track a franchise agreement with our noble Federal Parks Program."

The professor rolled to a close. "Yes, ancient vistas and famous events will soon be available at nominal cost to our families and youth. I do not mean a virtual experience, distorting eyewear, or drugs. I mean real, live time travel. I am not kidding around. *When have you ever seen me kid around?*"

He glowered and gleamed, towering beyond their reach.

The class roared – every one with passionate intensity – "Never!"

King grinned, tilting his head boyishly. "This lecture will be followed by a rigorous final exam, cumulative, on material you have come to know and love," he said, glancing at his teaching assistants.

"Then you will travel with me to the center of power. As interns in person and onscreen, you will see me open up this new world to everyone, and take care of America's business. Yes, asses will be kicked along the way. That I promise! Thank you, every one."

Professor Thomas King stepped away from the lectern and left the building for a waiting car, as the exulting class drew a deep breath following tumultuous applause. Some wept.

Senator Liz Maximus's office, Capitol Hill, Washington, D.C.

Senator Liz Maximus of Massachusetts leaned back in her chair as Sen-Ellis muted the screen following King's lecture. She looked at Zanetti, who was wondering if he could sue King for libel.

"The only good reaction is a suitcase full of swearwords, so I won't say anything at all," Maximus said, grinning. "Like my dear Oklahoma grandma used to say, 'If you can't say something nice...'"

She shook off her dismay. "Ravi, what have you learned from Ed, here?" Sen-Ellis had not slept since hearing Zanetti's revelations the night before. He was in a state of ecstatic awe, transfigured.

"Ed knows better than anyone, ma'am," he replied, glancing at Zanetti, who smiled at the precocious new student of his lifework. Sen-Ellis went on, "The facts are these. Over the past twenty years, 10.4 billion dollars secretly funded his Parks Program/Homeland office for temporal transfer programs." Zanetti's smile slipped a bit.

Sen-Ellis read from the program's most recent annual report, "'Throughout this period, the Parks Program has maintained a science-based, conservative research program focused on detecting and measuring the environmental impacts in the past and present that result from our presence there.'" He handed a copy to the Senator, and continued reading.

"'Opened ten years ago as a high-end theme park experience for visitors, the "Pleistocene Place" site at Kentucky's Ten Thousand Secrets National Park is the program's one fully functioning, long-term field research site to date. There have been numerous other temporal field trips, and our Venice 1959 program – '"

Maximus gestured gently for a pause, and turned to Zanetti.

"Doesn't the Kentucky park have caves?" she asked.

146

Zanetti nodded, "Longest known cave in the world is there, yep. But Homeland convinced the Federal Parks Program to revamp several national parks into money-makers with historically evocative entertainment themes, food and hotels, and casinos." With a pained expression, he continued, "Senator Styce was Homeland's champion for this change in Congress. In return for gutting the Parks Program's original mission, he got the Pleistocene attraction for Kentucky."

"The park that blew up in Nevada – " began Maximus.

Zanetti replied, "The Historic Red Light District & Jazz Casino National Park. That was one of the big new moneymakers." He shuddered, thinking about the fully legal red light district "experiences." In a national park.

"Good riddance to bad rubbish?" prompted the Senator.

Zanetti replied carefully, "We suspect that competing global casino powers are responsible for the blast, which killed three Homeland consultants and leveled the casino and burned down the…er, red light facilities. To answer your question, yes indeed. Good riddance – just between us."

Maximus kept private her thoughts about Zanetti: "What a tool. How can he live with himself, agreeing to these vicious travesties of the federal parks program, in return for so-called science? This temporal transfer stuff must really have a pull on some people," she reflected, glancing at Sen-Ellis. He was pallid with fatigue and glowing with joy.

"I have to get downstairs for a hearing," said Maximus. "Ravi, what can you tell me about Professor King's plans, in two minutes?"

Sen-Ellis rapped out, "He's removing all long-term employees from temporal transfer programs, and turning the programs over to Whetstone Consultants of Iraq War fame. There are two goals – one, to militarize the past in our national interest. Two, to franchise time travel trips for the public at Ten Thousand Secrets and other federal parks."

Maximus's eyebrows rose and she said, "But surely, everything we know – well, let me change that to – our popular understanding of time travel says you must not, maybe even cannot – do that kind of thing without repercussions. But, I suppose there's always parallel universes?" She beamed at them with apologetic amusement – speculative fiction was not her strong point.

Zanetti replied, "That overriding concern is the basis on which we have carried out our painstaking research. We did not want to open the past to heavy use until we proved that we could visit and not, like Ray Bradbury warned, kill a butterfly long ago and alter today."

"And what do you conclude, after twenty years of costly, painstaking research?" prompted the Senator, looking at her phone. Sen-Ellis gathered up papers as Zanetti continued.

"We have developed BMPs – Best Management Practices – to exclude impacts, such as our policy of taking tours to the Pleistocene on the same day. Over and over." In response to their puzzled looks he went on, "That's the Groundhog Day BMP. We adhere painstakingly to these practices. No mistakes are made, and no sloppiness is tolerated."

Zanetti grabbed his coat, adding, "Our number one BMP is, 'Determine if this temporal transfer is absolutely necessary, via a full-scale Environmental Impact Process conducted fearlessly and completely. No temporal transfer is the default outcome.' That means we almost always advise against temporal transfers. The risks are just too great."

Despite her overall support for Zanetti, Senator Maximus had a sneaky feeling of empathy for the explorers and promoters held back by this cautious approach. The three walked into the echoing marble hallway.

Keeping pace with the fast-striding Senator, Zanetti finished, "Last year, King issued a top-secret report saying that he traveled back and killed his grandfather, and is here to tell the tale. He says the past should be open for business, pleasure, and what he calls 'historical adjustments in the national interest.' So they put him in charge."

Sen-Ellis said, "I'll fill you in on that part, ma'am." Zanetti nodded goodbye as the private elevator door closed. Emerging several floors below, Senator Max, as the media called her, had a couple more minutes to spare as they pressed through crowds toward the hearing.

She asked Sen-Ellis, "You said you have information that Zanetti is unaware of?"

"Yes," he said, opening a door for her. "But I just got a whisper. There is an unauthorized program going forward. Unauthorized by Zanetti, that is. It's a secret survey of possible 'naturally occurring' access points to the past around the U.S. These would be used to bypass the BMP protocols Zanetti described."

"Run by who?" asked the Senator, as she settled into her seat at the table in front of the microphones and cameras, Sen-Ellis behind her. They were in a public space.

Sen-Ellis said, "The professor. So – " as the Senator turned toward the lights, "may I have that overdue leave, please, for a short trip to New York State?"

Ten Thousand Secrets drops to 9,999.

Down the flowing escalators, past the banks of cameras, across the gurgling stream and through the hand-hewn doors set with sparkling panes of artisanal glass, senior staff in the Office of Questions Asked & Answered were having a rough night shift. The Parks Program phone and email system had collapsed, overwhelmed by thousands of contacts from angry citizens demanding their time travel rights – now.

Three deeply rattled humans huddled at the long desk, each talking to distant offices while together viewing a screen. It displayed harried employees at Ten Thousand Secrets National Park struggling to maintain pre-dawn order in the Visitors Center, where a line of ticket purchasers stretched from the desk out the door. In the darkness beyond, security lights illuminated a parking lot swarming with arriving vehicles.

"That's right, ma'am," the harried ranger told the lady at the head of the line, her family of five bunched around her.

"We only offer one trip per day, and yes, $150 is the per-person ticket price. No child discounts, that is correct. We suggest you take advantage of our deeply discounted Casino Secrets & Joy Rides five-day resort and spa package, see the kid-friendly Secrets, and I can book you now for the Pleistocene, on your final day." The ranger looked up hopefully, but the woman shook her head, lips tight.

Her fiancé leaned over the children's heads and snapped, "We told you, this is our one day off, and we've got our rights, same as those fancy-pants over-educated free-loaders." Raising his voice for the crowd, he shouted, "You're ripping us off – " gesturing to the glowing trips and attractions price list – "on something us taxpayers already paid for." People shouted in support. Their angry voices filled the screen in the distant Answers Given office, deep below the restored prairie of central Ohio.

"Open the gate and let us all in today!"

"You've had twenty years, now it's our turn!"

"It's a cover-up – time travel is a lie – they're hiding U.N. troops over there!"

Two miles away from the Visitors Center past the glitt'ring Casino and Pleasure Domes, crowds milled around the locked gates to the Pleistocene Place building. The "Gone Fishin'" sign was back in place. Families shined flashlights through the gate and compared rumors. Most had walked over from their Pleasure Dome hotels and were shivering in resort-wear outfits.

A thick mist rose from the Green, Green River, snaking along the autumn-hued river valley, as dawn crept into the cloudless sky. Sleepy people crowded the riverside observation deck, staring at the time curtain along the far bank as it shimmered and warped like the aurora borealis. Cameras blinked. A little boy stood with his family, wearing sandals and a bathrobe over his pajamas. He held onto his mom's hand.

He said loudly, "I want to see the dinosaurs. You said we'd see dinosaurs." The crowd chuckled.

His mom murmured, "Honey, we'll come back later on." She said to her son and husband, "Let's go eat at the Hideaway Café & Curiously Satisfying Breakfast Buffet." Her husband was happy to depart. He did not believe in time travel.

"Just another Park promo," he thought, gloomily counting their vanishing vacation dollars, as his family walked up the slope toward warmth and comfort food.

Janet faces a new day.

Waking before dawn, I heard the rumble of traffic headed toward the Visitors Center. Office gossip said that a bigwig professor had revealed our park's biggest secret yesterday on the Internet, and thousands were heading here. A good day to be far away from monitoring visitors, managing overflows and fistfights and lost children.

I had to focus on my plan, get it rolling before the new hyper-vigilant Defense Department management team arrived. They would sniff out and eliminate the holes in Park security that I had found.

Sipping coffee, I reviewed the places underground where I needed to make measurements and calculate the...fatal dose. The date was fast approaching for its...administration. The park season wound down to a bare minimum during the winter months and human traffic would be at its lowest ebb, assuming this present ruckus died down. The tricky part was to make sure Lena was far away on that date.

A caffeine-aha moment struck: She would be with me. Damaris and Ron went back to college this coming weekend. There was no knowing Steve Roberts's schedule, but I'd go with the flow and protect him as best I could. As for the rest of the big shots, they'd survive, but their precious money-maker would pre-decease them.

The sky outside brightened, and I turned on the Internet news while getting ready for work, where today we would review the final protocols for our upcoming field trip to 1959 Venice. The Park may have given me this job to distract me from Hugh's death, but my skills were of real value to the trip team.

The newswoman burbled, "Not since cave explorer Floyd Collins's death in 1925 has the Ten Thousand Secrets region seen such a sudden influx of visitors. Vehicular traffic is moving slowly in the park, and I-65's approach roads are backed up for three miles in both directions." The screen showed car lights delineating the roads, then cut to the professor who had started this, yesterday afternoon. He stood at a lectern in a college classroom.

The reporter said, "Professor King, after his electrifying reveal yesterday of the time travel program, run in secret for twenty years by our own government, announced a leave of absence from his teaching position. He is headed to our nation's capital as the new head honcho to overhaul the time travel program." I finally realized that this professor and my new boss were the same guy, and put down my bag to watch.

King said, "Effective immediately, I am director of a Defense-Homeland program to usher temporal transfer – time travel! – into the public arena. Mistakes and defeats will be corrected." He was on fire, consuming himself before our eyes. This, then, was Hugh Hynes's murderer!

He waved a report, saying, "The American public will be time traveling soon, once we fast-track a new franchise agreement with our noble Federal Parks Program."

I powered down the laptop and headed out. Time to get to work – and to get moving.

Chapter 8

Ravi heads to upstate New York.

Brian was getting ready for his meeting with Maeve and Gregg at the highway project site, when Harris gave him a call.

"There's a weird wrinkle," he said. "A total stranger just called to ask if he could go along."

"No," Brian said, reflected, and went on, "Who told him? Who is he?"

Harris sighed. "He went to college with Rita. She gave him my number. He works in D.C. and is doing a survey of federal research projects, and wants to see how our federal dollars are being spent. Doing local field-trip checkups. 'Fact-finding mission,' he called it."

Brian said, again, "No."

"Look, man, he'll be there today. He called Rita to ask her about local projects and she told him about your federal grant work for that, umm, community. You really can't keep him out. It's the government's money, our sacred taxpayer money."

Brian swore.

Harris said, "Pliss come get me, I haff donuts undt I know how to use them. Look, this guy sounded OK. He's our age, and his name is Ravi, with a double-barrel last name. Might be helpful. He'll know the right questions to ask about the highway project."

Half an hour later, Harris and Brian arrived at the gravel pad. The old tree trunk had been moved atop a mound of dirt, rocks, and plants. The ground was scraped clean and piled high with road-building materials. In the field beyond, the yellow bulldozer was grunting to life between the two rows of orange flags. Harris brushed sugar donut debris off his lap onto the car floor, where it vanished into dog hair and candy wrappers.

He and Brian stared at the threesome in the parking lot: Maeve, waving at Brian, her long black hair sorting and settling in the breeze; next to her Gregg, in khakis and blue button-down shirt, glasses on a string around his neck. Behind was his white pickup truck, gleaming, new-washed. Gregg was talking to a tall, lithe guy with a mop of black hair, dressed for hiking, pack on his back and binoculars around his neck. Maeve walked toward Brian's car.

Harris said, "She likes you, Brian, I can tell," and they climbed out of the car.

"You know what," he added quietly as they grabbed their bags, "my he-male intuition tells me that you better not mention Rita to Maeve, OK?"

Harris was immune to women, but tall, dark Ravi was a different matter, so he headed over to get acquainted while Brian spoke with the others.

"Brian!" cried Maeve, as Gregg mustered a near-smile.

"This nice young man, Ravi," said Maeve, gesturing, "is visiting from your – "

"Our," corrected Gregg quietly.

"...capital city, to learn about the improvements we are making here." She took Brian's arm, hugging it to her warm side. But her eyes were stern.

"Who told him about us, dear?" she asked. Brian looked up to see Ravi winking at him. He hoped it was a good wink, not a bad wink.

"It wasn't me," Brian replied, but Maeve stepped away, chin up.

"We have a quiet, traditional community here, and do not like, what was that word, Gregg darling?" she asked, turning his way, as Brian closed his eyes against her onslaught on his senses.

"Snoopers," said Gregg firmly.

"Yes, what a silly word, sss-n-ooopers!" laughed Maeve as sunlight topped the hills and illuminated her pale, heart-shaped face. She was in her own land, drawing on its strength, careless of her visitors.

"Maeve," Brian said, "your grant money came from his office. Our papers were sent to them. The money they sent you comes from us, the taxpayers. The government has a right to see how its money is spent – "

"That is exactly my point, acushla," she replied, her Irish roused. "We are not taxpayers here! Why should we have to put up with snoo – " Gregg cut short her pretty speech.

"We need to get going. We're glad to have Mr. Sen-Ellis with us, but I have a road to build and can only spare an hour."

Ravi said, "From everything I have read, Ms. Maeve," (aha, he didn't know her last name either), "yours is an exemplary project, for which you should thank Brian Owen here, who guided you through the government paperwork." He shook Brian's hand and gave him a massive grin.

Maeve cocked her head, replying, "Will you go back to your capital and tell them that everything is fine here, and leave us alone?"

"Yours is one of several projects I am tasked with reviewing, ma'am," Ravi said. She wrinkled her nose at the old-lady form of address.

"I'll be gone before you know it," he added. She nodded sharply in agreement, glancing at Gregg, who smiled. Harris was pulled forward for introductions. He did not offer his hand, and Maeve looked from him to Gregg, Brian, and back at Harris.

"This one is different," she said to herself, then addressed Harris. "I have met your sort before, of course," she said. "I can see you are hardworking, with a diamond heart, but a man who prefers men is of no use to me." Harris bowed, not wanting to get any closer to her than necessary.

Maeve dusted her hands together dismissively and said, "Shall we walk?"

The awkward group trekked across the golden fields ahead of the bulldozer, which was snarling and puffing as it tore open a strip of brown dirt and glacial rocks. Goldenrod, asters, and bird nests piled up in its churning wake. As Maeve and Gregg led them counterclockwise around the white spire, the bulldozer noise and orange flags faded away.

Now they walked along a narrow, newly paved country road, more path than highway, toward an open-paved parking area. Brian allowed himself a moment of pride for a consulting job well done, and stole a glance at Harris. He was staring at Brian, wide-eyed and pale. This was different from the last time.

They walked past the sign "Special Heritage Area Parking" and into the open-paved parking lot, white flowers twinkling between the pavers. The group was quiet, following Maeve toward the bronze autumn slopes, her upland home. Smoke rose from the cottage chimney atop the little hill, but no one emerged to wave. Ravi and Harris looked around, probably trying to figure out where the music in their heads was coming from. Ahead, Gregg's stiff back signaled irritation at this waste of his time.

Brian broke the silence, if not the spell. "Ravi, we entered the official project area a few hundred feet back. The sign, parking lot, and improved facilities ahead – " Brian gestured to where a red neon light gleamed, "are central to the community-based improvements." Ravi looked back and forth along their line of travel.

"So," he asked, "we stepped over the border, just like that?" Harris was still staring at Brian, mute and appalled, his science-based brain in turmoil. Finding Ravi's choice of words odd, Brian wondered if they contained a warning, or information, and replied carefully.

"We are now in the grant project area, yes."

Maeve led them onto the green road, lined with purple asters and goldenrod, winding upslope across the meadow.

In project mode, Brian continued, "Ahead is a restored stone structure, perhaps an old dairy, with modern amenities that I like to think have a gently ironic feel." Ahead, Gregg stood under the neon ENTRANCE sign, hands on hips. Harris was failing to get a sign of life from his phone.

On her own ground, Maeve was easy to look at, impossible to handle. "A pretty young lady was with you here the other day," she said to Brian. "I do not see her today."

"She had to work," Harris replied, watchfully.

Maeve's laser-sharp baby blues were fixed on Brian's face. "Is it because of her attractions that you did not come to visit me?" Maeve was actually pouting. Brian wanted to reassure her, but Harris's glare stopped him.

Gregg said, "Maeve, our other visitor will be here soon. I gotta get back to the truck to meet him. You OK with these punks?"

Distracted from her prey, Maeve replied, "Oh my goodness. We need to be on our best behavior for this important man, Gregg. Yes please, treat him with every courtesy." She explained to the others, "A new patron is paying us a visit. A very rich man."

Gregg said, sharply, "Maeve, much as I love you, I suggest that you not talk about that." He turned back on the path, adding, "Lunch is set for noon at the Inn, right? These guys specifically excluded." Maeve nodded, and the three young men followed her into the tunnel, under the glowing red ENTRANCE sign. The music quieted; they looked around at the vaulted roof and stone walls.

Ravi said, "Brian, you termed this a 'dairy.' Tell me more."

Brian said, "Maeve, can you tell us about this building?"

Oh," she sighed, "it comes and goes."

"How do you mean?" asked Ravi, gently but persistently. They paused at the tunnel's midpoint. Their voices were muffled, and the air was still.

"You can probably feel it, even you humans, at this time of year?" She was whispering.

"What I feel is claustrophobic," Brian said. "Can we keep going?" Maeve remained still, listening.

"Sometimes it replies, today not," she said. "It does not answer. We brought these stones and timbers when we came here, those few centuries ago. Here I may listen to my home, and – other places." Ravi ran his hand along a wooden beam that curved from floor to ceiling.

"No, no," said Maeve, "not wise, young man. It is not yet fully the season. Soon enough, taxes are due." Ravi pulled his hand away. Following Maeve out the far doorway, the three exchanged wondering glances. Harris shut his eyes tightly, shaking his head, finger to his lips. The fresh air was welcome and Brian breathed deep. The music returned, humming a wordless story about the golden hue shimmering around them.

"Feels like the poppy-field scene in the old Wizard of Oz movie," whispered Harris. "Nasty."

They crossed the bridge on the green road, and passed the trickling waterfall. The creekside dell came into view, with the cottage Brian remembered from his first trip.

Maeve turned to smile at Brian. "Your friend, our Board Vice President, is feeling shy today, and won't be joining us." A window curtain twitched, and Brian waved. They soon entered the woods, up the slope toward the crossroads. A crow flew overhead, cawing, and Brian waved at him, too.

"I don't see the flags," said Harris to Brian. "I just don't get how this works."

Ravi said, "How about if I ask." He addressed Maeve, "What time is this place?"

Her eyes flew to his face. "My time," she replied. "The time I brought with me." They stood at the crossroads, the handsome sign pointing ahead to the Inn, aside to Apple Island.

"And what time is the highway project?" Ravi continued, as if he knew what he was talking about.

"Oh, that noisy thing, that is in your time," she said, shrugging a pretty shoulder. "I don't know how you humans put up with things like that." Harris snorted, and she shot him a glare. Ravi nodded.

Maeve went on, "They are paying us a grand fee, in gold dollars, to use our land in your time. I will spend it on improvements for my old-fashioned community in my time, with Brian's help." She smiled warmly at him, and his body responded.

"I must hasten to the Inn," she went on, "to make sure the feast is ready for our new patron. I trust you can find your own way back." She looked at Ravi and asked, "Have some of your questions been answered?" Maeve found him impressive. Best to treat him with caution.

Ravi was looking at the Apple Island path.

"What's down there?" he asked. Harris shut his eyes again. Maybe he thought that made him invisible. Maeve's sweetly gurgling laugh, surely aimed at Brian's ears alone, followed them as she walked away.

"Don't waste too much time on Apple Island — nothing ever happens there. Such a dull place, such boring fuddy-duddies. Brian, I'll be in touch, dear." She was gone, and the golden day dimmed.

"Sheeew," whistled Harris through his teeth. "Fairy queen. Where the bee sucks, there sucks she." There was no love lost between Harris and Maeve.

Ravi grinned at his tart words and said, "This community of hers is not in the U.S. Census. It does not exist."

"Who the heck are you, and why were you asking those questions about time?" Brian asked him, as they watched Acton approach along the Apple Island path.

Ravi said, "You deserve to know. This is a naturally occurring time opening. There are probably others. Do you know when she 'came over here'? That's probably the time of this place."

Brian said, "From Ireland, a thousand or more years ago, is what she told me. You *believe* that stuff?" Ravi smiled and shrugged, turning to shake Acton's hand.

Introduced, Acton said, "Ravi has found the words of your world to explain the situation. And Brian, you have the key: go counter-clockwise around the church. Otherwise you come here in your own time, and find the highway project."

Harris shook his head in disbelief.

Glancing at his dead watch, Ravi replied, "Back at the bulldozer, the important visitor has arrived. Not someone I want to encounter here."

He spoke to Acton. "Maybe you can show me Apple Island, while Mr. Big Shot goes to the Inn?" Acton bowed, gesturing down the path.

Harris finally spoke. "I want to see the big shot. Let me guess. It's the professor who was mouthing off across the Interwebs yesterday."

Ravi gave him an admiring glance and said, "Got it in one, sir! Bravo." Harris returned his grin, with interest.

Brian tried out his new time vocabulary on Acton. "So, what time is Apple Island, Acton?"

He replied, "It is your time, Brian Owen. Time for you to join us. But not today." Brian felt a shock of recognition, and fell silent.

To the group, Acton added, "Apple Island is a day in time. One day and one night."

Ravi said, uneasily, "I bet they're at the tunnel. Let's go," and he and Acton headed away.

He called to the others, "Catch you later at that pizza place, OK? Six p.m. – our time!"

They waved and walked back toward the tunnel and parking area. Harris filled Brian in on Professor King's wild rant, which he had missed. Ahead they saw a small group led by Gregg and a tall, imposing man. Behind them trudged a third, carrying a bag.

"There he is!" hissed Harris in a thrilled tone, and the two hastened to meet them.

Brian said, "Remember, I'm the boss. You are my assistant. Stay quiet and pay attention – OK?" He glanced at Harris for reassurance, because he sometimes played to his own rules and screwed stuff up. Eyes fixed on Professor King, Harris grinned, showing his teeth.

"Ah, here you are!" called Gregg heartily, as if meeting them were part of the official script.

As Brian and Harris came up, he said to King, "Sir, may I introduce you to the consultants who have been working with the community to develop these initial amenities. Rick," – to the bag-carrier – "these are our project colleagues."

"Sheeeew," Harris whispered again as King looked them over, and they returned the inspection. Powerful shoulders, clad in costly expedition togs, set off his large, noble head. Dark, deep-set eyes were framed by expensively cut white hair, gilded here and there. A sensitive mouth below a long upper lip, aquiline nose, and deep creases of experience all suggested a guy way out of Brian and Harris's league.

"Hello," Brian said, pushing past his nerves, stepping forward with his hand out, to no response. King's gaze stared through him.

Brian let his hand drop, continuing, "It's an honor, sir. Yes, I and my assistant here helped Maeve and her Board develop these improvements, and we hope to continue, in partnership with Gregg and Rick – "

King shrugged, said to Gregg, "Let's go," and they sailed past, toward the bridge over the creek on the path to the Inn, where Maeve's luncheon awaited them. Brian had eaten other people's dust before, so he swiveled on his heel and trotted toward the tunnel, Harris fulminating obscenely next to him.

Walking fast through the tunnel, Brian said, "Keep it down. It doesn't feel right to be swearing in here."

Harris snapped, "Au contraire, pal. This is a nasty place, and swearing clears the air." They were halfway along, daylight shining through the doorway ahead.

Harris went on, "Why the flying hell" – Brian really did not like him saying that – "did you say you were working with those f-heads?" The light in the tunnel dimmed for an instant, and they walked faster. A chill, garbage-smelly breeze sprang up. Ahead, a circular dark area appeared on the floor. They veered to the side of the tunnel and ran like deer under the EXIT sign, out into the warm day, down the slope to the parking area.

"What was that?" asked Harris, shaking with horror, as Brian unlocked the car door. The thick golden sunshine and strange music faded as they drove clockwise around the roundabout and back to the highway. The bulldozer had made further progress in tearing up the field.

"That tunnel is bad news," Brian said. "I hope Ravi gets back all right."

Harris said, "He's got those two forest guys to protect him, he'll be fine. They'll give him a little apple sprig for his pocket – " he paused, as Brian accelerated onto the highway. "I can't believe I'm saying these things," he muttered, subsiding into silence for the ride back to town.

Just the facts, from Ravi.

Only one slice remained of the second extra-large mushroom, peppers and anchovy pizza, extra cheese, when satiation finally slowed down the foursome. Ravi was all over the local root beer.

"Can you get this in D.C., I wonder?" he asked, pulling out his phone. He glanced at Rita, Brian, and Harris, saw in their solemn faces that it was not cool to check on root beer availability while the fate of the Earth hovered in the balance, and put his phone away.

Mushroomy Fields Forever was a repurposed farm stand, uneven walls painted in wild murals. It held a dozen tables, right now occupied by ravenous climbers, hikers, beer drinkers, and genteel Sunday walkers. Dogs and toddlers were underfoot, local photography for sale on the walls.

Rita had emerged from her grad student den to join them, and sighed as she set down her beer.

"Oh my gosh, what a horrible week," she whispered soulfully. Harris was eyeing Ravi, glancing from him to Brian, ready to talk.

"So you work for a Senator," Brian said. They had gotten that far before the pizza arrived.

"Yes," resumed Ravi. "Not gonna say who right now, no need. I did some research, and learned about a twenty-year top-secret project between two federal agencies, Homeland Security and the Department of Interior, to study and develop temporal transfer, or time travel." He leaned in and lowered his voice, drawing them all together above the remaining pizza slice.

Harris said, "There's been rumors about it for a long time in the engineering world."

He gained an interested glance from Ravi, who went on, "The Park Service project leaders were very cautious in their approach to using time travel. The military finally lost patience, took over the project, and now Professor Thomas King is the time travel czar."

"But why is he bothering us here?" Brian asked.

"Yeah, and how come they can put a highway into a nature preserve without public oversight?" chimed in Harris.

"I did some digging on that," said Rita to Harris. "Someone, I guess it must be Maeve, has a lot of local pull with our Congressman, and at his request the nature preserve status here was swapped with a remote location upstate."

"Wait, what?" squawked Harris. "You can't do that! There's a law!"

"There *was* a law – " replied Rita, ready to launch into chapter and verse. Ravi knew from their college days that she was a full-blown policy wonk, and deftly regained control of the conversation.

"King is looking for unregulated, naturally occurring time openings, so he doesn't have to bother with the federal rules and regulations." Ravi said this like it was *true*.

"Oh thank gawd for science," said Harris. "It's just good old fact-based time travel, not the magic fairyland that Brian dreamed up." He glanced at Brian, adding, "You can relax, old buddy."

"I'm not so sure about that," said Ravi. "I wouldn't throw out any good working hypotheses about what's going on." Brian sat up straighter. If *Ravi* thought it was possible, then maybe Brian was not nuts.

"Those woods guys and that island were pretty strange. I suspect that Maeve is even stranger," went on Ravi, glancing at Brian, who nodded, wordless on the topic of Maeve.

"Whatever we disturbed in that tunnel was not 'temporal transfer,'" Brian said.

Harris nodded in agreement and asked, "Did that tunnel give you any trouble, Ravi?" Ravi shook his head, patting his breast pocket and the sprig of apple blossom there.

He said, "I did exactly what Acton and Greenwood told me. The walk back was quiet, harmless."

Harris said to Rita, "Before I forget. You gotta steer clear of Maeve."

Rita nodded. "We have multiple working hypotheses about what's going on," she said, "and one of them is that Maeve is a dangerous and vengeful lady, and does not like female competition, am I right?" Harris rolled his eyes in agreement, finished off his beer, and looked around for the waitress, switching to coffee.

"I'm heading to Ten Thousands Secrets National Park next," said Ravi. "This is a fact-finding trip for the Senator, and I need to find out what King plans to do there, now that he's told the world that the Pleistocene theme park experience is the real deal."

Rita replied, "People are swimming the Green, Green River to get there, I heard on the news today."

Harris chimed in, "Thousands are swarming the park, demanding their 'time travel rights.' And my engineering office got a couple calls, people wanting to cash in on time travel tech, you know, instant-aging cheeses and whisky?" He met puzzled looks and subsided, sighing again.

Brian said, hesitantly, "My mom works at Ten Thousand Secrets," and continued in the instantly attentive silence, "I haven't been in touch with her for a while, but I know that much." They saw his sadness.

"Sure thing," said Ravi, gently. "You think I might encounter her? What's she do?"

"Not certain," Brian replied, "but knowing her, she's in the thick of things. I need to call my sister and find out what she knows. It's been a while." Glancing at their kind faces, he went on, "We were all shook up when that Nevada park blew up. My mom barely escaped. She's kind of withdrawn from us, and her old friends."

Brian looked down at the table, then at Ravi, saying, "Maybe you can say Hi for me."

By the time they reached the crossroads in the woods, Gregg had run out of polite conversation, which had been met with dead silence. Cat King did not like the out-of-doors, and was focused on the meeting ahead. He glanced at the sign and down the trail toward Apple Island.

"What's that?" he asked.

"It's geologically complex down there, sir," said Gregg easily. "And people have been playing around, building makeshift stuff over the years. We're going to blast out an old dam, to get the creek running better." Gregg gestured to the trail ahead, onward toward the Inn.

"You can't see it in this time, but the highway corridor crosses our path here, down the slope, crosses the creek, runs along its banks, and then heads through the hills a ways downstream." He smiled at the impassive King. "Really neat project, sir. A five-mile shortcut for gas field service traffic."

The trio emerged from the woods and walked along the green road between the small farms. Ahead, the Inn snuggled beneath giant holly hedges against the rising hill. The small ponies in their pastures had their heads down, nipping at the short grass, warming their flanks in the autumn sunshine. Perched on a fence-post, a crow watched them pass, bright eyes gleaming. On a cottage porch sat an older woman in a pink tracksuit, watching them, stroking the black cat on her lap whose golden eyes followed the walkers. A piglet in a pink bonnet lay stretched out at her feet, slumbering.

King emerged from his reverie and said, "Gregg, I haven't met Maeve."

Gregg responded eagerly, "You're in for a treat, sir, she is a remarkable woman – "

King brushed this aside, continuing, "But those guys we just met have to go. There is no place here for that 'community development and public access' bullpucky. Not with me in charge."

Gregg replied, "Isn't that kind of up to Maeve, sir? This is her time and her neighborhood, after all – "

"Back at the parking lot, we are in the USA, and I am now in charge of an important part of our nation's security," snapped King. "How dare you speak to me like that. This place, and whatever time it is, is ours, and I make the rules." King turned to the third person in the group, Gregg's foreman for the highway project.

"Your name again?"

"Ricky Jones," the man replied, shifting the heavy bag of display materials from one shoulder to the other. Ricky was small, wiry, with short pale brown hair under a well-worn cap bearing the Walden 2 company logo.

"Ricky, Gregg here is too busy to get the work done," snapped King, as Gregg's face filled with dismay.

"You heard me say, 'Those guys have got to go,' right?" continued King, stopping to emphasize his words and intent.

"Right," said Ricky.

"OK?" said King.

"Got it," said Ricky. As they neared the Inn, Maeve came out on the steps to welcome them.

Widdershins around the traffic circle, up the green road and across the darkened country as the crow flies and cat prowls, the old Inn glowed with candles and lanterns. Passing foxes glanced up at the shining windows and at the figures within and crept by cautiously, into the open country and starry night beyond.

Indoors, Maeve sipped her wine as the bartender plied Gregg with another helping of local viands. Across the old wooden table was Tom King, his harsh features limned in lamplight and shadow. He too was nursing a glass, mellow for a moment.

"I can never get enough of your cooking," Gregg gushed at Maeve and the bartender, who smiled a wintry smile. "I think about it when I'm back home," Gregg went on. "Can't wait to get back here for more."

He sipped the local dark beer, and dug in. Maeve was pleased at his acquiescence, and at how well he was fattening up. But she was watching King. They had already disagreed politely. He seemed to think he had authority here, which puzzled her. She ventured a remark, bait thrown into the pool.

"Cat, if you send this team, as you call it, where would they live?"

"No need to worry, Maeve, they will come in on day trips. They just want to map the place, make an inventory." He looked at his watch, remembered again that it did not work here, and glanced out the window at the starry night. Even iron men like King get tired.

"Time for bed," he said. "Got to get back to the car and head out first thing in the morning."

He caught Gregg and Maeve exchanging glances, confirming his suspicion that they had a thing going on. Not very professional, but what can you expect, he ruminated. She was pretty, in that Irish hippie chick way. Not his style. Whoever she was – and he did not believe for a moment in fairies – she knew her way around this naturally occurring temporal opening. She would be treated carefully, until his guys figured this place out, and how to manage it. So she could have her fun with Gregg.

For her part, Maeve was not about to argue openly with her new patron. Gregg had promised that King had the treasure of nations at his fingertips. She could bide her time, until the payments ended. And these "teams" – surely they would not miss a man, here and there. What good fortune all this was, for her community.

On the other hand, King did not know how lucky he was, to go free. Maeve eyed Ricky Jones, who was eating fast and staying out of trouble, over by the kitchen door. He and the bartend knew one another, somehow.

"Probably not worth the effort," she thought. And thus do the Ricky Joneses slip through life's traps and prosper.

"But before I head upstairs," King went on, "a few more things, so I don't have to bother you in the morning." Maeve gestured for the bartender to pour a final round of the amber liquor, and waited.

"Those boys I passed on the path today."

"Yes, Brian and Harris." She neglected to mention the one who had gone down the hill to Apple Island.

"They are no longer allowed access here. They are fired. We can't have civilians like that, snooping around. This is a secure area now."

Maeve replied, "But Brian has helped us, and we will pay him to do more, to bring in money to build a trail, a festival center – " King stood up, done here. He'd send in a team to deal with her.

"Just keep in mind, Maeve, we have real money, not the spare change that punk brings in. And let's skip the public access b.s. Think about how much cash you want, to start. Once I'm in D.C., we'll set up generous, regular use-fee payments." He headed for the stairs, not looking back. His guys would handle the money.

Climbing the creaky staircase, candle illuminating the hallway to the room with the big bed and down coverlets, King did not see the expressions that flickered across Maeve's face. Greed – excitement – regret. She would miss Brian, but only for a moment. Many nice young men had come and gone. Along with Gregg, Brian would amply complete the year's tax payment. And the years ahead would be even better, with money and new men flowing in. Maeve felt good – her burdens lessened. She could have fun tonight. She sent Gregg a thrilling glance. He ate the last bite of his locally sourced peas, contemplating dessert.

Chapter 9

Janet and Steve adjust to a new work environment.

Top-level staff in the Homeland-Interior complex below the restored Ohio prairie-savanna have high-ceilinged, sunny offices. A $10 billion DARPA product pipes in a sunlight mixture from numerous time-locations. New to his Time Travel Development & Exploitation office, Steve Roberts realized after a few days that he could adjust the sunstat. I listened to his gripes about his new-office perks as we started our screen meeting on the final details for the Venice 1959 field trip.

"I toned down 'central Sahara February 1900' and adjusted 'mid-latitude mixed palette of Pennsylvania clean air series April 2014' and 'Paris, France January 1882 cool white art garret.' The 'warm notes from Georgia American heritage June 1835' I left alone. And then there's this desk. It gives me vertigo."

He could not figure out how to adjust the stand-up desk with sensurround immersion communications for face-to-face holo-meetups with his new team. Zooming in and out of offices was dizzying, so he was wearing sunglasses in case that helped. This fancy technology was not available at Ten Thousand Secrets National Park, where I sat at my wooden and metal desk.

We were running down a checklist about Venice, reviewing safety procedures for quick evacuation to the present.

"I'm sure you know how I feel, Janet. BMP number one all the way," said Steve, referring to the temporal transfer program's #1 Best Management Practice: "No temporal transfer advised."

He and I were comparing each event step to the Temporal Transfer BMPs, and cross-checking each across three possible trip scenarios ranked from No Problems and Problems–Continue Transfer to Problems–End Transfer. We used the Travel Outcome Odds calculator, which models the cumulative temporal-impact-safety of each trip decision. Each TOO calculator outcome is accompanied by several accuracy estimates.

A separate Ohio-based work team was modeling participant safety, for each member of the travel team and the team as a whole. Our final joint meeting would be held the following day, and the trip had to take place within 48 hours of that meeting to stay within potential neo-shift parameters.

This was painstaking work, not attractive to either of us. Sent a new set of BMPs that morning fresh from Tom King's D.C. desk, we saw that he was eviscerating the safety features developed by Ed Zanetti and staff over the previous two decades.

Steve spoke openly about King's intentions, careless of surveillance because he expected them to fire him soon.

"I think King wants to omit TOO from the trip planning process, but he knows that tough legislators like Senator Maximus are reviewing his changes. So he's holding back for the time being. I hear he's interviewing modelers willing to adjust the odds toward less impact and more trips."

We read through the new #1 BMP: "Unless strongly counter-indicated, go Full Speed Ahead (FSA). Counter-indications will be found in less than 1% of all trip proposals, and generally can be ignored."

On to the new #2 BMP. The original read, "If a decision is taken to carry out a temporal transfer, a full, rigorous, multi-year Environmental Impact Process must be undertaken and completed ahead of the proposed transfer, all agencies included. A separate full process must be undertaken to determine if foreign and local governments should be included in this process, and if so, to what extent." The new BMP #2 read, in full, "A summary Environmental Review will be adequate for 99% of all temporal transfer proposals, with no-impact outcomes assured."

Steve swore pungently for the record about new BMPs #1 and #2.

I reminded him, "Do we care if this meeting is being reviewed and evaluated?"

"I don't care," he replied. "I am filing a complaint that these new BMPs allow and encourage time travel under dangerous conditions, with easily measured, I'd say *obvious*, steep consequences for local time events during and after the trip, *and* probable profound negative consequences for the time-event downstream into the present day." He wiped his hands down his face, trying to keep a lid on his rage.

"Tell us how you really feel," I teased him. I could not afford to lose my own position for a few more days, when everything would be set. Until then I remained a model employee.

"Sure, OK, I *will*," said Steve. "I suggest that this dangerous situation is a temporal impact outcome of Tom King killing his grandfather and living to tell about it. I would further suggest that he did some other things while he was on that trip, and I'd like to see a full Congressional investigation."

I admired Steve's courage, but needed him to stay on task right now and not derail my plan via a political scandal. Fulfilling my own mission would do a lot of damage to King's plans for the short term. It would also give more time to those who worked through conventional channels.

I said, "Steve, we're on the final series of cross-checks. Let's get it done. I will recommend to the work group that we hold this trip to the old standards, while taking field notes on where the new ones come into play, and their effects downstream. I think that's the responsible way to proceed, for this trip."

But Steve wanted to get on the record. "You know what they're planning? They 'fully anticipate a positive outcome for the final Venice pre-trip transfer' and say it is 'the kickoff for a full schedule of trips to that time/place destination, available to the public next year at six of our federal entertainment parks.'" He glowered at me via the screen.

"I understand your dismay, but let's keep going," I said, hoping he would be done ranting soon.

"I'm sorry," he said. "I don't want to get you into trouble. What's next on the list?"

After the meeting with Steve, I had lunch with Lena in the staff room. She shared her almonds and raisins, and asked how my morning had gone.

"I've had better," I said. "Steve is not happy about the new standards for time travel trips."

"From what we've heard, they are really lax," she replied.

"Your duties are present-day science monitoring only, right?" I felt alarm at the thought of her on one of the new, high-hazard time trips.

"For the time being," she replied, tucking a strand of hair behind her ear. "But they say that 'steeply streamlined' monitoring standards will free us to re-train as TimeTrip Sherpas.' "

I kept my fears to myself, saying only, "Maybe it's time for you to get going on those grad school applications."

"Oh MO— Janet!" my dear daughter exploded. "I can decide for myself! Of *all* people to lecture me on safety, you – " but up came Damaris, smiling, and Lena changed gears.

"In fact," she said, "Damaris and I were discussing the pay and benefit cuts that come with switching to the Sherpa program."

"Kind of insulting," Damaris said. "I don't know if I'll come back, if that's all they offer me." She started in on a plate of rice and beans. "You can't pay off student loans at minimum wage."

"By 'steep streamlining,' they mean cutting the science staff to one," said Lena. "I guess that would be me, if I'm lucky." She made the quotes gesture around lucky, and sipped her tea.

"At least we have that trip during break to look forward to," I said to her. She smiled and nodded but said nothing, I guess not wanting Damaris to feel left out. Damaris and Ron's seasonal employment ended that week, as the park shifted to its reduced winter season. They and other seasonals headed home until spring.

During the lull, with staff on leave and park activity at its year-end low, Steve had invited me and Lena on a cave paddling trip to his old underground haunts. I suspected he wanted to pass along his knowledge before he was fired. To camp overnight, on the banks of a cave river – that worked well with my plans, and that would be the night.

Looking at the capable young women, chatting about where they would meet during the winter season, I felt affection, but was distracted. My final trip underground to set things up was tonight.

Damaris shot through her lunch and departed. As I gathered up my stuff, Lena put a hand on my arm. "I just want to get caught up on some – " she looked around – "family matters." I leaned in closer. "Brother has been in touch!" she said, smiling at me. After the Nevada disaster, my son Brian had been angry – I think he suspected me – and we had not been in contact. Since then I had known only that he was working in the Northeast.

"He has a day job and a little consultant thing going, in central New York State, and he wants to get back together soon," she said, with hope in her eyes. "I thought maybe during break, after our trip, we could join him for – " I felt nauseated; must have gone pale.

Lena asked, "What's wrong? You OK?" I could not say that she would not be seeing me again, for a long time, after our cave trip. That was the night I had to go, to vanish. She would be safe; Brian would be safe. But this time, the authorities would know who was responsible.

Best to pretend. "Sure, tell him we can see him for the holidays, but let's keep the dates loose until we know our schedules a bit better," I said. "This new position of mine is unpredictable."

"Oh, good," she replied, eyes watchful. "He's working with a local community there – says they come across like fairies, very weird people. He thought you'd enjoy that." Lena saw I was getting up, and crammed in the rest quickly. "He says there's an island, that sparkles – he wonders if is the same kind of sparkle that he read about for the Pleistocene, here."

"How could that be?" I asked, as we walked down the hallway toward our offices.

"Yeah, I know," she replied. "The sparkly effect here is a top-secret high-energy process, held in place by the coal-fired power array down on the sinkhole plain."

"Tell him to be careful," I said, smiling. "He never listens to me, and I am no exemplar, but tell him anyway. And tell him I love him. Maybe we can learn more when we – we all meet." We waved at one another and parted for the afternoon.

I sat on my couch that evening as the autumn night deepened. Everything I needed fit into my cave suit pockets and a small backpack. Timers, one set for 2 a.m. on the night of our canoe trip, to trigger an explosion that would stop the big fans. A second timer allowed 30 minutes for gas buildup from the leaking well pipe, and was attached to a second charge to ignite that gas, and the well. Bye-bye pleasure domes. Between now and that date, I would disable the park's alarm system for that time period, to prevent anyone rushing in to fix the fans.

I had not planned to move this quickly, but King's security team was arriving January first. They would plug the holes I had found at this trusting, open, kindly place. I had to do it *now*. We three would be safe on our canoe trip in a distant part of the cave, and Brian was in New York State. The park staff and patrons of the entertainment zone would be at their annual low point.

And I no longer wanted to do it. I had interesting work, at long last. No other job like it, anywhere – or any time. With my new salary I could buy a house, and Lena and Brian could...the demon visions of security and comfort and family life ran through my head. The wall clock emitted its antediluvian digital ticks. Streetlamps came on, shining through the curtains. A line of light illuminated books, dishes, tablecloth. Pinecones I had piled there. Halloween, the election, and the holidays coming up.

My determination was fading in the face of human kindness and daily routine. Rage had been easier to find in that dreadful bogus desert park.

"Maybe we achieved enough by blowing up the first park," I thought, recalling my comrades there, now scattered and silent. Eventually I came back to the oncoming disaster here at Ten Thousand Secrets and elsewhere. King was taking control of the past from these gentle scientists, who fussed about harming a single blade of grass. King would plunder time, militarize this park, drive away and kill those who got in his way. He would change history, altering and maiming the present and future.

The comfortable, well-managed situation at this federal park was about to be wiped out by King and his thugs. But my small act would slow them down, shine a spotlight on the situation, and give others time for political and legislative action to protect the rest of our parks from vile exploitation. This was not hubris or mania on my part, it was necessary. I stood up and went out my door, snicking it locked behind me. Staying in the shadows, I walked down the stairs and into the laundry room, to the wall cabinet, key in hand.

Ed Zanetti is not coping well with change.

Ed Zanetti gazed out of Congresswoman Anna Holm's office at the grey D.C. day. Try as he might, he could not morph the traffic noise to a waterfall as a stress releaser. He knew he should pay attention to the interoffice negotiations going on around him. He had become a pawn. No longer a player, nor knight.

"Fool, maybe," he brooded, envisioning a multi-pointed cap on his head, bells jangling. His kids would like it. There, that helped.

Holm was taking a time-out from talking to King's office, where a team of young staff huddled around the screen, Cat's Whiskers every one. They were negotiating conditions for King to obtain Zanetti's temporal transfer programs information, demanding a free-will waiver and full brain scan. Holm conferred by phone with Senator Maximus and Ravi Sen-Ellis.

"Easy," said the Senator, in response to these proposed conditions. "Just say no. Ed was hired before that technology was available. His contract does not require any free-will waivers. He is exempt." Holm looked at Zanetti, who shut his eyes while nodding agreement with the Max.

He brooded to himself, "Can I play this as a holy fool? Skate through it in a state of bliss? Capitulate, be home tonight for the boys' holiday show at school? What does it matter, anyway."

"Ed, get the hell over here," snapped Holm, patting a chair next to her. "You have to engage. For the future of your programs, and national security. For heaven's sake." Sen-Ellis watched Zanetti move nearer, struggling out of his protective fog.

"Right, the Senator is right," said Zanetti. "But what if they fire me?"

"Lawyers," said Liz-to-the-Max. "Months, years of lawyers. Just tell them no. They know they can't get this." Sen-Ellis whispered legal precedents in her ear.

"So," said Holm, "Offer them one-on-one conversations?"

"Good," agreed the Senator. "Two in-person one-hour talks between Zanetti and King, with scheduled and as-needed breaks, and a two-person team behind each guy." Sen-Ellis would be on Zanetti's team, a bank of lawyers on call. Holm and Maximus looked at Zanetti.

"You have to locate your spine, Ed," said Maximus. Sen-Ellis winced, Zanetti looked wounded.

The Senator went on, "King wants to know how you think, and where you planted booby traps within your science programs."

"Time bombs," offered Holm agreeably.

"I only wish I had known to do that," said Zanetti. "But it's just the science, and instructions, and protective language, and in-depth monitoring of impacts downstream from each transfer. And data. Reports, documents, and raw data. No traps. I don't even get what you mean."

"Yeesh," said the Senator, recoiling from his naiveté, thinking, "There is no hope for a guy who brings genteel academic standards to an interagency knife fight."

"Scientists," said Sen-Ellis, with admiration. He indeed regarded Zanetti as a holy fool, and knew that King would eat his science for breakfast – disembowel the data, hollow out the procedures, and replace the delicate balance with tech-trained, amoral consultants. Heavily armed.

The screen rang. Holm clicked off evident links with the Senator's office, returned to the screen call with King's staff, and addressed the young faces there.

"No," she said. "No free-will waiver, no brain scan."

From the other end of the call, King had a view of Holm's office window, across the intervening boulevards and majestic open spaces surrounding Capitol Hill. He was monitoring the negotiations from a quiet chamber in his new office suite. His staff had not yet gained direct surveillance of Holm's office, which remained fully cyber-protected. They did not even attempt to test for holes in Senator Max's office protections, because there would be immediate sharp complaints and legal saber-rattling.

King spoke into the Cat's Whiskers' ears, "OK, OK. Tell her I will talk to him. I don't care. Zanetti's a charter member of the too stupid to live club – I bet he left the work wide open. I just want the temporal maps, inventories, interaction histories, any and all data, so we don't have to reinvent the wheel."

King had given these interns the easy stuff, a teething ring for serious matters later. Good kids all, with Rand, Machiavelli, and *Economist* values burned into their DNA. He cut the connection – let them do the details. He smiled in satisfaction at having terrified Ed Zanetti, definitely the afternoon's high point. Zanetti was the ultimate tweedy professorial weakling, with his trust in science as truth, the value of good manners and correct behavior – all extinct as the dodo. King would eat his brain and run him out of town.

And now he knew who Zanetti's protectors were in Congress. Maximus and Holm were not touchable now, but after January they might be. All eyes were on the re-election next week of Kentucky Senator Harlan Styce, who continued his death grip on the fulcrum of Republican power. If the Presidency went as expected to the Democrat, Styce would have to hold the line against permissive whiny liberals like Holm. Maximus, not so much. She was a contender, no doubt about it.

Reaching for his phone, King noted the play of reflected light on the ceiling of his office. Outside, the westering autumn sunlight bounced off windows and mirrors of passing traffic, a brief message of delight for thousands trapped in their offices. It reminded him of the sunlight and shadow at Open Site #1, a.k.a. Hollymount. That walk had been good, the meal memorable, and he had not slept that well in years. He would have to go back to look at the stars, last seen in a distant suburban boyhood. Maeve's pull on human beings takes many forms, some gentle, at first.

Cat King spent thirty seconds of his afternoon in reverie, shook himself, and entered Styce's personal number. The call connected right away. King thought about how sweet it was to have friends in high places.

"Styce here. Hi, Cat."

"Senator! Always a delight. I'm calling with an update."

"Those assholes from the parks program gone yet?"

"Once I clean out the top guy's mind, they're all history. Ha ha, a little joke there, sir."

"I don't get it. When do the public trips start?"

"By February we'll be booking trips to famous time-places, at the top six entertainment parks. Venice, Italy; Ancient Greece; and Philadelphia in 1776 are the first three. A bit pricey, though. So, we're repositioning your park's Pleistocene Place at $10 a head, with two hundred people per trip. That's family-friendly fare, if we can subsidize it with that NOAA money you mentioned."

"Get me re-elected, and the funding is clear sailing," said Styce, chuckling at the thought of losing. "That little girl they put up against me is cute, but she's not ready for the big time." He switched gears.

"No details over this phone, but the military side – everything OK?"

King replied, "Test runs in six weeks, sir. The infrastructure is at your park, so that area's gonna see a lot of growth. We're buying up warehouse space along the Kentucky interstates all the way to Fort Knox and Bowling Green, and moving modular housing into the park. I'll be down there installing my team next week."

King had not yet told the Senator about the open sites survey. Ard Sprinkle was playing dumb tourist at a likely one in Florida, due back that night.

Styce reminded King, "Don't forget our loyal supporters, who want to see historical indignities corrected." He smiled, thinking about his Confederacy-focused friends back home. Bourbon sipped, country ham served on the finest plates, crystal and silver gleaming in old homes on high ground above the Ohio River where it approached the Mississippi. Wrongs to be righted, history restored to its rightful course. Old dreams come true. Money in the bank.

King and Styce ended the call following mutual declarations of admiration and affection. King sent a reminder to Sprinkle to make sure his gifts were up front at the Senator's victory celebration the following Tuesday night.

Part III
What Could Possibly Go Wrong?

Chapter 10

A grant proposal is reviewed, on Halloween.

Brian's car was in the shop, so Rita drove him over and pulled in next to Gregg's pickup. The tree trunk was gone, replaced with concrete curbs, asphalt lot, and a shiny trailer with a wooden staircase, surrounded by white pickup trucks and fake military vehicles. The blue port-a-potty huddled behind the trailer, and the yellow bulldozer was noisily clearing a hole in the treeline past the church.

"Were you out here with Harris?" Brian asked her, about the protest the day before.

"I waved a sign, sure," she replied. "Harris is horrified at how fast they're moving. He can't get answers out of any office. And not many people showed up. They're all fixated on the election." She handed Brian his daypack through the window.

"You sure this is a smart thing for you to do?" she asked. They had already gone over it.

Brian replied, "I'll see you tonight at the party. I'm just reviewing the proposal with Maeve and Gregg, and we'll be done well before dusk. I'm only going to that cottage on the far side of the tunnel. Harris is picking me up here at 4 p.m. So – what are you coming as, tonight?" Rita loved Halloween even more than food.

"I'm teaming with my office-mates to go as the English School of economists. It's a bit old-fashioned, but my department will love it." She thumbed the ignition on but did not budge.

"What do we do if you're not here at four?" she asked.

"I told Harris. Wait an hour, try my phone. Do not use the widdershins entrance after dark. But that's just in case. This is way too much drama over a simple business meeting."

"It's Halloween night, Brian. 'The fairy folk ride,'" she quoted from an old song.

"Rita," he said, "for pity's sake, be rational. This is about a grant proposal for a needy community."

"Bat poop," she said, backing up the car. "It's that Maeve. She's sucked you into helping the road construction company fulfill their contract. Harris told me about your creepy fascination with that woman, or whatever she is. She's female, that's for sure. Wake up, smell the coffee – and be here at 4 p.m.," she called, driving off.

Harris and Brian had planned more than what he'd told Rita. If there was trouble, Brian would head for Apple Island, where Acton and Greenwood would protect him. Harris would call Ravi the next day – that guy could fix anything.

Right now it was 10 a.m. on a sunny Friday morning. Brian planned to be at the cottage in the dell in a half hour, carrying his lunch and water bottle. Out by 2 p.m., Maeve had promised via email. Lots of time to spare for complications.

Well, some things must be learned the hard way. No substitute for experience, they say.

The grass crunched underfoot as Brian walked widdershins around the church, bulldozer noise fading. He strolled down the lane to the parking area. With each visit, Brian noticed the surroundings in greater detail. The meadows were bright green, dotted with briar thickets, ferns, and bushes with yellow and purple blossoms. Birds called and sang a pretty melody, weirdly in harmony with the low murmuring music that seemed to come from the landscape.

As Brian crossed the parking area, the hill cottage door opened. The small lady emerged, waved, and hurried down the steep path. Brian waited for her arrival, and bowed.

179

"Will I see you at the meeting, ma'am?" he asked. Her hair was neat in a small bun, a clean white apron featuring Hello Kitty over her ankle-length dress.

The little lady's bright eyes gleamed. "I'm just the greeter, lad," she replied. "I live on both sides," she went on, patting her apron as evidence. Bowing farewell, Brian turned to the green road and tunnel, which he wanted to get over with. But she had more to say.

"You are unwise to be here today," she said. "You think you know the rules, but this day is different."

Brian replied, "I'll be in and out as fast as possible, ma'am. Thank you for your concern."

She watched him walk toward the tunnel. Soon he was beneath the neon ENTRANCE sign. Steadying his breathing, Brian walked straight down the middle of the tunnel. The muffled silence was as before, sunlight gleaming at the far door. He held a steady pace until just past the middle, where he felt – watched. Heard. A chill flashed down his back, and he jogged forward, out into the thick golden air. The musical tinnitus resumed. Shrugging off the icy chill, Brian headed up the green road.

Behind his back, the neon sign above the tunnel switched from EXIT to NO EXIT. At the parking lot end of the tunnel, the sign switched from ENTRANCE to NO ENTRANCE, and a heavy wooden door slammed shut across the opening. Harris and Rita found it like this when they arrived at 4 p.m. They could not get through, or around. They went home to await daybreak.

The old lady shook her head, sighed, and walked slowly back up to her cottage.

Brian hastened along the green road and over the bridge, rounding the bend toward the creekside cottage with time to spare. The dell came into view across the creek. A large white tent stood next to the cottage. Beneath it was spread a carpet, set with table and chairs – and Maeve, waving at Brian. Gregg sat near her, sipping from a delicate teacup.

The cottage door opened, and out came the kindly gentleman who had been nice to Brian on his first visit – whom Brian had made uncomfortable. He carried a tray laden with food in colorful dishes, and gave Brian a nod and smile as he walked across the lawn to the tent. His beautiful black tail curled around his legs, as did the tawny tail of the handsome lady with faded red hair, who emerged from the cottage behind him. She sat down at the table, fluffy tail curling into her lap. She rested her hands upon it, as her partner poured tea into her cup and placed baked morsels on a matching plate.

"Welcome, Brian!" said Maeve as he approached, staring at the decorations. The tent's outer edges were festooned with autumn flowers and greenery. Flower-filled green vines wound across the ceiling, blossoms glowing colorfully: pink, purple, yellow, blue. Their radiance lit the tent. From the curling vines hung ripe gourds and squashes in fantastic shapes and colors. Papery brown grapevines interlaced the green, and from them dangled luscious handfuls of small ripe grapes. Gregg reached up to pluck and eat a few, Maeve beaming at him.

Brian felt uneasy, slightly nauseated. It was garish. Giant carved pumpkins – jack-o-lanterns, grinning and aglow, brighter than the morning sunlight – held up the posts at the tent's four corners. The posts were live trees, branches and twigs interlaced to support the tent canopy above, roots growing down the sides of the big pumpkins into the ground. This was not the humble kitchen table community meeting Brian had expected. The chill across his back returned, and he stepped away from the tent. Maeve came forward, taking his hand in hers – Brian did not dare look her full in the face.

She said gently, "Tea, Brian?" The old gentleman moved to pour tea into the nearest cup, but Brian placed his hand over it.

"Thank you, I prefer water," he said, setting his water bottle on the table. Maeve shrugged and took a tiny pastry from the array piled on a golden platter.

"I'm not playing the poorhouse, this year," she said quietly, "for we have enough, and to spare. The year ends in plenty." Brian looked at the platter under her hand. The tiny pastries were shaped like oak leaves, milkweed pods, lily blossoms, acorns. They looked delicious, crispy brown, tinted with shades of wine, pumpkin and butter-yellow.

Bowls filled with chunks of honeycomb stood by a forest-green tureen in which steamed a hearty stew; a long pewter dish held small whole smoked trouts, scattered with nasturtiums. These and other platters and bowls marched down the table, among clusters of wine glasses interspersed with pitchers of drink.

Gregg walked along the table, filling his plate. "Let's eat!" he said. Brian noticed that he had gained weight since they first met. Gregg looked as if he had slept poorly, eyes red-rimmed, hair uncombed.

"Work deadlines," Brian wondered – "or something else?" He stole a glance at Maeve, who was greeting the lady in her pink tracksuit and the small black-haired gentleman with sparkling black eyes. Her Board of Directors was assembled, and the meeting could begin. Maeve wore a high-necked long black dress and jacket, colors shining through: flashes of green, scarlet, a smoky deep umber, shifting as she moved. Her black hair was piled high, bound with a net of tiny gems. She felt Brian's gaze on her white neck and turned, their eyes finally meeting. Hers were cool, businesslike.

"That's good," Brian thought, "I'll be out of here ahead of time."

"Ready for the meeting, Brian?" she asked with a smiling glance at the pen and notebook next to his empty plate and trusty water bottle. Maeve lifted a brimming decanter from the table, and poured each guest a tall glass of pale yellow wine. Its fragrance met Brian's nose, challenging his thirst and longing. At Maeve's gesture, all lifted glasses to her toast, Brian his water bottle.

"Today is the culmination of our year, and we now commence our grandest festival and ceremony. To a sacred day and night!" They drank deeply. Brian inhaled the heavenly scent of the wine.

"Maybe later," he thought, "after the meeting is over. But maybe not."

"Brian and Gregg," said Maeve, "at the start of our most joyous day of the year, we also celebrate the events that brought you into our humble community." Gregg beamed, and Brian picked up his pencil.

"Your work on our behalf has brought us a new prosperity, not seen in all the long and often lean years since we came here from across the seas." She smiled at her Board, saying, "For some of us, it seems like just yesterday."

"You are ageless, lady," replied the small bright-eyed man in a croaky voice.

"You have transformed us, and our quiet country lives," agreed the tawny lady from the cottage. Brian's mind wandered to her tail, concealed by the tablecloth.

"She's more like a fox than a cat," he thought, struggling to focus on the meeting. The music was rising, and the birds singing in harmony clustered overhead in the golden autumn trees.

Maeve replied, "We are ending this year well, with good years ahead, promised by our new patron. We can discharge our annual debt with ease. And now to business." She drained her glass, as did the others. The black cat – or was it the old gentleman? – refilled them, golden glassfuls sparkling with sunlight, reflecting the jack-o-lantern glow. Time must have passed; the sun was overhead.

Brian addressed the group, "I have a list of suggestions, with dollar amounts and preliminary proposal language, for your consideration." All watched him except Gregg, who was fiddling with something next to his plate.

"Whatever you want, Brian, we're all for it," said Maeve, spearing a trout onto her plate, her gaze on Gregg.

"We've got a month to the deadline, plenty of time to pull in the partners, get a letter from your Congressman, and submit the package," Brian went on, with some effort, through the music and deepening delicious odors. He was incredibly hungry and thirsty, but how was it already time for lunch? He pulled out a sandwich, munching as he read to the group.

"A gravel-paved walking trail on the Apple Island Trace and downstream along the river, back up to the Inn road, at a location to be determined; a small Visitors Center at the parking area; preliminary planning for a Festival Site; and picnic facilities at the tunnel." Someone giggled, and Brian looked up from the list, which swam before his eyes.

Across the creek, the path to the tunnel was lined with glowing jack-o-lanterns. Opossums, rabbits, skunks were emerging from the woods, some walking on their hind legs, each carrying a gleaming vessel, from acorn to wild apple in size, befitting their stature. After setting their tiny lanterns in place along the path, the animals came across the bridge to join the party. Larger lizard-like creatures were carrying big orange pumpkins down the path, around the corner out of sight, toward the bridge and tunnel beyond.

Brian glanced in the other direction, uphill toward the Inn. The green road was unlit and dim, the air rapidly darkening, dark clouds spreading across the sky. A dusk had fallen.

Jumping to his feet, Brian grabbed his stuff. "Gotta go – sorry," he said, and saw that Maeve and Gregg were sharing a massive joint.

"What's the hurry, man?" asked Gregg, blowing a cloud of green fragrant smoke at Brian's face, where it hovered and aggressively sought entrance into his mouth and eyes, nose, and ears. The Board members were conversing with their friends, the animals who had joined them at the table. Everyone was eating, drinking, laughing.

"We've got all night to get the work done," Gregg went on, and Maeve laughed deeply, leaning against his shoulder. All at the table lifted their full glasses in a toast "to the night," and Gregg waved the joint, drawing green smoke tracers in the air.

"It's almost time," said Maeve. "Isn't it, path-watchers?" she called to the leathery creatures across the creek. Their orange eyes gleamed at her. The jack-o-lanterns at the tent corners were red-hot, lit by shimmering fires that flickered green and blue. It was warm under the tent. Brian stepped away from the table into the cooler evening air, walking toward the bridge. They could party on – but he knew he had to go. Harris must have been waiting for a long time already.

Crossing the lawn between the cacophonous party tent and the creek, Brian glimpsed cold stars through bare sycamore tree branches. New-fallen leaves crunched underfoot. The leaves had been golden on their branches this morning – how much time had passed, since he had sat down? His mind clearer, Brian walked back to the table and touched Gregg on his shoulder. He bent his head back to stare at Brian, eyes unfocused.

"Time to go home," Brian said, shouting over the din of animal languages and Maeve's deep laughter. Brian glanced at her, and caught her eye. She was surrounded by her friends, a chipmunk on her bare shoulder whispering in her ear. Her arms were wrapped around her furry and feathery Board members, and amber gleamed at her throat.

Maeve said, "Yes, you're right, Brian! Time to go. Let's pay the piper." She walked around the table toward Brian and Gregg, animals hooting and chanting happily from their perches on chairs, benches, and tabletop.

"Dears," she addressed them, "I regularly pay my taxes, so that our lovely life here together can go forward untouched. You stay here and enjoy yourselves – I'll be back shortly." Glasses were lifted, a chattery squirrel toast was made by the several in attendance; what seemed like "Don't be long," was called out in several animal lingos.

Maeve came close, entwining her arm in Brian's. He smelled her skin-warmed scent of pine and honey wine, then felt her strength, and was unable to free himself. She dragged Gregg backwards out of his seat at the table, chair toppling into the grass. He stumbled to his feet as she marched the two men across the lawn toward the bridge. An owl hooted overhead.

"They're mine now, go home," she shouted to the owl. The leathery creatures threw creek rocks at the owl, which circled, hooting.

Maeve said to Brian, "Your people have a saying," as they lurched across the bridge, creek tinkling below. "'The only certainties in life are death and taxes.'"

Gregg was awake now and said, "I told you that one. I couldn't believe you'd never heard it before." He stumbled again as they walked fast down the glowing pathway. The heat of the larger jack-o-lanterns scorched Brian's legs.

"You walking us back to our cars, Maeve?" Gregg asked. "That's really nice of you. I promised my nieces I'd take them trick-or-treating tonight. I sure hope I can drive OK."

Maeve ignored him, whispering to Brian, "Here the saying is, 'The only certainties are taxes and renewal.'" They rounded the bend, and across the bridge was the tunnel, mouth glowing red. Bats flew overhead, cheeping and swooping, grabbing the season's final bugs. Brian turned his head to look back, and found the leathery creatures crowding their heels. Their orange, non-animal eyes stared into his. They walked on two legs and four. Their iridescent scales took on the colors of the jack-o-lantern flames that towered overhead as Brian and Gregg were dragged toward the tunnel.

"Maeve, hang on, slow down, I have to catch my breath," Brian pleaded.

Gregg said, "Yeah, wow, slow down, babe," as she halted at the crest of the bridge.

"What's that mean?" asked Gregg, staring at the neon sign above the glowing tunnel entrance: NO EXIT. "You turned the tunnel into a Halloween haunted house?"

He glanced at Maeve for reassurance, but she was looking at the tunnel mouth. A large living shape hunched there. It rose tall on two legs, outlined in the red glow, and bowed, beckoning. Maeve stepped forward – and Brian broke free. She screamed, clutching at his clothes, tearing off his jacket. She did not let go of Gregg. Her scream shook the woods and hillside. It ate the night.

"Stop him!" came her wail – but the creatures scattered as Brian turned and ran back along the path. This was her job, not theirs. Several of the pumpkins had toppled, and flames caught in the dry pathside grasses as Brian tore back around the bend. Across the creek the animals at the party table sat silent, staring as he ran past. He saw them flee. Squirrels ran up the trees, chipmunks bolted for their holes, birds flapped to their nests, out past bedtime tonight. A mass of opossums, raccoons, and skunks dashed over the lawn, down to the creek, up the bank, and across Brian's path, as he ran headlong.

Maeve's voice was at his shoulder. He ducked away, then kept running. It was only her voice.

"Brian!" she said, and he heard her fear. "I'm coming to get you. Stop and wait for me. This is a great honor for you and your kind. And we are eternally grateful." Brian tripped over a black snake and dodged a doe, her eyes reflecting the jack-o-lantern flames. Brian ran uphill, through the woods, full-tilt, skidding left without pause onto the Apple Island Trace. He heard an owl, in flight ahead of him.

Two barred owls, now, calling, "Who-cooks-for-you," pulling Brian on. He ran full speed along the path in the dark as it sloped steeply downward. Her voice, nearer now, was in the woods to his right.

"Brian! You silly boy. I am almost there." He had to slow on the steep slope, moving fast, grabbing trees to stay upright and on the path. The welcome sound of running water rose up to meet him – and there under his feet was the log bridge spanning the creek to Apple Island. Brian looked up to see the outline of the apple trees, bright stars gleaming above in the moonless sky.

"Brian, sweetie, I'm right behind you – " her voice was shockingly close – his heart leapt in fear – and then he was across the bridge, off the logs into soft green grass. The leaves on the apple trees stirred in a soft breeze, wafting their blossom scent to Brian. He could no longer hear Maeve – just the sweet trill of spring peepers. Walking over to a pine tree by the fire ring, he sat down with his back to its rough trunk, thinking, "If Maeve follows me here, I'll do my best."

But no one came. He was on his own in the springtime evening with the apple orchard in bloom, a star-filled sky overhead. The pines sang quietly in the breeze. Brian's breathing eased, his heart unwound its tightness. He wondered how much and what kind of an idiot he had been, wishing he could get some advice – a reality check. No sign of Acton and Greenwood. Had they sent the owls to look after him? *Were* they the owls?

With this sketchy idea, normal thinking returned. Running was ended, for now; Brian needed to calm himself, make a plan for getting out and back to town. What was the first right step? His sister had told him that sleep heals. Brian wondered if he could sleep in the open, unprotected by walls and locks. The pine tree was warm at his back, and a thick layer of brown needles carpeted the ground. Relaxing, Brian wept, a few tears. He looked at his phone – dead as a doorstop.

Brian wiped his eyes, needing to talk to his mom, isolated from him for a year; his sister, his dad, his friends. He walked up the slope to look out over the orchard. A faint glow illuminated the sweet green meadow beyond the trees, edging the surrounding lake. Spring peepers and the gurgle of running water were the only sounds. Drawing a deep breath, Brian determined to wait out the night here. He was in the open, and could see anything coming.

Maybe Greenwood and Acton would return with the dawn. He wanted to ask Acton what he meant by saying that it was time for Brian to join them. That sounded good. Close up the apartment, make his excuses, take a break. Get this strange business figured out.

After walking back down the slope, Brian settled between the curving roots of the big pine tree, on the soft fragrant carpet. Not bad. He took out his dead phone and, for comfort, typed in a message to his dad, "Miss you. See you soon," pressing the screen where the "send" button would be. Nothing. Shutting his eyes, Brian drowsed, woke to put the phone back in his pocket – and on the screen was a reply in dim letters, "Miss you too. Love." Brian slept.

Waking deep in the night, Brian saw stars twinkling through the pine boughs. The fat streak of the Milky Way gleamed brightly. Starshine painted the pine grove in pale shapes, with a tranquil view to the island's edge, the stream speaking gently under the log bridge. On the steep slope beyond, the hemlocks stood still. The peepers were quiet. Brian drifted back toward sleep, snug among the tree roots, pulling the blanket to his chin. Blanket? What blanket...

Brian heard, "Wake up, asshole," and opened his eyes to find Gregg's assistant standing over him. Ricky. He had kicked Brian awake, who sat up, letting the green blanket slide off his shoulders. Standing, he held onto it.

"What the he – heck, man?" Brian asked, shocked to see Ricky here. The sun was rising on the cold spring morning. Brian pulled the – yes, cloak – onto his shoulders, fingers finding the fastener, the green garment falling around him in warming folds.

"Where the fuck is Gregg?" Ricky growled.

"Go ask Maeve," Brian snapped, warming quickly into anger at his intrusion. "How did you get here?" he asked, edging past Ricky to cross the log and pee.

"I walked in on the highway right-of-way," Ricky replied, "same as your royal self. Where'd everybody go? You were meeting with them yesterday. Gregg didn't come home. His family sent me to look for him."

"I last saw him on the bridge by the tunnel, with Maeve," Brian replied, returning to the island. Ricky stood still, waiting for more, so he added, "Last night – not sure of the time." What a glorious morning. Birds sang, the chill vanishing as the sun rose to shine into the pine grove. Brian needed to think about what to tell Ricky, and walked up the slope. Ricky followed closely.

"Seriously, what are you doing here?" Brian asked. Their breaths steamed in the sunlight.

"This is part of the project area," said Ricky. "We've mapped every inch. See that dam over there?" he pointed across the pinks of the spring orchard and lake to the waters lapping at the autumn orchard. The bent old apple trees were rimed with glittering frost this cold autumn morning. November one, Brian thought.

"We're taking out that dam. Restoring the original stream flow, stabilizing the highway bed downstream. This is gonna be a really nice roadside rest stop." Ricky smiled broadly as Brian stared at him in stunned astonishment. Ricky gestured to the orchard below.

"Yep, parking there, with a few trees left in the dog walk area, and a historic marker. Building over there with toilets, some kind of heritage design. Like it, asshole?" he asked, with a nasty grin.

Thinking wildly, "Gotta get back and tell Harris," Brian turned and walked along the spine of the slope toward the shore, to get around Ricky and back to the log bridge. But Ricky dogged his steps. Brian scrambled over a stone wall, stepped around blooming daffodils, and onto the lakeshore. Ricky moved faster, trampling the plants, standing between Brian and the way out. He had a bad look on his face, flat and mean. Brian was a college boy, not a fighter, but he knew that look.

Ricky stepped closer and said, "Not a smart place to be standing, asshole. We lost a guy there." Brian looked around at the open ground, the flowering slope, the still lake. Ricky jumped close, pushing him back hard, with a stiff hand.

"We GPSed the spot. Whoopsie-daisy," Ricky said, with a second hard push. Brian fell backward, waiting for the ground to take him. But he kept falling.

"Bye-bye, no hard feelings," Brian heard Ricky say.

At the sound of pounding feet, Ricky spun around. On the far side of the log bridge stood Harris and Rita, panting heavily. Arriving at daybreak, they were still blocked from the tunnel entrance, so they had driven back clockwise around the roundabout, parked at the construction pad, and run. They kept to the highway right of way, around the roundabout clockwise, and across the meadow between the orange flags. Up the hill and through the autumn woods they went, fleet as young deer, finally plunging down the steep slope to find Ricky standing alone.

Harris glared at Ricky. Rita was distracted by the sight of springtime on the far side of the log crossing, and pushed Harris to cross the bridge, but he stood his ground. He did not want to overuse his privileges on Apple Island.

"Where is Brian?" called Harris to Ricky.

"Fuck if I know, man," Ricky replied lazily.

"He's supposed to be here," snapped Harris, "and you should *not* be here."

Ricky replied, "I haven't seen Brian. You seen Gregg?"

"No. They both took the other route for their meeting yesterday, and you can't get in there today," said Harris.

Rita spoke up, "Brian said if there was trouble yesterday, he would come here. How long have you been here? We figured he'd be waiting for us under these pine trees."

"Nah," said Ricky, stepping onto the log bridge. "Nobody here except us tadpoles," he called, jogging past them up the slope into the hemlock woods, toward his car. Harris and Rita walked slowly into the orchard to look for Brian, but they did not find him anywhere on Apple Island.

Chapter 11

Actions and consequences.

Steve Roberts and Ed Zanetti rested on the bench and gazed at the long-ago French countryside. Not even the serene summer day could ease their modern woes. Large birds drifted on hot air above the flower-filled fields.

"What's that bird?" Roberts asked.

"How the heck would I know," said Zanetti. "I don't have time for birds. I have bird experts." He heard himself whining and adjusted his attitude. "It's probably just as well I'm getting out of this job. It affects your mind. Kind of demoralizing."

"Not sure what you mean," said Roberts, elbows on knees, watching the birds. The two men had been sitting under the tree for about twenty minutes, safely in the past for a private meeting. Zanetti needed his friend's advice before the final de-briefing session with King. There were things – such as here – that he did not want to reveal. Could he, *should* he, keep his mouth shut? Roberts had made suggestions on what to give up and what to hide.

Zanetti was a different can of worms. He thought that secrets made bad science. Shouldn't he tell King everything, and rely on truth to prevail? They were taking a break from this ancient debate, which had veered into Marx, over to Chomsky, Assange, Snowden, Picketty, Thunberg, and back to their present dilemma.

"About the only real perk I got out of the past twenty years was that two-week trip to Pasadena, 1910," Zanetti said, watching the birds drift, rise, circle.

"Birds don't have a care in the world," he griped inwardly, self-correcting to, "Ecologists say that the birds are working, struggling to survive...just like me?" Shaking his head to cut the self-pity, he spoke aloud.

"I got back from there-then just as this whole thing started. We were testing the feasibility of time vacations, using homes that we knew to be empty. I stayed in a bungalow under cottonwood trees, with a lawn, and palms, and trees with ripe grapefruit I wasn't allowed to touch. We knew from the records that the family was in Europe." Zanetti sighed, remembering the walks into town, the markets, hikes into the hills, that two-day trek to the beach; the infrequent open automobiles, horses, the clean-air sunshine. He had got caught up on his reading and missed his family.

"The new time-sharing, you know?" he said with a brief grin. "I packed in food and water, packed out my waste. Slept in a hammock that I took along, and used our experimental vacuum cleaner – selects for waste deposited from a specified time period, weighs less than a pound, cost us $4 billion – to clean up when I left."

"What's not to like about that?" asked Roberts, glancing at Zanetti, then back at the view. There was something wrong in what he was seeing, but he couldn't figure it out, and did not want to disturb his friend's reverie. Zanetti, not usually a man of many words, continued his reminiscence.

"I loved it, but the whole time I felt a sense of doom." Roberts raised his eyebrows encouragingly, so Zanetti went on.

"Just think about it! Southern California then, and now? They had a paradise on Earth, and they ruined it. It was called the Garden of the West. Even the L.A. River ran free!" He shook his head, adding, "That neighborhood was obliterated by Interstate 210."

"You were living a life of privilege," replied Roberts. "I don't know much about the specific regional history there, but that was hard times for a lot of folks, especially the Native tribes, the immigrants – "

"OK, all right, don't you think I know about all that," snapped Zanetti. "After the first few days when I saw how good it was then, and knowing what was coming, I considered what would happen, if I walked into town, and tried to warn someone. But I stayed away."

"Wouldn't have made an ounce of difference," said Roberts. "It has already happened. You cannot touch the outcomes."

"Oh ho," said Zanetti. "So that's how you roll, huh! I am nursing a viper in my bureaucratic bosom!" He shook himself out of his bad mood and grinned at his friend.

"It's what Douglas Adams says," replied Roberts absently, staring at the scene. He sat up straight, saying, "But I don't know for sure. Hey, it's the same time and date every time we visit here, right?"

"Yes, of course," replied Zanetti. "That's BMP number 7, the Groundhog Day Best Management Practice. My idea." He looked around and asked, "What's wrong?"

"Where's the painter?" asked Roberts. They both searched, their eyes returning to a particular place. The distant man in his smock, standing at his easel, paint palette in hand, was not at his time-defined spot.

"Abort," said Zanetti (BMP #2), and they ran back up the path to the present. Through the portal, down the hall, back into the underground research center. They each used the men's bathroom and returned to populated corridors near the dining area, slipping into the stream of staff. Walking toward Roberts's office and the escalator to Zanetti's department, they breathed more freely.

"Maybe it'll be OK," said Zanetti. "I'll have to file a report, though."

"Of course it's OK," said Roberts, watching a security officer walk past in the post-lunch crowd. The man stopped, cut through the walkers, and put a meaty hand on Zanetti's shoulder.

"Your security is expired, sir," he said. "You have to leave at once." The crowd flowed around them.

Roberts said, "This is Ed Zanetti, outgoing Homeland-Parks liaison. He's been here twenty years. Take your hands off him." Zanetti's face was pale as he stared at Roberts.

No sir," said the officer sturdily, guiding Zanetti toward the nearest escape hatch. "Effective just now, this guy is barred from entry. Security breaches, personal spending of project funds, possible treason. Watch the news." He forced Zanetti into the lit space behind a blank door, which hissed shut. The elevator shot up, opening on the escalator plaza. Zanetti stepped out. He would not have to worry about that final meeting with

King. Far below, Roberts slipped away from the security officer into the crowd, heading toward the news screen in his office.

Long ago, an obscure French painter lay dead in the meadow, throat slashed by a futuristic knife. A courting couple found the body. No newspaper notice honored him, no one mourned his death, and his savings were spent on a modest burial. His paintings may be found in flea markets and thrift shops.

The Venice field trip, 1959.

The narrow vessel chugged forward, morning sunshine dissolving thick fog. Standing at the stern, I tasted salt and smelled ocean in the boat's diesel exhaust, white wake burbling into green seawater, seagulls crying overhead. The five others were clustered forward under the awning, watching our time-skipper navigate the poles and buoys, easing past treacherous shoals in the shallow waters around Venice. He was using 1959 charts only. No electronic gear was allowed – it might disturb nearby Cold War listening posts. The impact scenarios for that possibility yielded dire results.

I heard shouts, and knew from my immersion time-training that we were approaching the quay near Piazza San Marco. We watched a vaporetto depart, carrying workers and early rising tourists up the Grand Canal. To our right, a fleet of gondolas bobbed along the Molo. As we looked for an opening, a white speedboat emerged from the fog and cut in ahead of us to the dock. Fashionably dressed men and women emerged, sunglasses at dawn, kerchiefs on the ladies' heads.

"Late night out for someone," whispered Ravi Sen-Ellis in my ear. Men unloading their gondolas and small boats whistled at the women and shouted rude comments to the men. The glamorous group had probably come from the Lido – the offshore island with its beaches and mansions – and soon vanished into the fog toward Harry's Bar. My Venice 1959 geography implant was working.

Two days earlier, Ravi had appeared in our park office and demanded to be added to the trip. We were united in saying No, but a personal call from his boss, Senator Liz Maximus, changed our minds. Who can say no to her?

"He has more temporal transfer experience than most of your staff," she said, "thanks to a top-secret investigation now under way." We got nothing more from her about the secret work, but she accepted all liability for his safety and lack of familiarity with our programs, BMPs, and standards.

"He has to be bombarded with information for the next two days," Sally Drew warned the Senator. I liked Sally's crisp Ohio efficiency, so different from my daily chaos. We worked well together, planning the final details of this trip.

"He's a quick study," the Senator averred. Ravi sat across the table, mild and cool.

"I bet you five dollars that he'll do something really helpful during the trip," the Max went on.

"Not taking you up on that, Senator," replied Sally. "You might have transfer outcome information for this expedition that we are not privy to." Senator Maximus laughed at this fishing hint.

She replied, "Let's just say that our work protects what you have developed. I respectfully request that you trust Ravi to be supportive and helpful."

"Who cares," I thought. "Let's get the trip over and done with." One look at Ravi, tall and impassive, showed that he was an asset. No need to quibble. The clock on my own plans was ticking toward zero, and I wanted to get through these final days with my chess pieces in place when the time came, two nights after the Venice trip. That would be Election Night, a good time to send a message, and only a day ahead of King's invaders. Empty rooms in staff housing were being prepared for their arrival, prefab housing assembled at an old work camp. Trucks unloaded shipping containers in the overflow parking lot, and armed guards were on patrol.

I was tense and nervous, with a continual headache. Unable to sleep. Thank goodness, Lena was away visiting her dad's family. She would return for our Election Night cave river paddling expedition with Steve Roberts. Those were my two local chess pieces. Son Brian was safely in New York State, and the Park and entertainment zone staff was at the annual low point. These thoughts recurred ceaselessly, so I forced myself back to the meeting.

Sally ended the call, face shining after talking to her heroine.

She said to Ravi, "We have to cram a lot into you over the next forty-eight hours."

He bowed his head, replying, "I'm ready and willing. What's first?" He smiled at me, Sally and Jinx Barker, the time transfer program's historic veracity expert. With Ravi and two of the full-time park rangers, our expedition would number six, dressed as American tourists, circa 1959.

Jinx spoke up. "How are we going to dress him?" he asked, looking from Ravi to Sally.

"Same as the rest of us, of course. Except bigger!" Sally smiled at Ravi.

"But he's – " replied Jinx, with a meaningful stare at Sally. A silence fell. Ravi's expression was impassive, and I waited to see how Sally would handle Jinx's attitude.

She said coldly, "Ravi looks like a professor. Dress him as an American professor, summertime, 1959."

"But, in 1959 – " said Jinx.

Sally snapped, "Today's representation and inclusion rules and standards apply. That's BMP #4, remember? We have been remiss in our diversity to date, and this is a great opportunity." She stood up to end the meeting. Ravi shot her a look of approval, ready for his speed indoctrination.

Jinx departed muttering, "Need his sizes, gotta get his pack assembled."

We disembarked without fanfare and the boat retreated offshore to wait our return. Emerging from the waterfront Piazzetta, we walked across the enormous ancient space of Piazza San Marco. Sally led the way, dressed as an American tour guide. I held the rear, clad in a short-sleeved shirt, sweater and capris, feet in sneakers and a rucksack on my back. Fog muffled the many ringing church bells; the Campanile tower rose beside us, top hidden in the gloom. We took a two-minute pause, body cams recording sight, sound, and air quality. I looked into the

Basilica's arched doorway. Golden beauty shone within, and an odor of stone and centuries enveloped me.

"I came here on a cruise ship two years ago," whispered ranger Val, clad in a blue windbreaker and white sneakers. She gestured to the waterfront. "It docked out there. This piazza was jammed with people, everywhere, long lines for everything. But now – then – is so empty, and quiet," she said, as we turned to view and record the vast space. Cafés were opening, waiters shaking tablecloths, arranging chairs. Old ladies sold packets of bird feed to early tourists, who threw cracked corn to the legions of pigeons that swarmed around their feeders. There were three billion people total on the planet, this date.

"I keep thinking it should be in black and white," offered Wilson, the other ranger. He had developed time-sickness, so he sucked a sedative/anti-nausea lozenge. Each person's pack or purse contained a survival pouch with essential medications and compact foods, water in a period canteen, water filter, and one survival pill, for use in case of stranding.

These precious capsules, $9.8 billion to develop, each contain a quickly restorative mix of vitamins, minerals, amino acids, mega-probiotics, 500 calories, caffeine, inflammation reducer, vaccine boosters, a mild pain-killer/sedative, and several other goodies to protect a stranded traveler. The survival pouches were the only modern items allowed (BMP 9.1.a., "Life-sustaining and protective items may be allowed at the discretion of the trip planners. See Appendix C.").

I had slipped private items into my rucksack, using my status to avoid the pre-trip inspection. Jinx had also handed me a metal-zippered pouch full of women's cosmetics and other unmentionables common to American women of the time. Arguing against these useless, heavy items, I was stopped by his strange logic.

"What if a pickpocket grabs your purse? We don't want you to stand out in anyone's memory, or to introduce modern items."

Ravi walked ahead of me, jaunty and watchful, cool and fine in a seersucker suit, no tie, camera around his neck. In this ancient meeting place of the world's peoples, he blended in, unlike the American tourists around us, with their loud clothing and voices. They were our protective cover.

"No chit-chat," called Sally, and Val covered her mouth guiltily (Ref., *Manual of Basic Trip Procedures*, 3rd edition, page 77, "Non-period conversation forbidden; keep conversation minimal."). Jinx shook his head at Val. We walked quietly past an American family, the mom calling encouragement to her daughters as the dad filmed them feeding the pigeons. His silver 8mm camera whirred as the two little girls shrieked, pigeons swirling, landing on their shoulders and arms. The smaller girl strewed corn on the pavement, closed her eyes tight, and smiled, jumping up and down, pigeons alighting on her sweater.

Our itinerary was simple. Take the Merceria Orologia route to the Rialto Bridge, pause for two minutes, and return along the Grand Canal, Calle dei Fabbri, and other streets past American Express and Harry's Bar, to the dock. We'd have up to five minutes in the waterfront Palace Gardens if time allowed, then take the boat back into the fog to the re-entry point. One hour. Any disturbances in this plan meant immediate departure.

My job was to stay at the back and keep an eye on the group, anticipate problems, and call abort if needed. Appropriate for my hyped-up state. I could not glance around, though I knew where we were at every moment thanks to the geo-implant. This was research, preparing for the looming launch of Venice TimeVentures Trips at several entertainment parks. Tom King was rolling out recreational time access trips while moving his military strategists into place. Win, win.

As we walked down the narrow streets in sunshine and shade, over canal bridges and past smelly, picturesque alleys, team members snapped photos on authentic heavy cameras in leather cases. These contained black-and-white film on 200-shot rolls instead of the usual 36. Each person had an assignment: quality of pavement; number of stairs (ensuring accessibility for modern travelers); building facades and shade (possible vacant property accommodations, indicators of environmental comfort); free public seating (almost nonexistent, in Venice); crowds and foot traffic; gondola, motorboat, and vaporetto traffic on the canals; and more.

These data, along with eye-videos and air quality sensor readings, would inform our research archives about this era and particular day. Someone would look for that dad's home movie, age the family's faces to find them in the present day, search U.S. records for families of four there on that date.

Captain Bill Adwell sat offshore in the small fishing boat, fog-penetrating binoculars aimed at the landing area, hoping for a scheduled return, but ready to move in momentarily.

Emerging into daylight at the Rialto Bridge, we rested in a shady alcove behind a busy market stall, standing in trash and discards, eying one another wordlessly. No one paid us any attention. Strollers ambled past the closed storefronts on the bridge, rosy in the warming sun. The four park employees took photos and whispered comments for their eye-videos.

I looked longingly at a café, people seated at small tables in the warming sun, drinking fragrant espresso. That kind of fun would be experienced by travelers after us. Our tight work schedule allowed no time for reflection or fear, although Sally and I exchanged glances over Wilson's continued unease. Sally checked her period watch (wound by hand, daily!). We walked along the canal, turning left at the Calle dei Fabbri into the warren of streets and canals toward American Express and the waterfront. We were on schedule to the minute.

For decades, every American visitor to Venice visited American Express, to cash travelers checks, call or telegraph home, and to pick up mail waiting there. The street outside was filling up with tourists, hustlers, pickpockets, and beggars. Our cameras clicked as we walked slowly past, Sally guiding us around stationary pigeons, avoiding the trajectories of others, not disturbing conversations. The program would gain a wealth of information from the faces and groupings of people there that day.

In the building's shade, young people slouched along the walls, disheveled and needy. A pale young girl rested, pack at her feet. She looked thirsty. College-age white boys clustered around a map, next to a man wrapped in a dirty green blanket, head down. I saw how white and wealthy these traveling Americans were. Ravi did stand out, here. I eyed him as we walked slowly past the crowd. He felt my gaze and returned a smile.

A voice called out his name: "Ravi!" He turned slowly, because surely it was a different Ravi. But I turned fast – that was my son's voice. The young man wrapped in the green blanket had his head up, gazing at Ravi, who now looked back – at my son, Brian. I was smacked by a physical shock and almost called his name – but stepped behind Ravi, out of sight.

Sally stopped and the group halted. She looked back at me, eyebrows up. This was not a scenario we had planned for. A trip participant identified, called out in public by name, years before he was born? This should be an abort – but it was not on the list. Ravi walked over to Brian. They spoke briefly.

Ravi walked over to me and whispered, "That's your son, right?" His knowledge shocked my eyes wide open. I stared at him wordlessly.

"It's OK. You have to trust me," Ravi said. "He's in bad shape. I'm going to give him my survival pill and water. Help me figure out how to get him out of here." Ravi walked back to Brian, pulling things out of his rucksack, and I gave Sally the five-minute signal. She shrugged, holding up her watch. We would have to ditch the side trip. Who cared? My beautiful boy was not far away and safe, but right here, and very ill. His head lolled, his eyes glittered, body sagging against the wall.

Ravi offered him water bottle and pill, but Brian was too weak to take them. Ravi gently poured water into his open mouth, along with the pill. As I watched him swallow, my mind began to work again.

Ravi came back to me, carefully walking around pigeons and chatting tourists.

"How long does that take to work?" he asked, then, "What's the plan?" I saw, over his shoulder, Brian rising to his feet. It works fast.

"He's part of your secret project, and got stranded during an investigation," I heard myself saying. "We'll bring him back with us." Ravi's eyebrows shot up.

"I like it," he said, "but you have to make Sally believe it."

"Tell him to join our group – don't mention me. I'll tell Sally," I replied, as Brian walked toward us, combing greasy hair with his fingers, rubbing dirt off his face. I did not want him to speak my name, *Mom*. I edged past the wondering others to where Sally stood, jittery and glaring.

"Ravi was sent here to find him," I said inventively. "He got stranded on one of the Senator's secret missions." Sally nodded, obedient to her heroine's interests.

She said, "Back to the ship," and I returned to the rear. There I watched, relief turning to horror, as my boy, tall and renewed, face shining with health, clapped Ravi on the shoulder, shook his hand, and walked away into the teeming city, long ago. He was lost to my sight immediately. I could not breathe.

Ravi stepped back in line, and the group walked quickly through the alleys toward the dock. I followed slowly, my heart breaking, then walked faster to hear Ravi, speaking to me over his shoulder, breaking the rules.

"He said he knew where he came in, and was going to go back there and get out on his own."

"That's crazy," I said. "How does he know – "

"He's been here five days," Ravi went on, as Sally shot back a warning glance. Our group hurried across a canal bridge, around a corner into a narrow street with lace shops, nearing Harry's Bar. The air was cooler, sea-salty.

Ravi said, "He drank water from the public wells and got sick. Could not get anyone to help. Did not understand where he was. I told him the year, and he said he knew where to get back. I told him about our boat."

I stared at Ravi's big back, made my decision, and stopped. I would go find Brian. The group was quickly distant, moving fast-forward toward the dock. Ravi did not notice my absence. Turning, I surveyed the crowds and city labyrinth, thinking about the items in my rucksack, wondering if they could locate a time-entrance here. Fuck the rules. Fuck my plans. Surrounded by crowds, I was alone – wonderfully alone – and would find my son.

"Ravi!" came a distant voice, far back in the crowd.

"Ravi!" it came again, closer. I stood, transfixed. Here came Brian, green cloak streaming behind him, fleet and young, easing through the crowd, running toward the waterfront. He was staring ahead as he ran. Then he saw me. Oh, such a smart boy.

He stopped, grinned, said, "I should have known!" and swept me up, turning me to run with him toward the dock, arm around my shoulder. He was laughing.

"Oh my God, I feel better. I was really sick. What's in that magic pill? Mom, it's so good to see you." We ran together for a minute, nearing the dock, where Ravi waited.

"I was being stupid," said Brian to Ravi.

"Hurry," Ravi replied, "the boat is here." Sally and the others glowered at me and stared at the laughing Brian, as we waited to board.

I unbuckled my pack, removed a certain item, clicked it on, and put it in Brian's hand. "Put this in a pocket," I said, as Ravi stepped onboard and we waited our turn. I whispered, "You don't know me. Act sick and stay quiet." He nodded as we stepped down ancient stone steps, across the churning saltwater gap onto the boat. I sat on the wooden bench, Brian beside me. Eyes closed, he leaned back and sighed deeply. I saw his filthy neck, realized that he smelled bad. My heart pounded with pity. Captain Adwell pulled the boat away from the dock, and we chugged slowly into the thinning fog. My next, right step – what was it? I felt blank, empty.

Ravi sat across from us on the facing bench, leaning forward, elbows on his knees. He smiled at me. "Close call, huh?" he said. I shook my head, unable to speak, emotions wild and unruly.

"Put him on the bus, get him out of here," said Ravi in a low voice, as our boat chugged toward the portal. Brian's eyes opened wide. We both nodded, as Sally sat down next to me.

"What the hell," she started.

Ravi sat up straight and said, "Not your business. He's our business. That was a near miss. The Senator would have been very sorry if we lost him." Sally nodded, leaning back and shutting her eyes against the disorientation of the time change. I put my head down, squeezing Brian's arm. Then we were through, into a cool autumn day on the Green, Green River.

"Pizza," whispered Brian. Ravi and I snorted with laughter. Our tiny vessel slipped into the time-departures boathouse at Pleistocene Place.

"All right," said Sally, standing up, as we gathered our items and stepped off the boat onto the narrow walkway. "Let's debrief, then go to lunch," she said. Cameras twinkled at us from the dark corners of the boathouse.

"Sorry, got a plane to catch," said Ravi, with an apologetic smile. "I'll be in touch tomorrow. Great trip! Thank you very much – I'll tell the Senator all about it." He turned toward me, away from the cameras, and shoved a wad of money into my hand.

He whispered, "Pay in cash for a bus ticket – tomorrow morning. Send his crazy ass straight home, no detours. Don't talk to anybody about it."

I smiled at him and said, "I'm ahead of you on all counts. Won't show up anywhere." Ravi shot me a surprised look.

He said, "Oh ho, you got one of those, huh? You both reassure and worry me!" and departed, chuckling. I spoke to Sally, the group, and other eyes and ears.

"I'll see you all later. That was a super trip, and I think we're looking good to launch soon!" I grabbed Brian's arm and followed Ravi out.

Brian and I emerged from the building onto the park pathway. I put finger to lips and we walked silently together through the woods, across the road, and down the path to my apartment. Inside, I kept the lights off and removed another tool from my pack, as he watched. There was no contamination of the rooms by anyone other than myself, so I turned on the lights.

"Weird welcome!" said Brian, smiling and pulling off his cloak. "I need a really long hot shower, and my clothes are gross. You got a bathrobe I can squeeze into?" He headed into the bathroom.

I called after him, "That device – keep it turned on, and within three feet, at all times."

"Sure, whatever!" he called over the shower's hiss. I surveyed my pantry, because there was no pizza in Brian's immediate future. The park's snack bar and restaurant were shut down, and the entertainment zone was closed for rest and repair. Yes, the casino's lights blazed, the Family Secrets Dome still open. Tonight, as on every night, the lights pulsed into the sky, laser-spotlights visible for miles around, calling to customers from atop this old sandstone plateau. No, we would not go there for a meal and a mother-son evening with the slot machines.

Nonetheless, we had a long, rolling feast. When he emerged pink and shiny from the bathroom, wedged into my ratty bathrobe, swathed in a red towel kilt, I pointed to cheese and crackers on the table. He went to the sink and drank water, three long, cold glasses-full, then demolished the first offering. By early evening he had worked his way through a pot of rice and beans, paused to sauté a wilted half-bag of salad mix with nuts and corn, topped with pan-crisped sardines – two cans. On to mashed potatoes, embedded with savory items from jars in the refrigerator door.

A frost-bitten half-gallon container of maple walnut ice cream, purchased for a meal with Lena two months earlier, finally slowed him down. We rested on the couch side by side, talking happily. The dryer rumbled below, readying his clothes and cloak for next day's bus ride.

"So, we can talk, right? *Mom*?" he asked.

"Sure, in here." I replied. "Tell me about that cloak."

"That's as far as I got, during the rice and beans," he replied. So far I did not know what to make of his story. Surely normal science had an explanation for these strange events and bizarre people. I had met women like Maeve, and morally suspect consultants like Gregg were a dime a dozen. But it dismayed me that Brian had had direct contact with Tom King. A mother wants her children to stay away from monsters.

"When I woke up in the night, it was draped over me," he said, polishing off an expired blueberry yogurt. "And in the morning, Gregg's assistant Rick was there. He *kicked* me awake! I tried to stay away from him but he pushed me – and I fell back – and kept falling. It felt like it did when we came back on the boat today. Then I was in an alley. I mean, later on I realized that. It was nighttime, and a motor boat was going by."

Brian smiled, shaking his head. "I thought I was still on Apple Island, somewhere I hadn't seen. So I waited – I dozed, with the cloak around me – but when dawn arrived, well, I knew something bad had happened. I tried to wake myself up, all that kind of thing." He cleaned out the remaining nuts and raisins, and looked around my comfortable room.

"Nice place here, Mom. This is a better fit for you. Lena told me you got a promotion, too."

I did not want to mar the evening with lies and evasions, so I pressed on about his story.

"What happened between then and when we found you?"

"I remember the first couple of days, but not much after that. I mapped out the surroundings in my head. I thought I was in a theme park, but I couldn't find the edge or the exit, you know?" He shook his head in wonderment.

"So I decided to temporarily accept that I was in Venice, Italy. But it was so weird. It wasn't normal, even for a foreign country. No one had cell phones. Everything was old-fashioned. No computers, no cash machines. No convenience stores, no fast food, and you had to pay to pee. The clothes and hairdos were dismal. And everyone smoked! I saw a date on a newspaper and got scared. Not many people spoke English, but a nice guy pointed me toward American Express." I listened, fascinated and horrified.

He continued, "I went in there, but they couldn't help me. They said it was 1959, and asked me for my passport. I showed them the American coins and five dollar bill in my pocket and they stared at me reeaaaally strange. They treated me like I was crazy, and asked if I wanted to see a doctor." He leaned against the couch, fading toward sleep.

"How, 'crazy'?" I asked.

"You know, they talked gently and slowly, staring into my eyes. I was also starting to feel sick because I drank from a public faucet, the second day. A guy tried to stop me, but what the heck! I was thirsty and hungry, I didn't have any money, I was just a beggar like the others. The restaurant waiters shooed me away."

He stared into his memories. "And then it gets kind of blurry. And really nasty." Shaking his head, Brian tilted toward a prone position on the couch.

"So, you gonna stay here awhile, Mom?" he said, smiling, letting me know that I had not distracted him.

"Not sure," I hedged, thinking about the timers belowground, counting down my remaining hours here.

"Lena thinks you're up to something," he said, watching me as I stuffed the couch cushion into my spare pillowcase and placed it under his head, arranging sheet and blankets for my boy.

"Right now I am up to getting you a good night's sleep, so you can be fresh for the bus ride. You should be in New York City for the upstate transfer by – "

"Lena tells me that things are going much too smoothly for you. She says you can't stand that. You're going to fuck stuff up. How you gonna do that, Mommy dear?" asked Brian – and then he was asleep. I pulled the blankets around his chin, tucked them in around his feet, watched him sleep for a long while, and went downstairs to pull out his dry clothes and soft green cloak.

The next morning, he stirred grated cheese and pickled jalapeños into a bowl of oatmeal, my cupboards now bare. We waited for the Bowling Green bus outside the casino entrance.

"This casino is as crazy as the one in Nevada," Brian said sleepily, craning his neck to stare up at the glass façade and gargantuan antebellum plantation home pillars, which changed color every few seconds. I bought food and bottled water from the lobby vending machines.

"What's in my pocketses!" he chortled, as the purchases slid neatly into capacious inner pouches of the cloak.

I said, "Hold onto that other thing until we get you onto the bus." He gave me a sharp look, but did not return to our earlier conversation. The roar of a big truck came through the trees, climbing the road from the Green, Green River landing. Gearing up as it rumbled past, it was already breaking the park's sedate speed limit. Brian paid no attention until the fourth identical truck roared by, and then he began to count.

"Eight big trucks, heading past us at dawn," he said, as the noise from the last of the behemoths finally died away. "They're water trucks." He looked at me enquiringly.

"Those are frack water trucks. They filled up at the river," I replied, and he recoiled.

"But that's illegal – " he said.

"In New York, sure," I answered. "But here it's business as usual."

"In a *national park*?" he asked, his voice rising.

"This is not just any old national park, it's Senator Harlan Styce's national park," I said, trying and failing to keep anger out of my voice. "The nearest frack well is less than a mile away, in the woods over there past the casino," I said, waving in its general direction. "That's how they got the casino and entertainment district in here. It's an experimental fracking site, exempt from environmental laws and review, using the

Halliburton Loophole. The casino and all that got built in the exempt area."

"How come we haven't heard about this in New York?" Brian asked indignantly, as our bus came into view.

"There's lots of things you haven't heard about, in New York," I replied tartly, then put my finger to my lips as the bus stopped in front of us. We climbed aboard the green park bus, which rattled along the road onto Wilcher Boulevard, down the steep slope to the sinkhole plain. As daylight grew, we passed Buchanon Memorial Airport. Out on the runway red and blue emergency lights pulsed, figures hurried. Our bus driver remarked that a sinkhole had opened up under a landing plane.

"Not the first time, either," the driver said chattily, "but you won't hear about it on the news, nossir." We drowsed past the guarded industrial park that housed the park's time-servers, around the village of Oakland, merged onto I-65, and neared the ambitious little city of Bowling Green.

"I'm sorry to go so soon," Brian said, "but I'll be glad to get back home. I need to talk to Acton and Greenwood. I want to work with them." He looked at me, maybe seeking approval.

"Don't quit the day job," I said. "Eco-warriors in the woods don't earn rent money. Those guys are probably eking out a living on a grant, eating kale and oatmeal. Maybe it's time you go back to school for that next degree."

"I'm not sure about Acton and Greenwood," he said. "They are not regular guys. Let me think how to put it." He closed his eyes and furrowed his brow to make me smile, but he was serious. "They don't seem – mortal." He looked at me, eyes wide. "There you have it. Not human. Not quite."

"Maybe they're some kind of time traveler," I offered, "Like Doctor Who?" I smiled to show that I was joking – while trying to understand what he meant. He rested his head on my shoulder and laughed softly.

"Aww, Mom. Love you."

I patted his face and said, "I love you too, you know that." We rode in comfortable silence to the bus station. The clerk did not want to sell me a ticket for cash, but got over it after conferring with the manager. I bought

Brian a bag of fresh donuts and a cup of coffee, and he gave me a fierce, long hug.

"Please, Mom, this time, stay put. Give my love to Lena, and I'll see you both soon." He handed over the device, and climbed on the bus. We waved goodbye through the bus window, and it roared out of the station, headed north. I was *not* crying. I clicked off the device and walked back inside to wait for the next casino-bound bus. There were plenty.

Chapter 12

Pastorale.

Election Day dawned windy and mild across Kentucky, with rain in the forecast and colder weather on the way. A mile-long convoy of big trucks wound west on I-64 from secret Virginia warehouses, headed toward the seasonally empty parking lots at Ten Thousand Secrets National Park Casino & Entertainment District.

At the park, beds and giant flat-screen TVs were assembled in the prefabricated man camp housing on Joppa Ridge. The ten interlocking bunkhouses and administration units off-gassed fresh plastic into the warming dawn air, caves below providing quick septic hookups for toilets, showers, and labs.

In the suburbs around Bowling Green, realtors for the area's gated housing developments headed to the polls early to vote for Senator Harlan Styce. His final pre-election mailing promised that he, single-handedly, would fill the hundreds of mansions, unsold and empty since the '08 crash, with highly paid executives and consultants for a top-secret Homeland-Defense project headquartered at Ten Thousand Secrets National Park. Active and furlowed employees of military services and contractors from Kabul to the Carolinas googled "Bowling Green, Kentucky."

After voting, the realtors attended a joyous prayer breakfast buffet hosted by the local conservative think-tank, The Bluegrass Center for Policy Concerns. Fortified by spiritual uplift served with biscuits and gravy, realtors lined up in the lobby to sign lucrative long-term leases for hundreds of homes, partnering with an unnamed government entity.

Long-moribund bank accounts showed new activity. The caves beneath the rolling golf courses and tattered strip malls would soon roar to bacterial life when toilets flushed and washing machines drained, delivering their fresh loads into cave rivers flowing to drinking-water springs.

By early afternoon, the convoy's lead trucks were exiting I-65 at Oakland onto Wilcher Boulevard, passing Buchanon Memorial Airport (still closed for runway-collapse repairs), then heading uphill and into the federal park.

In Washington, D.C., Thomas King, administrator for the American Way Temporal Transfer Program, gave his two floors of employees the afternoon off to vote, on condition that they show up at Styce's election headquarters by 7 p.m.

In nearby Silver Springs, Maryland, Ed Zanetti voted according to his conscience for the first time in twenty years, and cooked supper for the family.

In New York State, a young man drowsed on a bus winding its way north and west up Route 17 through the headwaters of the Delaware and Susquehanna rivers toward his apartment and friends, who were planning a big welcome with pizza and beer. He was dreaming about apple trees, and the good boots he would buy with the cash his mom had given him.

Not far away, a badly beaten fairy queen wrapped thickly in soft spider web lay curled around the central stems of a protective briar, sleeping until spring brought healing. She had taken the full punishment for underpaid taxes, to spare her woodland friends. No hard feelings toward Brian, but he was a marked man. Within her pain and coma, Maeve grew goals for the new year: money and staff. It had been a long time since she had talked to her Old World cousins. She needed their help to take care of her land and community.

In the deeper woods, owls conferred with crows.

The buds of next spring were forming on the autumn trees.

In a quiet corner of Ten Thousand Secrets National Park a mother, her daughter, and their friend, clad in caver outfits and carrying overnight packs, walked into the deepening autumn dusk under big oak trees and through a tall green stand of Kentucky cane to a dark, fern-decorated opening in the steep limestone bluff. Illuminated by the final rays of sun, the cave entrance popped into prominence, rock glowing warmly around the dark opening. The man switched on his headlamp, bent low, and crouch-walked inside. Mom, then daughter, followed. No cameras noted their presence and disappearance. Woodland animals, incurious, continued about their private business.

The underground river.

A hundred feet in, the cave opened up and we walked easily along a narrow canyon between water-sculpted stone walls. My headlamp showed the roof rising above, thick with water droplets that reflected the light. Big cave crickets wiggled antennae at us. Our boots shifting the loose rocks underfoot made a musical noise, as the cool outside air of the entrance was displaced by the muggy warmth of the cave.

The passage widened and we came to a hole in the floor where a deeper canyon dropped away below. We climbed down, ledge by ledge, another thirty feet. As we stepped onto a sandy floor at the bottom, I heard the tinkling of running water, loud in this small space. Silent, wrapped perhaps in memory, Steve led us down a gentle slope into a big room. In its dark and rocky center ran a sizable cave river.

Steve looked around and smiled. "What a relief. I was scared something had happened to it." He clambered up the slope to a stony ledge, saying, "The rafts should be right here." He triumphantly waved a square package, then a second.

"Our own little flotilla!" he crowed, slithering down to the riverbank and tossing one of the packages to Lena. He ripped off a thin covering from the other one, unfolding and shaking the bundle, which popped and puffed to full inflation. Lena inflated the second boat while I pawed around on the ledge to find four folded plastic paddles. Steve was settled into his watercraft, holding it against the muddy bank, as I handed him two.

"Always have a spare!" he chirped light-heartedly. Lena wedged our packs into the front of his boat. We settled gingerly into the other, and pushed off onto the river. Our headlamps illuminated the walls and the slow current that swelled into the dark passage ahead of us.

"I've only done this afloat once before," said Steve, "ten years ago, right after they dammed it. We've got a good current for a while, until the water backs up behind the decorative waterfall."

He corrected his craft's course and went on, "About an hour ahead there's a beautiful side room to visit. We'll camp on the bank a ways beyond that. Then it's about forty-five minutes to the Casino landings. We'll get there in time for breakfast at the Hideaway Café & Curiously Satisfying Breakfast Buffet. Tomorrow is their last day of the year."

We glided between straight-sided stone walls, the flat ceiling overhead glistening with moisture droplets. I felt as if we were paddling down a flooded hallway.

"Is it like this the whole way?" I asked as we rounded a straight-walled bend, across from a muddy beach that receded into the gloom.

"Not hardly!" snorted Steve from behind, as Lena pointed with her paddle at the rapidly lowering ceiling ahead. A few paddle strokes carried us under the lower roof, two feet over our bent heads. The current seemed to slow, and our wakes lapped both sides of the narrowed passageway. I felt a tiny spark of apprehension, which Lena and Steve both must have divined.

"It opens up!" said Lena.

Steve echoed, "It opens up again just ahead," their voices loud in the small space. Not far downstream the roof rose to hover a comfortable fifteen feet overhead. We paddled and glided in contented silence for a while, then floated into an intersection. A higher, dry corridor extended at right angles from our lower stream passage.

"Here we are," said Steve, gliding to the bank. We stepped into the water, dragged the boats onto a small gravel beach, grabbed our packs, and stretched. I wrapped the boats' bow-ropes around rocks.

"You don't have to do that, you know," said Lena.

"Yeah, it would be a dire disaster for the Casino's business if this water level deviated by more than about two inches. This water isn't going anywhere," agreed Steve.

"Well, you just never know," I said, as they smiled gently at my apparent fussiness. Behind my mild claustrophobia, I was thinking that maybe I had gone about this whole thing the wrong way.

"What would happen if the dam, ah, developed a sudden major leak?" I asked, as we scrambled up the slope from the boats and entered the oval-shaped side passage.

"That won't happen," said Steve, absorbed with adjusting his shoulder pack. I felt Lena staring at me. They started along the passageway among the boulders that lay scattered on its flat floor, but I stood still, wanting a reply. Illuminated by my headlight as he rounded a corner, Steve decided to take my question seriously.

"If the dam popped a leak, this artificial river would be reduced to its natural trickle," he said. "It would become a walking passage again, as it was when I first found it, except there would be a two-foot layer of mud to wade through. The Casino riverboats downstream would run aground."

"Why mud?" I asked as Steve turned to follow Lena around the corner. His voice floated back, echoing.

"Dirt has washed in from the surface, off the land cleared for parking lots and Casino development. And there's a lot of worse stuff that has washed in, like farm chemicals and fracking fluids. But come and see a secret place that has been left alone."

I scrambled to catch up. Past the corner I saw their lights bobbing off the walls of a rounded, attractive passage. Soft brown dirt lay between the footpath and the red-tinted walls that rose to the ceiling. I say "footpath" because, unexpectedly, it was lined with carefully placed small rocks. Steve and Lena's headlamps swung toward me, pausing to let me catch up.

"Stay on the path, and watch your head," said Steve.

"Why? What's the matter?" I asked, puffing slightly, but they had gone around another bend. When I too rounded it, I saw the reason for his warning.

Lit by our headlamps, glittering crystal patterns stippled the walls and ceiling; and gleaming, asymmetrical formations hung down toward the floor – weirdo mutant chandeliers. The stone-marked footpath skirted these beauties and wove among the crystalline, multi-colored stalagmites that rose from the floor toward their partner stalactites, hanging from above.

Lena and Steve were leaning in close, beaming their lights on a cluster of transparent shapes that emerged from the wall at chest height. Slender, twinkling white sugar-sticks hung at twisted angles, each several inches long. Above them hovered a curving flower-shape, made up of shimmering transparent filaments, delicate as a butterfly wing. I held my breath, shining my lamp on and through the cluster to admire its pallid, gentle forms.

"Don't worry, it won't melt," whispered Lena.

"On the other hand, don't touch," said Steve. He shined his light along the passage, revealing a blaze of gleaming, silvered shapes and curves emanating from the walls and ceiling. We had entered a sort of fairyland.

"Gypsum crystals," he said, answering my unasked question. "The water that seeps through the walls is saturated with gypsum, and dries into these fantastic shapes. Drop by drop. Takes many years for them to grow, and a second to obliterate them."

Lena had continued along the footpath as we talked, and called back to me.

"Mo— Janet, come look!" Steve glanced at her and then at me, but said not a word. I stepped forward, then stopped, seeking the balance needed for each careful footstep, to avoid crushing these treasures. To my right and left rose two- and three-foot-long stalagmites of dim blue-grey, shining with water dripping from stalactites above. A forest of slender white hollow tubes hung down from the ceiling in clusters of hundreds or thousands, thankfully a clear ten feet overhead. Our lights glanced and rippled through their gleaming arrays.

"Soda straws!" breathed Lena. "Come look!" she repeated. She was hunkered down, feet carefully placed in the established footprints. I edged forward through this dainty garden of young, living stone, putting one foot in front of the next, noting that damage had been done even to create this single footway. Crushed tubes and deep footprints marred the shimmering surface.

"Why are we even here!" I cried out. Steve was waiting behind me for his turn to move forward.

He commented, "Well, well, all kinds of things are revealed away from our intrusive and controlling overseers. You are capable of actual emotion! Who knew!"

I ignored his outburst, itself unexpectedly emotional, to hunch down next to my daughter. Her light was focused on the floor.

"Look!" she whispered, "cave pearls!" My light, added to hers, shone on a cluster of gleaming white small, perfect globes, shimmering, nestled in a round stone bowl filled with clear water. Our lights picked out other small pearl-filled pools, situated at the bases of the surrounding stalagmites.

Steve said, "C'mon, move along, let me have a look, it's been a long time," and we rose carefully – Lena reaching out a hand to steady me – and edged forward to a drier area where we could look around, less fearful of each footfall. I glanced back along the curving passage, through the silent tangle of shimmering shapes. Steve was hunched over the pools of pearls, in a quiet moment of reverie. Ahead, more gleams and shots of crystal were revealed by our lights, but with reduced intensity.

"This is the heart of it," said Steve, not looking up. "But the passage goes on – it's booming borehole." I raised my eyebrows at this strange phrase and he said, "A big walkable passage – go ahead and look."

Lena and I walked along the handsome passage as it ambled forward in genteel limestone curves, a smooth strolling surface underfoot. But Steve did not follow, so we soon turned back. He had retreated to the far side of the decorated area and was gazing closely at an intricate crystal puzzle.

With Lena leading the way, she and I threaded the perilous steps among the treasures – with a long stare at the pearls in their pools – back to his side. I guess I was relaxed, because I broke a personal security rule: I asked another question on the same topic.

"How high would the water have to get, to reach this?" – realizing instantly that I had broken the brief spell of our camaraderie. Lena turned to stare at me, her young face's features glowing in the soft light of our headlamps. Steve frowned and shook his head.

"It would never happen," he said. "If the dam went, the water would flush down the big culvert to the Green, Green River. It wouldn't back up into this passage." He adjusted his pack, then swiveled around to look at me, shining his headlamp full in my face.

"What's on your mind, anyway?" he asked, as we began the short walk back to the boats. I grimaced at the bright light and turned away, fumbling for a soothing response, and failing badly.

"I just wouldn't want to ever see this disturbed," I said, adding tartly, "We shouldn't be here in any case."

"Heck," grumbled Steve, "it's been ten years since anyone was here. And I thought you'd like it." He stumped silently along the passage, wide shoulders stiff with irritation. We soon were back in our boats, wordlessly paddling downstream.

The tension among us vanished as we became captivated with the beauty and singularity of our trip. The river passage remained high and wide. We moved slowly, often letting our boats drift forward in the gentle but definite current. We slowed down to glimpse side chambers and small side passages that sent back messages of unknown frontiers to our eyes.

I felt the three of us bonding in the peaceful darkness, out of time and place within the deep Earth. I regret the brevity of this time together, and will hold it with me forever. I learned things on this trip that I now wish I had known before; but it was already too late, and it is all behind me now.

We paused at a rock-rimmed inlet to eat candy bars. Steve shined his lamp down into the clear water, illuminating small, pallid eyeless crayfish scuttling across the muddy floor. He reached down, deftly plucked a crayfish out of the water, and held it under my headlamp. His firm two-fingered grasp was just below the creature's claws, which snapped and waved. It had no eyes, but two spots were light-sensitive.

He turned it over and Lena said, "Look! Eggs!" A small cluster of white balls clung to its underside.

"That's a nice thing to see," said Steve, gently placing the female back into the water, where she hustled out of sight under a rock. "A healthy and reproducing crayfish population means there are good conditions for cave life to flourish." We all smiled at his ponderous words. In a friendly manner Steve bumped my shoulder with his and went on, mimicking my voice.

"*If* the water came surging back up here, then drained away, these little guys would be in big trouble. *And* your next question is, 'How fast would the water drain away if the dam started leaking?'" He grinned at me, waiting to see how I would react to his teasing. I had been wondering this very thing, but had not asked, for fear of them glaring suspiciously at me. Lena tucked candy wrappers and water bottle back into her pack, and spoke in tune with our relaxed mood.

"How do we get around their stupid fake waterfall between here and the Casino riverboats passage?"

"Their 'stupid fake waterfall,' my dear girl, what a shocking lack of respect you reveal for our beloved Homeland-Park Service overlords and superiors," said Steve, laughter indicating his true opinion, expressed freely in this private place. "There's a built passage we walk through to get around it, Lena. No worries."

We paddled on, Steve in the lead. He chatted from time to time, giving us a guided tour of the water, the rocks, and his long history of exploring and mapping these passages. I had never seen him so relaxed.

I said to Lena quietly, "He's different down here."

Steve heard me and replied, "We all are. You two, for example, are behaving much more like the mother and daughter that you are." He did not look at us when he said this.

He called back, "We can be ourselves down here. No one to listen or pry. The cameras and microphones don't start up again until just above the falls. I know, because I helped install them." The water widened and slowed; we had to actively paddle to keep moving.

"From here on, it's dead water backed up behind the dam," Steve said, as a sandy beach appeared on the right, picked out from the gloom by our headlamps.

"Here's our five-star hotel!" he added, and we pulled our boats onto the shore. It was 7 p.m. outside. Seven hours to go. The dark water curved out of sight, downstream and upstream. An oval rock ceiling arched overhead, hung with water droplets that gleamed in the light from our headlamps.

"Our starry sky," said Lena, arranging three sleeping bags on a tarp. The stony cave ceiling curved above our little camp. Improbably, it felt cozy and safe. And private. A person did not have to watch herself so closely, down here. Because no one was watching her. Into my apprehension at what I had set in motion, and what would soon happen, came a warm feeling of personal peace. A candle was lit within me, as Lena lit a candle lamp and placed it to illuminate our bivouac.

I thought, startled, "This could have been enough. Had I only found it sooner." But years before I had given up on seeking and hoping. Hope had been replaced with rage, and rage-based action. Rage at impotent government, and at the vicious, heedless business interests that feed on apathy. And action, to match the mindless destruction. It was a bitter moment, rediscovering hope here, as the clock ticked toward 2 a.m. Too late now, for me and what lay downstream. I had to stop these thoughts. Focus on keeping those I loved safe.

I watched Lena's face in the glow of the candle lantern as she coordinated her tasks with Steve. They were at ease, comfortable here in this silent dark realm. Steve set a gas stove on a rock and assembled a selection of ready-made foods. Water was boiling. Lena found a seat-spot, patting for me to sit next to her.

"First up, a cup of tea," Steve said, handing us each a fragrantly steaming small mug.

"Oh, that's lovely, thank you," said Lena, holding the cup beneath her chin to breathe in the jasmine scent and warmth. Steve turned back to the stove, added more water and stirred in the contents of several packets.

"Men's bathroom downstream, women's upstream," he said. "Use containers as needed. Standard expedition policies in place." That answered a prosaic question!

The mood lightened as a gorgeous odor of vegetables and stew filled our campsite. Two bats flittered past.

"Must be a hole to the surface somewhere nearby," said Lena to Steve.

He replied, "Yeah, there's a couple of woodchuck-sized entrances on top here. We made a voice connection back twenty years or more. But all the exploration stopped ten years ago, when the powers-that-be made this into an entertainment park. I had to stop caving and focus on protecting what I could." He shook his head and sighed, a big sigh of sadness, speaking as he stirred the stew.

"Those bats need to start their winter sleep. I hope they're healthy. Maybe we can have a look at those woodchuck holes, once we get past this next work push. When Damaris and Ron come back, next March." He looked at us as Lena handed him our bowls.

"We could start a dig project. It's like old times, with all you young people, and your tough mom, here." We did not reply. I for one was famished, focused on the food. Lena passed around a plate of bread and cheese chunks, as I slurped ravenously at the vegetable-laden, gorgeous stew. We ate silently, mopping up the stew and cheese with the bread.

"Seconds!" Steve cried, passing around the now-cool pan, and we each scraped out a final portion.

"Lick the bowls and spoons," chimed in Lena. "We're not washing dishes. And no one can see the food on your chin."

"It's official park policy!" agreed Steve, as we leaned back on our rocky seats and contemplated the candle lantern, satisfied and cheerful, taking in the deep silence. A steady water drip could be heard in the darkness. Lena pulled chocolate bars from her pack.

"Dessert!" said Steve. Lena flashed the labels with fancy flavors.

She said, "I got your favorite, Mom," broke off a big chunk of the one with sea salt, and handed it to me with a smile.

"That's more like it," said Steve, "and I like that flavor. Let's snarf down that one and start on the next." I did not want to offer explanations, and Steve asked for none. Lena had confirmed his suspicions, and he no doubt figured he had all winter to find out more.

We enjoyed the cave chocolate, went off to our separate bathrooms, and got ready for bed. Clothes on, jackets off, caps on our heads, boots off and lined up nearby, headlamps at hand. I took the middle sleeping bag, giving the inflatable boats one last glance as I settled in to my bag. They were up on the beach, away from the water, paddles inside.

Lena blew out the candle lantern where the kitchen gear was clustered. Our headlamps went out and the darkness and quiet took over. I could see nothing, hear nothing, except the rustling of our sleeping bags and Lena's soft breathing. She curled up and was quickly asleep. On my other side, Steve was still awake.

"Oh, this is nice," he said. "So totally peaceful and safe." I sensed his face turn toward mine, and he went on, "Maybe this is the start of a beautiful friendship."

"Maybe so," I said, "but right now it's the start of a beautiful night's sleep." And just like that, he slept. His breathing slowed and smoothed. I lay listening to them sleep, hearing the water drip, and gazed wide-eyed into the dark. Every once in a while I allowed myself the luxury of checking the time on my glowing watch dial. Fifteen minutes would go by, then another. Steve rolled over, snoring lightly, and flung his arm across me. A privilege he had at home, I thought wryly, but it felt nice, just the same. In that tranquil place I too fell asleep.

"What was that?" asked Steve sleepily. I checked my watch as we sat up. It was 3 a.m. My eyes went wide.

"The boats are on top of us," Lena said, her headlamp revealing the inflatables lying across our legs.

"The water is flowing!" said Steve, out of his bag, grabbing headlamp, pulling on socks. I moved cautiously, listening to the water. The stagnant pool had developed a slow current.

"Was the dam scheduled for repairs?" Lena asked. She shoved the inflatables aside, got up, and sat back down, still sleepy.

"That's gotta be it," said Steve. "They're dropping the water level up here so they can get at the dam. But you'd think I would have seen it on the duty roster." He stood at the water's edge, watching the pool's quickening current.

"I guess we're getting up now," I observed, and put water on to boil. Something occurred to both of them.

"So why – " said Lena.

"Yeah," Steve said, walking up the slope for his boots. "If the water level is dropping, why did the boats climb on top of us?" We went off to pee, up for the day, some more eager than others to find out what had happened downstream. I made tea and handed it around, not saying much. Lena rolled up the bags, stashing them with the tarp in Steve's boat.

"I'm awake enough to think," she said. "The water must have surged upstream, to push the boats uphill onto us." She turned to me and in a low voice added, "Funny coincidence, considering your questions last night." I put away the kitchen gear, not saying a word.

"What could cause that?" asked Steve, dropping his backpack into the boat, ready to go. He gazed thoughtfully at me. I placed my bag next to Lena's and fastened my boots.

"I guess we'd better go find out, huh," was all I said, collecting their empty cups. Ten minutes later we were paddling downstream, pulled by the rising current.

Behind me, Lena hissed, "Mom!" I knew that tone.

"Not now," I said, digging in my paddle to keep up with Steve, who was speeding toward the waterfall. We paddled fast and silent for a half hour. The water was dropping, and soon our boats were bumping along the river bottom.

"No need to damage these beauties," puffed Steve, stepping into the ankle-deep flow. "Let's walk." He grabbed his boat's rope and splashed downstream, tugging it behind him.

"Just a few more turns, and then it straightens out to the waterfall," he called, as we splashed after him.

"What's that smell?" asked Lena, as we turned a bend and encountered smoke. It swirled eerily in our lights. A boom and crash reverberated down the passage.

"Steve!" I called. "Stop. Wait for us. Let's stay together."

I did not want to lose either of them now. Staring downstream, he waited. His and Lena's faces were somber, eyes wide with worry. I hoped I looked the same. It was shocking, no doubt about it. But I felt a wicked surge of energy, and a rising sense of joy. And then, a rush of shame. My respite here had healed me just enough to understand how obsessed I was – but this was no time for reflection. Needed to get them out of danger.

We splashed together around the final bend, dragging the boats, and entered a straight tunnel ending at a big arched opening. Beyond it lay the entertainment zone and pleasure domes. Through the smoke we could see flickers of light, bright flashes, and heard rumbling crashes of big things falling. Steve began to jog, then run.

I called, "Slowly. Something bad has happened. Let's stay together and safe." The water was only a few inches deep, now. I would be needing my boat, so I took over pulling it from Lena. We walked up a concrete ramp to the arched opening.

"Maybe the gas well blew up," said Lena.

"Holy shit, I bet that's it," said Steve. "The Park warned that could happen, but the gas well was permitted anyway. Styce insisted. To please his energy pals in Bowling Green."

"I saw the air quality readouts from our last trip with Hugh," said Lena. "They were really bad. The methane coming off that leaky gas pipe was a lot higher than before. I sent in a report two days ago."

We stood in the doorway to the entertainment zone. There had been a metal gate: it lay twisted and broken. A rank odor of burning plastic came at us, so Lena pulled the bat-decorated bandanna from around her neck and tied it over her mouth and nose. Steve leaned against the arch of the opening, gazing into the chaos beyond. He looked drained, older. We could see one another by the ghastly lights ahead.

"Those damn fans were total bullshit," he said. "Not one sensible, science-trained person thought they would work very long. Another favor by Styce to a local company." He stared out at the ruins of the vast entertainment chambers, the drained Styx riverbed littered with debris and grounded boats.

It was time to part from their company, but first I needed to see them to safety. I peered into the gloom to see where safety might be found.

"Look, stars," said Lena. Overhead, a massive hole blasted in the dome's plastic ceiling was open to a dark sky filled with stars and clouds. Cold air blew in, clearing the smoke and fumes. To our left, water poured from the cave stream into the near-empty riverboat channel, flowing toward the busted dam and culvert to the Green, Green River – crucial to my escape. Spars fallen from the ceiling and walls pierced the hotel's windows, boutiques, and walkways. The Styx River Bridge was destroyed, an unmet half-arch suspended in the air above the empty channel. Chairs, tables, and glass were everywhere.

"Let's get out of here," I urged, as Steve pointed to a narrow metal staircase that dropped to the floor of the boat channel. We handed down the two inflatables and walked downstream through the fallen debris, still dragging our boats in the stream, looking for an escape route. A cold rain began to fall.

"Should we be worried about gas?" asked Lena.

"Probably the gas well fire is venting up and out," replied Steve. We crept past a riverboat hull as he spoke.

"Let's not talk until we're out of here," I said. "Pay attention." Wordlessly, we walked below the unbroken half of the bridge and found a staircase up to the boat landing. Beyond was the hallway to the Family Secrets entrance – our nearest exit.

"Leave the boats here," I said. We dragged them out of the water, collected our packs, and climbed the staircase to the main floor. Lena kept me in front of her, and I realized she had her eye on me. I would have to choose my moment to leave when she was distracted. Fires were burning in the hotel rooms overhead. We could see flames taking hold in the food court and Secrets attractions along our escape route.

"Maybe we better run for it," said Steve, as a small group of Park security staff emerged from the smoky gloom.

"Hey, guys!" he called, but they were already heading our way.

Lena stood next to me and said, "Brian will be worried when he hears. I'll let him know we're OK." She unzipped a waterproof pouch holding her phone.

"You seen anyone else in here?" asked the group's leader. Beneath his helmet and gear I recognized the guard from our Pleistocene trip – Lee Turner. He saw me, and in an instant, he – knew. He stepped forward, hand to the holster on the side of his bulky suit.

"I thought so," he said. "We'll deal with you later." He pointed to a man and woman on his team and said, "You two, escort these three out. Stay with them."

He divided the others into two groups and instructed, "We'll go upstream and you go downstream. Meet you back here in a half hour."

I stepped back, away from the group. Had I left it too late? I glanced at Lena, to see her bent over her phone, no doubt texting her brother. The phone light illuminated her face, one last moment for me to remember.

Steve said to Turner, "You don't need to go upstream. We just came from there." I stepped behind a fallen sign, then moved fast around piles of debris, dodging overturned and broken chairs and tables. I had a minute or two. Down the staircase to our boats. I took Steve's, with the tarp and sleeping bags, grabbing the rope, running downstream along the channel bottom into the smoke. I was heading for that culvert beyond the broken dam – it would take me out of the caves onto the Green, Green River.

The destruction on the main floor was worse here, closer to the blast – the buildings were burned-out skeletons. The roof was shattered, grey sky of morning looking in on the smoke and tumult. I gazed up at the side passage where the fans had been, toward the gas well beyond. Nothing remained except bare cave walls, the opening blackened by the two explosions and methane gas conflagration. I heard the well fire roaring, fueled by gas gushing out of the broken well casing. I wondered what it looked like on top, a jet of flame visible for many miles.

I came to the eight-foot dam and scrambled over collapsed rocks and cinderblocks. Beyond, the round opening of the drain culvert stood out in the cave wall, still taking in water. The water pooled as it approached the culvert, so I climbed into the boat. I did not hear the footsteps behind me until the boat jerked to a halt, mid-stream. Lifting my paddle to strike, I turned to find my daughter furiously glaring at me, eyes angry and full of tears.

"No!" she gasped, and climbed in, panting. "You can't go without us this time, Mom," she said. The boat nearly foundered in the shallow water, but we righted it. I settled her pack, handed her the other paddle, and we approached the culvert, blocked by a metal mesh, water flowing through into the dark. There was a gap at the top. We got out and shoved the boat through, scrambled after it, and climbed back in. The boat was seized by the shallow fast current, and we were on a steep ride down the silvery culvert to the river, daylight growing ahead.

At the riverboat landing, Lee Turner realized the two women were gone.

"Where'd that bitch – " he said.

Steve ran back into the smoke. Rain pelted down into the mess, raising giant gobs of hissing steam as he reached the ruined Styx River Bridge. He gazed carefully around for his friends. The riverbed was stabbed with steel beams. Around them flowed the shallow stream, mingling with heavy rain, dissolving plaster, and wallboard, carrying debris toward the broken dam and culvert. The half-bridge was shorn of its lamps, pitted with holes and piled with debris. Steve looked for the inflatable rafts below, and saw only one.

He climbed down the stairs and found a confusion of muddy boot prints in the dirt and debris around the remaining boat, empty except for one paddle. Two sets of footprints headed downstream.

Steve thought, "Their two packs are missing. They've gone downstream." He kicked the remaining craft loose into the water, where the rising stream took it. Spinning, it vanished downstream. The rain was already erasing the footprints.

"I would have guided them," Steve said to himself. He climbed up the stairs to Lee Turner and the others and threaded his way past them through the ruins, out the shattered casino doors into the rain.

CPSIA information can be obtained
at www.ICGtesting.com
Printed in the USA
LVHW031615080520
655240LV00004B/1135